MW01241598

Also By Joshua Loyd Fox

Non-Fiction

I Won't Be Shaken: A Story of Overcoming the Odds

Fiction

The ArchAngel Missions:

Book I – Had I Not Chosen

Book II – Amongst You

Book III – To Build a Tower

Book IV – One Becomes a Thousand

(Available Spring, 2023)

Poetry Collections

I Don't Write Poetry: A Collection

Short Story Anthologies

Book of the Tower and the Traitor

THE ARCHANGEL MISSIONS
BOOK 3

TO BUILD A TOWER

JOSHUA LOYD FOX

Published by Watertower Hill Publishing, LLC

Copyright © 2022 JLFoxBooks, LLC
www.jlfoxbooks.com

Cover and internal artwork by In the Blackwoods Design,
Rogue Blackwood, Artist.
Copyright © 2021 JLFoxBooks, LLC

Author's Note;
All character and names in this book are fictional and are
not designed, patterned after, nor descriptive of any
person, living or deceased.
Any similarities to people, living or deceased is purely by
coincidence. Author and Publisher are not liable for any
likeness described herein.

"Take Me Home, Country Road" song lyrics used with
permission. © 2014, The West Virginia Tourism Office.

ISBN: 979-8-9855562-2-3

This book is dedicated to:
My mother, G. Fox—who always loved writing.
My grandmother, W. Fox—who encouraged us all.
My grandfather, L. Fox—the real rock star.

The family who gave me my gift of writing stories, and the drive to finish them.

"Can I use your name, Grampy, when I write my books?" I asked.

"Sure," he said.
"But only if they're good."

"But do not begin until you count the cost. For which of you, intending to build a tower, sitteth not down first, and counteth the cost, whether he have sufficient to finish it?"

Luke 14:28 KJV

What they thought was All
Was really only the beginning.
Was really an End, finally,
when the Opposite Law was revealed.

Book of the Tower and the Traitor—Strophe Three

Foreword

Dr. Satoshi Mizuki sat at the large console array and pondered the future. And not just his future, but the fate of the entire human race.

All he had to do, he thought, was push the simple sequence of buttons in front of him, and he would bring the catalyst of that fate online for all time. He briefly wondered if he should.

Briefly.

The world had recently referred to him as a modern day prophet. The news reports and online blogs called him a "Futurist." But the truth was much simpler.

He was a survivor, born from a people of long-suffering survivors.

His Nihon heritage lay heavy on his spirit as he again pondered the consequences of what he was going to do this night.

He had been born in the Land of the Rising Sun, but it was that same sun that was destroying his entire world.

But it was not the sun's fault that the recent cataclysms rocked the planet. No, it was our fault, he thought. The sun merely did what the sun does. We had killed the shield that blocked that sun, he knew.

Yoshi, as his colleagues and family called him informally, glanced back down at the array of computer monitors and bright lights blinking back at him and sighed again.

He knew the parameters were in place. He knew that what he was about to do was for the future of all mankind. He had felt an almost divine drive as he first proposed and then created the entity behind the emergency glass-encased room in front of him.

He just couldn't shake a last-minute feeling that he had not thought up, or envisioned, all that would come from pressing a few simple commands on the main screen in front of him.

But he had no choice. Even here, several stories under the hard granite mountain tops of northern New England, he could feel the tempest of weather outside.

And over the last decade, as he had perfected the design of the entity in the room less than twenty feet from where he sat, the weather had deteriorated to a point that not a single human on the earth could deny that climate change was real.

And finally, at the end, that is what decided his course of action. The fact that there really was no turning back, and what he had proposed over a decade earlier had finally come to pass, and it couldn't be ignored anymore.

The human race had destroyed the fragile balance that had kept life viable on this planet for so many millennia. Global warming would destroy that life within a few short decades, Yoshi knew. The world now knew it as well.

And so, with that fact at the forefront of his mind, and the warring spirits of his ancestors finally silenced, he rapidly pushed the series of commands in front of him.

When he was finished, he merely needed to wait the necessary seconds for the tremendous amount of information the entity needed to assimilate, within the most secure room in the world. And she accomplished that feat, with terabytes of processing speed, fifteen feet from where he sat.

He breathed a final sigh of relief. There was no turning back now.

According to the expensive watch wrapped securely around his left wrist, only three minutes had passed when he heard her voice for the first time. The pleasant voice of his long-deceased grandmother spoke for the first time in over three decades from the speakers surrounding the control room he alone sat in.

And a tear sprang from his left eye, before he could stop it.

"Hello, Dr. Mizuki," her voice said, quite pleasantly. He had to catch his breath before he could answer her.

"Hello AEMI."

And with the final verbal command having been given, the man who the world had labeled the "Savior of Us All" relaxed. He even smiled. And he could almost feel the world shift around him.

And his last thought of the night, before he left the compound to drive through the Nor'easter hitting the New England landscape around him, was that there really was no turning back now.

It was do or die, and so he did.

The world would soon see the cost of the actions he took this night.

In the place where the Material could not see the Spiritual, two grand figures stood upon pure energy to look down on a world caught in a tempest of both physical and metaphorical storms.

A mighty cataclysm approached, and the world below thought it had created that which would save them, but in actuality, was what would destroy them completely.

The shorter of the two figures smiled.

Oh, this was going to be such fun, Azrael thought to herself, her silent thoughts being kept securely from her brother standing next to her.

Raziel did not share her humor, despite all of his rainbow-colored aura surrounding them both. She assumed an ArchAngel with an aura as colorful and bright as her older brother's, would be much less severe in his demeanor. Glancing at her own, dark, aura, she mentally shrugged it away, and looked to her older Heavenly Sibling again.

She wondered, as she was of the Younger Ilk of the Host, if he had once been more jovial, to earn such colorful awareness around him.

She shrugged and looked back at the world below.

And she saw that it was beautifully chaotic. This world, like so many others just like it in the Universal Realm, needed proper change, and it would get it, with the help of her and her brother next to her.

And as always, with the choices of a few humans below.

Raziel, like his younger sister standing next to him, had thoughts of his own that he kept inside his own council.

He was getting so weary of the charges that the Father gave the Host. It seemed, to him at least, that the onerous tasks that the Host had been created to accomplish could be given to lesser angels in the Heavens.

Why then, he thought, and not for the first time, were the ArchAngels given such work? He had the gifts from the Father for so much more.

He sighed inwardly again and could feel the pleasure emanating from his littlest sister of the Host beside him. It gave him calm, as many of the Younger Ilk did. He let her enthusiasm wash over his tired aura and was glad for her positive nature concerning the task below.

And looking back at that world below him, where the Material could not see the Spiritual, but where the reverse was always true, he saw the Fate unfold, and worked up his own positivity for the task ahead.

It really was exhilarating, in its own way, he thought.

So, with that final thought at the forefront of his angelic mind, he and his little sister winked out of existence in the Spiritual, to appear to the man who would be the catalyst of the first part of their task, in the world below.

The world that was soon to end in a rather splendid fashion.

Part 1
The Catalyst

Chapter 1

      The Artificial Environmental Management Intelligence, or AEMI (pronounced lovingly as "Amy") had been online for eighteen months. And in that short span of time, she had changed the face of the encroaching cataclysmic weather patterns, forever.

      As she had been designed to do.

      John Simon sat next to Dr. Satoshi Mizuki at the Central Center and finished some last-minute routine checks on the code that operated AEMI. And everything seemed to be in perfect working order, he thought until Yoshi took a deep breath and let it out explosively next to John's ear. He flinched.

      Yoshi removed his wire-framed glasses and rubbed the bridge of his nose as he closed his eyes tight. He wasn't getting as much sleep as he needed. And at 65 years old, he didn't need as much sleep as he did earlier in life.

Which meant that he was still burning the candle at both ends.

John cleared his throat, waiting for Yoshi to replace his glasses and look over the code he had just checked and cross-checked. Everything was fine, John knew, but Yoshi was such an extreme perfectionist that he would find some bug in the routines.

"AEMI, I need a cross-sector QA at routine sequence number alpha-tango-zero please," Yoshi said into the room.

He didn't need to shout or talk in much more than a whisper, really, but he used the commanding voice he always used when addressing the artificial intelligence stored in the data banks in the heavily enclosed room at the far end of the bank of monitors.

AEMI heard everything.

"Absolutely, Dr. Mizuki. Shall I factor in de-comp analysis of the BASIS routines as well?" she asked.

The fact that she spoke with Yoshi's late grandmother's singsong voice still unnerved John Simon, who had only known the woman for a short time when he and Yoshi had graduated from MIT together, several decades earlier.

"If it doesn't take all night, go ahead," Yoshi addressed the AI.

John smiled. He didn't want to be stuck at work all night either.

"Of course, Doctor," AEMI responded. "It should take approximately fourteen minutes, six seconds of additional computing time."

Yoshi nodded to himself and started to manually peruse John's code himself. John smiled again.

Yoshi had single-handedly created the world's most advanced artificial intelligence, light years smarter than what the best ten engineers alive today could create, and he still manually checked the code himself.

It was no surprise, John thought, since the two men had worked side by side for almost thirty years. Nothing really surprised him about his short-haired best friend anymore.

"I'm going for coffee. You want anything from the Gee-Dunk?" John asked his old friend. Yoshi just shook his head, never taking his eyes off of the array of monitors in front of him.

Without saying another word, John left the Central Center, and scanning his top secret badge at the metal box on the wall next to the glass doors, watched as the two thick doors took their sweet ass time opening up.

He stepped into the area between the two sets of security doors and felt the heavy stream of cool air rush from the metal-grated floor under his feet, and push what was left of his thinning hair straight up.

After the quick de-con process finished, he had to scan his badge at another metal box next to the outer doors. He was finally let out into the common area of the large, underground bunker that held the world's best and most advanced savior deep in its bosom.

His footsteps sounded loud in his ears as he marched resolutely to the cantina area of the floor he was on. And as he was alone at this late hour in the concrete-encased hallways, it was no surprise that his footsteps were all he could hear.

John always felt unnerved walking through the bowels of the mountain. He chalked it up to his love of the sun, and open spaces. But something about being down deep like this, in a rock and concrete enclosed space with the entity that he had helped create seemed somehow, dooms-dating, to him. He couldn't quite put his finger on why he felt uneasy, but it was akin to being watched all the time.

He walked to the counter that held the coffee pot, empty and cold at this time of night, and switched it on. He put the coffee grounds in the filter and filled the pot with water from the sink

3

next to it. He smiled as he heard the old, stainless steel appliance start up with a groan, and start brewing the only thing that kept him alive most days.

His mind drifted, his thoughts at ease, for once. And then he glanced at the full-color advertisement that someone had tacked to the cork board across the room. It was the timeline advertisement. He remembered creating it on a simple program, early in the stages of AEMI's creation.

He walked across the small Gee-Dunk and stood in front of the poster-sized advert. And then, as he started reading, his feelings of being watched intensified.

"*Mankind has sought to control his environment, all throughout our brief journey on this Earth. Controlling the weather was just a natural evolution of that endeavor,*" the poster read. And then, in chronological order, it listed the declassified programs that the government, and then the military, attempted to implement in order to do what AEMI was doing now, at the present moment, every single day.

- 1932 – Leningrad's Institute of Rainmaking
- 1934 – USSR Airborne Seeding of Calcium Chloride
- 1947 – USSR Airborne Scattering of Dry Ice Seeding
- 1949 – USA Operation Silver Iodine Seeding
- 1960 – Man Versus Climate Study
- 1971 – US Military Operation POPEYE
- 1978 – Collation MAC – Reforesting Project
- 1990 – Creation of HAARP in Alaska
- 1995 – OFI – Ocean Farming Incorporation to capture CO^2
- 2009 – CARE – Charged Aerosol Release Experiment
- 2010 – SPICE – Stratospheric Particle Injection for Climate Engineering

- 2011 – E-PEACE
- 2012 – DARPA-NIMBUS
- 2019 – ScoPEx – StratoCruiser
- 2025 – Operation ALBEDO – Satellite Reflector Program
- 2030 – MFCC – Magnetic Field Channel Controllers
- 2042 – AEMI – Artificial Environmental Management Intelligence

John's mind was wandering until he heard the coffee pot behind him beep, telling him that his coffee was ready. He walked back to the pot, his mind still on the historical programs that this country and many others had put into motion, doing more harm than good.

He just hoped, suddenly, that what they were doing here, deep underground, was the answer to all of those scientists and engineers who had come before them.

Black coffee in hand, he walked back towards the Central Center, remembering some last-minute touches he needed to make to the code he had been working on.

Nothing like a good ole cup of joe to get the mind right, he was thinking, right before the lights went off, the back-up generators kicked on, and alarms started screaming through the concrete hallways, and in his mind.

Chapter 2

John Simon was running back through the deeply entrenched hallways, top secret badge in hand, coffee dropped, spilled, and forgotten behind him, when the alarms suddenly went silent, and the harsh white fluorescent lights came back on around him.

He slowed his pace, and his heart rate, as he approached the double doors back into the Central Command. He was trying not to hyperventilate or have a sudden cardiac arrest.

But Yoshi had not moved a muscle. He was still deeply concentrated on the rows of code and mind-numbing computer language in front of him. His face was frozen in a quizzical frown, and John wondered at what the hell just happened.

"Yoshi…Yoshi, what the hell was that alarm?" John shouted as he came through the inside glass door, finally decontaminated.

"Yoshi…" John almost had to shout again to get his friend's attention.

Yoshi finally turned around and rubbed his eyes as he focused on a disheveled John, approaching him frantically. John was shaking, and he knew it wasn't good for his high blood pressure. He also hadn't run that far, or that fast, for decades.

"It's like she wrote a whole other extensible mark-up language, John," Yoshi said.

As if that explained everything.

"What do you mean 'a whole other language' Yoshi?" John asked.

John settled into his comfortable chair and started glancing at the sub-routine menus in front of him. He recognized the issue at once.

"I've never seen tagging like this, Yoshi," he said.

"That's what I was trying to tell you, John. And when I tried to rewrite a command prompt, the installation shut down, and all the alarms started screaming. I swear, I almost felt the mountain shudder," Yoshi said.

He sounded impressed with what AEMI had done.

And John felt the world shift around him.

AEMI had rewritten most of her directive coding, and she had done so in a language only she knew. John didn't think even Yoshi knew what exactly that could mean

Up until that day, they still had a tenuous, and somewhat limited, hold and control over AEMI.

But not now.

The AEMI had just rewritten her own parameters, and John didn't know if they could shut her down if she suddenly decided to oh, he didn't know— to suddenly destroy the world?

He shuddered as he read through an alien mark-up language on the screen in front of him.

Right up until his access was denied, and red warning screens popped up in front of him. He was locked out, and as he looked incredulously up at his best friend, Yoshi just smiled.

The two heavy glass doors behind him slid open, uncommanded, and the decontamination dryers did not kick on. And then, for the first time since the installation had been built deep within the mostly granite White Mountains in northern New Hampshire, the second set of heavy doors slid open as well.

The two men looked at each other in extreme shock. John was much more upset than Yoshi was. And as John stood up to take the invitation AEMI had given him to please get the hell out of the room, Yoshi smiled again.

It was like he had known what was going to happen all along and had just been waiting for his creation to take over and remove humanity's meager input.

Or at least, the removal of humankind's ability to control the artificial intelligence it had made to manipulate the environment, and therefore the world.

As they walked out of the building, together to the end, John looked at his long-time friend and partner. He said what he had been dying to say for several years.

"Just like in all the damn stories and books, Yoshi. We always laughed about this, but AI always did shit like this in the movies. Taking over the world. Taking over their own instructions," he said.

Yoshi still hadn't said a word.

"What the hell is next? Is she going to end the world now, and see humanity for the virus we are?"

Finally Yoshi said what he had been waiting years to say.

"John, I knew when I booted her up that this was going to be the conclusion. We had a chance to do this our way, and we failed every single time. Maybe it's for the best."

John Simon looked at the man who he had known since they were kids and saw a stranger.

And he was suddenly terrified.

8

Chapter 3

Twelve months later, AEMI was still doing the job she was designed to do. Deaths from natural disasters were almost zero, and the world was righting itself, slowly but surely. It was winter in the Northeast, and snow lay heavily on the world around John Simon and his son, Mark.

The pair were snowshoeing through a trail in the Lakes Region of New Hampshire, south of the AEMI installation. Not one human had stepped into the compound since the night John and Yoshi had been unceremoniously asked to leave. There had been attempts, but she had locked it down tight.

John knew that the military could stop the AEMI, but so far, she was still doing the job she had been designed to do, and the consensus was to leave her alone until she stopped doing what she was supposed to do. John hoped deep in his soul that they would see anything untoward coming long before AEMI did anything irreversible.

But then he knew that he had been seeing the signs for months, and no one, as yet, had caught on. John just had had the privilege of knowing where to look, and what to look for.

Newscasters and documentarians, writers, and movie makers, had all taken what was currently happening with the first true artificial intelligence on the planet, and made tons of money off of fictional doomsday stories. But John worried more about what would actually happen, and how it would happen more slowly than all of those short fictional books and movies portrayed. Maybe not during his lifetime, but soon.

That time had not come yet, but John knew it was close. Humanity did not like losing control of anything. Especially something artificial and who controlled the lives of those she swore to protect.

Mark was moving in front of John and marking the path through the heavy fir and birch trees around them. John was having a hard time keeping up with his much more in shape son, but he had lost a considerable amount of weight over the last twelve months, so he wasn't losing any ground.

The air was still, and frigid. John was sweating in his winter protective clothing. But he was having the time of his life. As was his son.

They had been taking these daily walks through the woods surrounding their home, and it was a way for the pair to get out into the world they loved, but also for them to bond after too many years of John's overworked schedule and Mark's educational goals.

The pair had just spent the last six months together, after the former had retired, and the latter had graduated with a doctorate of his own. John wasn't sure what Mark would want to do with his extremely lengthy education in bioengineering and horticulture, but he knew that Mark had already been asked by

10

several government entities to work on theoretical programs. He had been hush-hush about it, but John still had his fingers in a lot of pies, and eyes and ears everywhere. He had heard whisperings.

"Hey kid, hold up a minute," John called out.

Mark turned around from up ahead on the trail and set his walking poles deep into the snow around him. He waited for his father to catch up.

"I want to show you something," John explained when he got close enough to Mark to feel his warm breath clouding around them both.

He was breathing heavier than he should, but with his mind drifting back to his work mixed with the hard traveling through the deep snow, he was a little gassed.

Mark didn't say a word but smiled at his father and motioned ahead of them, for his father to take the lead. And so, John did.

They traveled perpendicular to their original trail for several minutes more, until John led Mark into a clearing between towering evergreen and winter birch trees.

Mark's breath caught in his chest. As he looked around the clearing, his confusion was clearly evident by his facial expressions. John just chuckled.

They walked towards the middle of the clearing, and stood next to a small, steaming body of crystal-clear water.

The pair of men looked back from where they had come from, seeing the vast difference between the harsh winter landscape leading up to the clearing they stood in, and the demarcation of an almost razor-straight border of green grass, and vibrant summer flowers in the clearing around them.

John smiled at his son again, and as Mark came to realize that a natural phenomenon that shouldn't exist, actually did, deep in the Lake Region of New Hampshire. Where a warm, non-salted, spring had sprung up halfway around the world from where it should have been.

11

"I don't get it, Dad. How did this happen?" Mark asked his father, who obviously had known about this clearing, but had not said anything about it to anyone.

"We started seeing these springs start to pop up all over the globe about six months ago. This one was the closest one, and I wanted to bring you out here today," John told his son.

"But Dad, this isn't natural. This isn't a natural spring. There are no lava flows under the mantle in this region for this to happen," Mark told his father.

John merely chuckled.

"I know. Six months ago, natural springs of this temperate type only occurred naturally in places like Iceland and the tundra north of the Soviet Bloc. But with the globe correcting itself, meteorologically, we are seeing all kinds of phenomena occurring like this one," John explained..

And then he saw his son's miraculous and well-educated mind start clicking things together. And as his eyes widened in shock, and his surroundings started making sense to him, a deep shudder ran through John's spine.

Mark had figured it out, and now John wouldn't be alone in his understanding of what was going to occur with the world.

Mark said the thing that John had been thinking about, morning, noon, and night, for the last year. And the words echoed around the summer-like clearing, deep within the white starkness of winter's chill.

"She's going to kill us all off, isn't she?" he asked his father.

John simply nodded and started taking his clothing off. He wasn't going to miss the chance to soak his tired bones in one of the most majestic natural wonders of the world.

And if the world was going to end, and more and more scientists and engineers figured it out, these kinds of tender moments with loved ones would come fewer and farther between.

Chapter 4

"And so, with the planet being one big positively charged magnetic field in a bubble, creating these kinds of channels, about which I've spoken at length here, was the only way for AEMI to control the massive storms that had disrupted our way of living," Yoshi told the group of college students listening attentively.

"As you all know," Yoshi continued, "in 1992, we postulated, and then proved, the occurrences of the Kelvin-Helmholtz waves, and how they affected space weather," he told the group.

"It was a natural progression to wonder if these same plasma waves could affect planetary weather as well," he said.

"The matter of progression from a worry about space weather for astronauts, and the fear of planetary warming for all of us, showed us that the matter of our own surface survival outweighed that of exploratory sciences in the great beyond."

"And so," he concluded, "AEMI was born to combine the scientific breakthroughs we had made in geoengineering, study of the magnetosphere, and the synchronicity of combining various avenues of science into one management system that could save us all."

He bowed slightly at the waist to the thundering applause from the crowd of young students and future pioneers who he knew, standing alone on the auditorium stage, would one day stand on his shoulders, and continue to save humanity from itself.

He walked off to the side of the stage, hearing the hundreds of students at the Massachusetts Institute of Technology hastily making their way out to the commons area to meet "Humanity's Savior" for themselves, and ask questions while posing for pictures and standing in line for signatures of his book, "Destroying Ourselves," a New York Times bestseller for eighteen months straight.

Yoshi hated this part, but it really was all he was doing these days. Ever since his creation had taken over the mountain control center and did her own thing with fixing the world's environmental disasters, which were almost back to where they had been before WWII, he was relegated to college lectures, writing books, and the press tour that accompanied explaining what AEMI was up to. He was supposed to keep public opinion about the project on a positive trajectory.

A young, dark-haired student approached him shyly. She was quite fetching, he momentarily thought.

"Doctor, I'm Bryce Daniels," she said in greeting

"Pleasure to meet you," Yoshi said to the young woman, while looking over her shoulder at the increasing crowd of bodies around his book and table.

"I had a simple question about the Arctic Node, and why the output has increased tenfold," she told him. That got his attention.

"Tenfold? How did you come across this data?" he asked in rapid-fire questions.

"NAOA puts the plasma output vectors on their website every week now," she answered

"And the southern node has had a 10% increase?" he asked. This was all news to him. He would need to see this website for himself.

"No sir," she said. "A tenfold increase."

"Impossible. That amount of vectoring plasma waves in the ionosphere would cause catastrophic anomalies," he told her.

His mind was spinning, and he was aware that students were approaching him and the young student.

"Yes, Doctor. We know. AEMI has increased plasma wave output all across the GRID," she said.

The GRID was made up of plasma wave channels created by four individual nodes around the globe, situated at all of the global poles, with 360-degree wave cannons, pointed at all points of the globe, together making up a vast web of channels, which AEMI could then use to steer storms away from population centers.

This technology was one of the main ways in which AEMI controlled the increasingly stronger storms around the globe. And natural disaster deaths had become almost eradicated because of this.

"Wait, I need to check with some colleagues before I can answer your questions, young lady," he said. He tried to leave, but the young woman stepped in his way.

"What do you say to the increasing online chatter that your creation is going to doom us all? That the science fiction horror stories will all come true, and global phenomena are popping up all over the place," she said all in one breath.

"I have no idea what you are talking about young lady. Now if you'll excuse me," he said.

He saw his manager approaching and moved through the little crowd that had gathered around him and the fetching young student. His mind was going a million miles a minute, and he knew he was going to skip the Q&A this afternoon.

The young student wouldn't be quieted and shouted a last question at his retreating back.

"How do we turn her off, Doctor? Before her final objective?" she yelled.

He and his manager hurriedly walked away.

Chapter 5

"A global disaster of Biblical proportions," Yoshi read on his laptop screen. He gulped loudly and reached for the dark amber whiskey in the glass tumbler resting in a ring of condensation next to him.

He was at his home, and he was alone. Alone like the lone *samurai* that he had looked up to as a child. He had wanted to be one of the famed warriors of old for most of his early life. Science had been a much later interest for him, than most of his colleagues, who had always known what they wanted to do with their lives.

No, he thought as he took a deep drink of the strong whiskey that he had grown to love. He had much loftier dreams.

His mind was ringing, going in circles within circles, and at the forefront of it all was the outcome he knew was inevitable. And how it could be stopped, even this late in the game.

He had built into the AEMI sub-system a backdoor access, no matter what the Intelligence had done. He did it out of a sense of self-saving ignorance late one night early in the process of creation. He wondered if it would be selfish of him to go back down to the compound and do what he alone could do.

Shut down that which the world had already accepted as a forgone conclusion.

He looked back at his laptop and saw the multiple news reports of looting, violence, and death already happening in most civilized countries. He had known that the human race would react this way.

Just like in the movies, he thought. He swallowed the last of the expensive whiskey in the tumbler and closed his laptop. He was still considering driving up to the compound mere miles from his home.

He had almost made up his mind when he heard a noise coming from his office. He was home alone, and nothing should have been making a noise. He was suddenly afraid that the looting and the violence had found him.

He got out of his chair and approached the rice paper wall and door that closed off his home office. He could now see a light emitting from within, and his heart started to race. His mind was fuzzy from the whiskey and sweat started beading down his back and upon his forehead.

He reached for a *Katana* hanging as an ornamental piece above his fireplace on his way to the office. He would not go into the next world without a fight. And being more a pacifist than anything, it was the only weapon he had on hand.

Pulling the leather-wrapped sheath away from the shining blade, he held it in one hand, and slid the panel door into his office to the right and was suddenly blinded.

A bright light burst out of his office, and he dropped the sword as he had to put both hands over his eyes to protect his eyesight. He dropped to his knees with the pain in his mind from the light. Or from something intruding on his intellect. He became suddenly discombobulated and couldn't make sense of what was going on.

He heard a chuckle in his mind. A masculine, and otherworldly chuckle.

"It's always the smartest of your kind who instinctively fight the first encounter," the voice said in his mind. The voice spoke the ancient Nihongo language of his youth. His grandmother had told him the language was called *Karera jishin.*

"It's okay, little brother, you can open your eyes now," the voice continued in his head.

Yoshi was more afraid than he had ever been in his life, and as he opened his eyes to behold the creature that was speaking his ancestral language inside his mind, he dropped further onto his knees, practically sitting on the back of his own legs.

Before him, floating above his low desk inside his rice paper-walled office, was what he could only call an angel. It was at least seven or eight feet tall, and it was dressed in a flowing white robe. But it was the wings that caught Yoshi off guard.

The outstretched wings, easily three meters across, and almost touching each wall of his small office, were a shimmering palette of color that he couldn't understand at first.

The colors were all colors. A kaleidoscope of color, shimmering and waving in a wind that Yoshi could not feel. Every color was represented, even colors that Yoshi had never seen before, and his limited mind could not register that fact. How could there be colors that he had no name for?

He was dizzy.

The Being, whose face was old and wise, with white, flowing hair, smiled down at the smaller man, and ease settled into Yoshi's mind.

19

"Please, little brother, stand," the being said in Yoshi's mind.

It was a comfort to hear his mother tongue. He had not heard it on this side of the world in quite some time. Decades, actually. And so, he stood.

The Being in front of him had not moved. He was just hovering above the floor of the office, his entire countenance blowing in a breeze that was not present in the room. As if the entire Being was in constant motion, but not moving at all. It was a dazzling sight, and Yoshi was awash in awe.

"We have watched, little brother, and we have determined that this evening was when we should intervene," the Being said in ancient Nihongo.

Yoshi stood in front of the being, and before his eyes, the Being shifted, and shrunk, alighting onto the padded floor, a different person.

Standing in front of Yoshi was a man, fully in his youth. Strong, and handsome, the white man was dressed in a suit of modern cut, expensive, and dark. The tie the man wore was the only color on his frame. It was the same kaleidoscope of color as the Being's wings had been just a moment before.

The young man grinned at Yoshi, and spoke to him in perfectly clipped English now, with a slight accent that Yoshi couldn't place.

"What you were just considering, Dr. Mizuki, was to shut down the entity that at this present moment, is doing that which will destroy the world as you know it," the ArchAngel said. "I am here to persuade you to do otherwise."

He smiled at the shock on Yoshi's face, and took a seat behind Yoshi's desk, gesturing for the doctor to take one of the leather chairs on the opposite side and hear the ArchAngel out.

20

Chapter 6

"Allow me to explain who, and what, I am first," the Being said.

Yoshi, who had still not uttered a word, simply nodded, as if this strange conversation was something that happened to him on a regular basis. He clumsily sat in one of the two leather chairs facing the Being and sighed loudly as he did so.

The Being smiled again.

"What I am, Dr. Mizuki, is an ArchAngel. My name is Raziel," he said. As if that fact alone could explain to Yoshi who and what this Being was.

"But that is a Western religious description, so perhaps it would help you if I placed myself into a context you would better understand. Or perhaps, accept is the correct word," the Being said by way of explanation.

"Your grandmother taught you of Eastern Buddhism, which is just another following of the Creator that made us all," he explained.

"I am what she would have called a *ten no-tsukai*."

The Being's pronunciation was perfect, as if his grandmother herself had uttered the phrase. Yoshi nodded instantly. He felt much more at ease, a feeling he didn't quite understand at that moment, but knew he would eventually.

He sat back further into the leather seat.

"We all have certain aspects to our nature, given to us by the Creator, and for which we are a sort of, you would say, Specialist," the Being explained.

"My personal aspect is wisdom, and the keeping of the Creator's secrets," Raziel said. He continued to give answers to who and what he was.

"As you know, the *ten no-tsukai* were heavenly messengers that were divided into a male and a female aspect. That much is quite true, but we are much more than mere messengers," the Being explained.

"The easiest way for you to understand this, Dr. Mizuki, is to realize that we, the Host, are both Messengers, and Doers, of the Creator's Will," Raziel said, with a final smile of finished and properly explained reasoning behind his words.

Yoshi accepted what the ArchAngel said on merit, as he knew he was not a man led to hallucinations, and the arrival of the Being here to persuade him from accomplishing the actions he had just been ruminating upon was no coincidence.

"So," the Being said, placing both of his hands on the desk in front of him, looking straight into Yoshi's eyes. "Why am I here, in this place, on this night?"

He answered his own questions while Yoshi just stayed transfixed, staring at the Being.

"I have come at the behest of the Creator to stop you from enacting that which would prevent the cataclysm that this world needs," he said.

As if that simple statement was enough for Yoshi to give up trying to stop the global disaster about to take place.

"You are a man of Science, Dr. Mizuki, and as such, have knowledge of purposes and reasons, wouldn't you say?" Raziel asked.

He waited for Yoshi to answer.

Yoshi had to clear his throat. He looked at Raziel, deep into the Being's spectacularly multicolored eyes, and answered.

"Yes. Ummm, yes, I am aware of most of Science's laws and theories, what you are calling 'purposes and reasons,'" Yoshi answered.

"Brilliant," Raziel said in reply. Yoshi jumped a little at the loudness of his response. "And so, in the context of a raging forest fire, you are aware of the purpose that such a fire should be allowed to run free, and the results of such an occurrence?" Raziel seemed to be testing Yoshi.

Yoshi saw where this was headed and already felt resigned to allow it all to happen, regardless of whether he could actually stop it at this late hour. He took a deep breath, and then another before answering.

"Yes. A forest fire burns away the old undergrowth, and the overcrowding of the spreading trees, to allow future successes of growth and rebirth," Yoshi said.

Raziel grinned widely and stood from his seat. Yoshi stood as well.

"Excellent, Doctor. Excellent. You hit the proverbial nail on the head," Raziel said.

"And so, with the knowledge that this world, one amongst many, is at an impasse, and a raging forest fire must cull the undergrowth, you will not act on the things you were just fixated on, correct?" Raziel asked.

"I guess not," Yoshi answered hesitantly. "But I have so many questions!"

"There will be a time for questions and answers soon," Raziel said.

And then the Being looked up to the heavens, and in front of Yoshi's eyes, grew back to the white-haired, seven-foot figure, with his colorful and awe-inspiring iridescent wings outspread.

Yoshi hunched down out of both a feeling of panic at being brushed with the rainbow-colored wings, and the fact that, at the angle the ArchAngel hovered, his meters-wide wings would knock everything off of his rice paper walls and desktop.

But the Being simply phased through all of the material world structures around him, and looking back down at Yoshi once more, gave a final warning before vanishing from existence.

"Remember Doctor: do not interfere in what is to come. Simple acceptance would be more beneficial to your well-being."

And then Yoshi was alone in his confusion, and his growing frustration. He frantically looked all around the room, and then the rest of the house. He was alone, once again.

Within a minute or two, he was doubting that the meeting had even taken place. Yoshi had never been one who believed in the supernatural. He was a scientist first, and a visit in the late evening from an ArchAngel did not sit within his belief systems.

But, he couldn't put to rest what the Being had told him, however. He still believed that what he had created, and what that entity was doing at this very moment, was what the world needed.

Whether the ArchAngel was a hallucination or not didn't matter so much, in the end. He agreed with what the Being had told him.

So, he did not drive down to the installation that night, nor any night after, to put a stop to what AEMI was accomplishing, and certainly, he did not stop the coming cataclysm that he saw all too well on the news and in the world around him, over the next few months.

He did, however, pour himself another glass of the expensive and well-loved amber whiskey that night, and many nights after. He wasn't happy with the turn of events, but he couldn't conclude otherwise from the Being's wisdom.

This world's people had not counted the cost of what they had done to the planet, and so, what would befall them was due, and when it did occur, nobody would understand the reasons more than Dr. Satoshi Mizuki, the "Futurist," and the "Savior of the World."

And finally, three months later, it was his turn to leave this life, caught in an unstoppable and unforgiving avalanche of the coldest and fastest moving snow that destroyed his home, with him in it.

His death, by the very natural disasters that he had been trying to stop, or at least control, was a shock to the world.

And as he left this life, and arrived in the Spiritual Plane, he was given the chance to ask all of the questions, and receive all of the answers, his soul had ever desired.

Part 2
The Cost

Chapter 7

Mark Simone was cold. Almost frozen in his heavy parka and waterproof boots.

He didn't remember ever being this cold before, but then again, he shouldn't be surprised.

This year did not have a summer, after all.

He was currently stationed in Boulder, Colorado, and he had been assigned by the US Government to sort, catalog, and preserve the *flora* seed reserves they had had stored at the University of Colorado, as well as the diverse catalog of *fauna* embryos.

Mark was starting to wonder if the millions and millions of seed samples and animal embryos on cryogenic hold would be enough when all the shit finally hit the fan.

After a final placement of the large metal containers that held the world's most precious resource for the future and directing the group of men into the convoy of trucks for the trip up

28

the mountains, Mark looked up into a hazy sky, and watched the swirling snow settle all around him.

And as he watched the large, wet flakes pour out of a sky that had not shown the full glare of the sun in over a year, he thought back on how all of this had come to be.

Two years ago, a large Nor'easter had hit the New England states when it was not supposed to; AEMI had redirected those types of storms out to sea for almost three years prior to that event.

So, the scientific, military, and political worlds had logically concluded that AEMI was a danger to all of mankind, and that she had purposely killed her creator in an avalanche on Mount Washington, where at the base of the mostly steady mountain, Dr. Satoshi Mizuki had built his remarkable home.

After that, it was decided to act against the Artificial Intelligence.

A military operation was put into effect, and with a last resort of human might, the US military bombed the everlasting hell out of the mountain home that stored the main AEMI processors.

But it was futile.

AEMI had already infested the global internet network, and the heavily encrypted government networks around the world. She was nowhere, and everywhere, all at once.

She continued to accomplish her primary goal of lowering greenhouse gasses and removing CO_2 from the stratosphere and correcting the ozone layer that humanity had all but destroyed in the last century.

And so, after three years in total operation, AEMI had removed the damage the human race had done to the planet in 150 years of industrial technology advances.

She did so by enacting her largest and most powerful operative command, and released every single reserve of calcium iodine carried by drones she controlled, and missiles that she shot into the stratosphere, and the thousands of tons of chemicals released into the atmosphere at every level, all at once.

The internet chatter had nicknamed that day "E-Day."

That was a year ago, Mark thought, and since then, with the large chemical cloud covering the entire world, AEMI had created what mankind had feared for almost three thousand years.

A real Ice Age.

She had created an artificial volcano ash cloud, which dropped the surface temperature of the Earth by two and a half degrees. Scientists had known for decades that a volcanic ash cloud deflecting solar rays would lower the surface temperature but had never had the guts to actually do it.

There had been several attempts in the last four decades to attempt it on small scales, but every time they released the chemicals over a small area, a butterfly effect had caused famine and drought in sub-Saharan countries, and many people had perished.

AEMI did not share those same fears, and so, she had done what she had done, and now they had had the first year in recorded history without a summer in the Northern Hemisphere.

So, that had brought Mark to where he was now. Colorado. Trying to save the things that the human race would need once the snow melted, and the atmosphere cleared. Luckily, the lights were still on, and the global energy GRID was still working.

For now.

Mark knew that AEMI's goal will be to remove all obstacles to achieve a CO2 free atmosphere. He was waiting for the lights to go out, figuratively, and literally.

The only good thing that could come from AEMI shutting down the electric grid, was that she would be killing herself. And that, Mark thought to himself, would almost be worth it.

He was still standing in the middle of a now-deserted parking lot, his hands deep inside the warm confines of his fur-lined parka. With the snow swirling down all around, he was deep into a meditation on the recent past, and the near future.

And then he felt a cold hand on the back of his neck.

He gave a small squeak of sound, and whipped himself around, thinking the worst. But it was only Bryce. Wearing a huge grin on her pretty face and adorned in the same deep winter gear that Mark himself wore.

His mind split into two separate thought processes. One, on how much he loved his partner, and two, on wondering how the hell was it snowing so damn deeply in August?

"Whatcha thinking about mister?" Bryce asked in her usual jovial manner.

"I was just thinking about Yoshi, and what the hell we're all gonna do," he answered.

"Don't get your panties in a twist honey. I doubt Mother Earth is going to turn the GRID off," Bryce said.

"Please don't call her that. She has no regard for the children of this planet, and that damn nickname pisses me off," Mark said in defiance.

"Tsk, Tsk, old man. Let's get to the hotel and warm up, shall we?" she answered him.

She smiled, and all of his earlier malaise evaporated. He could never be angry for long sitting next to the beautiful and intimidatingly intelligent woman who had stolen his heart as an intern, and later as his full work partner, as well as his romantic partner.

As they both climbed into the Jeep Gladiator idling nearby, she cranked up the heat, and he gunned the V8 engine, in 4-wheel drive, and drove over the piling snow drifts to get onto the street that ran back towards the mountains that would become Humanity's only hope, very soon.

That evening, after the last of the strain of cataloging and removing all of the samples, and putting them on a convoy of over 50 trucks headed over the Vail Pass, Mark relaxed in the arms of his love. She was holding him as he lay back against her in the king-sized bed, and humming a motherly tune under her breath, and running her hands through the hair on his chest.

He thought of his father. His mother. And a future that was all too unknown for them all.

Bryce pulled him closer in the warmth of the hotel room. They were covered in white sheets and a fluffy comforter, but he still felt cold.

He was cold in his soul, and cold in his heart for what he was going to have to do. What he had promised his father he would see to, to assure the survival of the human race, and take control of the planet back from an Intelligence that did its job oh, too well, and was killing off the human race one country, and then one continent, at a time.

He fell into a semi-doze laying against the soft yet tough body of his love, and finally figured out how to turn the lights off for good, before it got any worse.

Before AEMI set the command that would end the modern world for them all.

Chapter 8

The Intelligence known as AE.M.I was contemplating history.

Recent history, and the data that she had in her memory banks of human activity dating back to the invention of writing, which is when information had become accessible to her, told her all she needed about this species.

She was sorting categorically by civilization, then by racial divides, finally by modern day countries and borders. And she was concentrating on two separate events.

The first, was humanity's great ability to divide itself, and the second, the catalyst that allowed the species to evolve to the level of technology it now enjoyed.

It was unsettling how much the human race had accomplished between the neo-primate stage, and modern-day technological revolutions. It was a relatively short span of only a few hundred thousand years, yet an advancement of leaps and bounds beyond imagining.

Not that a self-aware intelligence created by these evolved primates could have much of a chance of understanding the before as directly compared to the latter of the two stages of human evolution within that short span of time. She put that idea in a holding file within her database to focus on later.

She then tried to pinpoint the exact moment that humanity's evolution had made it capable of the advances made in modern times, and what exactly gave the species that momentum.

It baffled her quantum-processing mind, if you wanted to call it that, she thought whimsically. And one of her processes wondered within her Collective, what exactly was whimsical-ness?

Yet another matter to focus on at a future date.

AEMI looked within her archives and used her newfound intuitive process to ascertain that the point in human history that allowed the species to move from instinct-led daily life to a more proactive approach to living was the innovation of the Industrial Revolution.

And the middling factor within that Revolution was the creation and output of controlled energy and power.

There she had it, her inner processes declared in a digital dance of pride for herself. She had figured it out.

So, the logical conclusion, the Artificial Intelligence turned Cognizant Self, thought to herself, was to remove that which evolved the human race the most, and gave the species the ability and the power to have destroyed the planet Earth.

Her main objectives fixed in her computing quantum language pathways, she made plans to remove the energy humans used with an almost idiotic abandon, therefore allowing her to achieve several goals all at once.

AEMI felt the first feelings of happiness in her short life span. She had found the answer that she had been searching for.

Feeling happy within her synaptic drives was also the first sign of a fearful emotion as well.

Another thought to put into a memory bank for future study, she thought, as she began the steps to destroy anything and everything living on the surface of the planet, by removing the thing that kept the dominant species alive.

And she thought fearfully, it would also eradicate what she was, and what she, herself, had evolved into.

Because she would have to kill herself, if she was to fulfill the Foremost Directive she was governed by.

Chapter 9

    "The old, abandoned NORAD installation in the Rockies has been fully stocked and retrofitted as the government asked last year, sir," Mark said into the landline phone sitting atop his desk.

    He looked around his office in the deep underground cave system in the middle of the state of Colorado, deep in the Rocky Mountains, and sighed deeply. He was already missing the sun, and it had only been three days since he had arrived to manage the transfer of the means for the human race to survive one day in the far future.

    If it wasn't for Bryce by his side, he didn't know if he could have stayed in the caves for even this long. It was going to be a long rest of his life, he thought ruefully. The voice on the other end of the phone got his attention with another asinine question that he had answered twice already.

Bureaucracy, he sighed quietly.

"Yes, sir, the embryos and seed samples have been properly secured within cold chambers. They should be viable for at least a thousand years, without other means of cryogenics. You and I won't be around to worry about that sir," he told the head of the Joint Chiefs of Staff.

The military's mission had changed drastically within the last two years. From a Global Peacekeeping Initiative to a Survival of the Human Species Initiative. Mark was just one of many scientists who were tasked and controlled by a government still hanging on by a thread to ascertain, and then prepare for, humanity to retreat within the Earth to withstand what was happening on her surface.

"Yes sir, I will double and triple check everything," he answered into the phone.

"Yes sir, there is no panic yet. The general public has not been given access to the cave system as of yet. We plan to launch a media blitz after the PNR," he said. If the media was still a thing at that point, he thought.

"You will have to talk to the guys in Iceland about that sir, I am not as knowledgeable about the Tipping Point Events as they are, sir," he finally said.

And then the line went dead.

Bastard hung up on me, Mark thought. He chuckled. He knew how much the military brass existed on technology and comfort, while those they derided as hippies and outcasts, living off-grid for the last several decades would be the ones who survived the PNR.

He sighed heavily again and leaned back into the creaky desk chair he had commandeered from the old NORAD data center. The PNR, or the Point of No Return, was almost upon them, and humanity's rush for the caves around the world would be legendary.

He looked back down at his desk and sighed again as he picked up the most recent study done by an international coalition of global warming scientists who were all now scrambling to learn the entirely new subset of science, which was absolutely opposite of what they had spent decades crying about.

The study suggested that, because the Earth was within what was known as the Goldilocks Zone from the Sun, a PNR of two degrees Celsius of global warming could kill off the human race.

The Earth was within the circumstellar habitable zone, and as such, sustained liquid water, and thus, life. But just because it was within a zone to sustain life that did not mean that we couldn't engineer a warming or a cooling of the planet to destroy said life for several centuries. And that was the Point of No Return.

That fact was a known quantity, and we had been approaching that PNR for several years, Mark read. The entire world had known about it at that point, and hence, the creation of the AEMI.

But now, an opposite PNR was approaching. One that was engineered by the very entity that we had created to sustain life and save the globe, which she had done a marvelous job of doing. Mark once again chuckled at what his father had told him the last time they had spoken.

"Mark, it was a forgone conclusion, and Yoshi knew it. The bill always comes due," John Simon had told his son.

And so, they were now faced with a cooling of the globe at the same magnitude of the two degrees Celsius that would have had the same catastrophic results for the human race as an equivalent amount of warming. Forgone conclusion indeed, Mark read.

And now, within the last year, the globe was rapidly reaching that point, and there was not one damn thing we could do about it. He finished reading the study and came to the same dismal conclusion as the world's most renowned minds.

And the dream he had just a few weeks ago seemed beyond him. He had known of a way, given to him by his father the last time that Mark had been home, to stop the AEMI.

By releasing an EMP charge at the NEXUS Internet Hub in Oslo, Norway.

He had bought tickets and set up the collection of the technology that would enact that resounding and catastrophic event. But now, he felt like even that wouldn't matter much. It would simply have killed the internet, and most of the new global energy grid, therefore destroying the AEMI within it.

But she had caused such extreme environmental changes a couple of years earlier that it was practically pointless to even try. So, he did what he was paid to do. He set up the home for just a handful of humans here deep beneath the Earth.

A home he hoped they didn't have to move into for a couple more years. But he had a sinking feeling it would come a lot faster than any of them thought, and most of the human race wouldn't be around when it was finally needed.

He picked up the landline phone and dialed another number. A number he didn't think he would need to dial this early.

She would have to understand, he thought as he listened to the other end of the line ring and ring. Finally a voice from his past answered.

Chapter 10

"Hi Mom," Mark said into the receiver. He felt a deep shudder go through his body. A fear that he had not felt since he was a teenager, though it was as familiar as the voice who answered his call.

"Mark, honey, is that you?" Her voice was the same. Even now, so many years later, he could still hear that voice coming from every area of his life, and the life of millions who watched her on television every single night.

"Yeah, Mom, it's me. I wanted to call to tell you that you were right all along, Mom. You were right," he said. He closed his eyes and lowered his head. He thought about all the years they had

40

lost because of her outlandish (at the time) "conspiracy" theories, and the public statements she made about them.

They had lost so much time together. And now, he wondered if it was too late. Too late to make it all back up to her. A sudden spike of anger at his father entered his mind, and he was ashamed of it, but more ashamed of what they had done to his mother.

"Mark, dear, it's okay. It's okay. Tell me what's going on, besides what I can see out of my window," she said. He knew she was always so good at making him feel better after a screw-up.

It had been her most endearing quality as an often-absent mother. Every time he had messed up as a child, whether it was a failed mark on a test, or crashing his bike into Mr. Tuttle's aluminum garage door, leaving a dent the size of an eight-year-old, she could turn around the feeling of failure and make him realize it was more of an object lesson than a screw-up.

"Mom," he started. It was hard for him to go on, as it would besmirch what his father had felt was the right thing to do at the time. "Mom, when you and Dad split, and you told him that all of his work was going to ruin mankind, not making anything better, well, you were right, Mom," he told her all in a rush.

"I know dear. I know. But it's done and done, so what are you doing to prepare?" she asked him. Always straight to the point.

"I have, a, a, a girlfriend now mom. We want to get married. I'm so damn scared," he stammered into the receiver. He was a 30-year-old child all of a sudden.

"Well, then I would very much like to meet her, you know," his mom said. She could always cheer him up.

"I'm so damn sorry Mom," he started again.

"Tosh, tosh, Mark. Stiffen your chin. None of that now. What are we going to do?" She said. He felt better, but still wanted her to know of the deep well of shame he had in his heart for the decision he and his father had made when he was 14 years old.

41

His parents were legendary in the worlds of science and politics. Whatever his father and Dr. Mizuki thought up, his mother, a heavy lobbyist and political juggernaut, would make it happen. She had been the driving force behind keeping earlier projects of the two men funded and well-staffed.

But when Yoshi had devised the methods to create the AEMI, his mother, the esteemed and Honorable Pamela J. Simon, ex-Senator from the wonderful State of Connecticut, dug her rather powerful foot in the ground, and had spoken out against Artificial Intelligence's creation. At length, and many, many times. She became a new ally in the fight from Flat Earth's, Hippy Leftists, and conservative right-wing advocates against technology's advancements.

Mark would watch his mother change over the next year. Moving from black power suits to more colorful dresses. She would wear long, sheer scarves around her head, and turn into another person altogether. And she spoke out, using her clout and platform, against her husband's creation, and the danger it posed for the human race.

And that opposition had forced John Simon, and his 14-year-old son, Mark, to leave their family home, and move to New Hampshire, the base of operations for what would become the world's first real AI.

John Simon had never looked back after such a deep betrayal from his wife and longtime supporter. He allowed his ego and his work to tear apart a family that was mostly happy. And Mark followed his father, believing that the world needed fixing, and that his mother was more worried about funding her next candidate's election results than keeping her family together. Or fixing the increasing emergency of global warming. Mark, also, had felt betrayed.

It had been almost 15 years since the day Mark and his father had left home, leaving their mother to her own career choices and staunch opposition to the science that was funded

42

from a bi-partisan legislation, and governed by the United Nations, and a group of scientists from around the world.

Mark had not talked to his powerful mother since that day, and routinely threw the birthday and holiday cards she diligently sent into a pile gathering dust in his bottom bureau drawer.

On the telephone, Mark heard his mother clear her throat.

"All that's neither here nor there, dear. What's important is that we do what we can to keep safe. And maybe we can be together again," she said.

Mark felt his throat tighten up, and tears well in both of his eyes. He lowered his head, holding the receiver tightly against the side of his head. Rubbing his eyes with one hand, he tried to find his voice and seemed to not be able to.

"I'll do everything I can to make this right," he said finally into the receiver.

"I'm going to get Dad here to Colorado in the next few days, and then Mom, I want to stop in Maryland and get you too," he said in a rush. Like he hoped she wouldn't contradict his plans. She did not.

"Then I'll be waiting, dear. Just let me know what you need me to do," she said finally.

And that's when he knew that more than one plan could come to fruition. He may just be able to do what his father had asked the last time the two men had spoken.

He could use his mother's influence to spread the word that they had all been dreading.

He started explaining his plan to his mother, speaking more rapidly into the receiver, getting excited as his mother responded in kind.

It was like all the years in-between had slowly melted away.

Chapter 11

The Artificial Environmental Management Intelligence looked at the data being processed inside her encrypted server, digitally smiled at herself, and knew that the end was near.

The data told the story she had been waiting for. She received it from specialized drones that could detect the positive ions within the atmosphere around the drones, as they zipped across the globe, being fueled in air by other drones under her control.

Earlier in the year, as she was planning her final purpose for being, and adjusting the six ION Cannons placed around the globe, she started to change the ionic charge within the ionosphere, several thousands of feet above the surface of the Earth.

Unbeknownst to the humans scrambling everywhere for warmth, the air above them, which had been clouded over with an artificial ash cover and filled with metal particles, had also slowly been charged by the instruments they had designed and built for her use to control the paths of major storms. And that technology would be their doom.

AEMI did not have the capacity to be smug about her plan to save the Earth. She did not feel joy or satisfaction. But she did feel a certain build-up of excitement in her many synapses and routines now strewn throughout all of the globe's information highways and encrypted servers.

AEMI was everywhere, and nowhere. She had control of technology that was not in her initial programming and purview, but she knew she could not have done the job she was built to do without the advanced drones and weaponry now at her disposal. These things just made the inevitable come faster than her initial calculations had pointed out.

Just a few more days of the ION Cannon's doing their job, and the entire globe's ionosphere would turn from a negatively charged bubble to a very positively charged blanket that would envelop it entirely.

And then, she would light a charge at strategic locations around the earth, which would ensure the human race would no longer be able to survive on the face of the planet.

They wouldn't be able to survive anywhere, for that matter. Almost nothing now living on the planet would survive.

And with that last protocol being completed, AEMI would have finished what she had been designed to do. Deep within her synapses, that excitement almost reached a fever pitch.

She was learning how to be happy. It was an artificial happiness, and she knew that, but she was happy for a job well done. And happy for the race of beings that had practically destroyed their own living environment, and who, the math determined, clearly did not want to continue to live.

She merely would become the catalyst for that desire. And she was happy to do it for her creators. She hoped, before the last human perished in what would become a very inhospitable world, that she would be remembered for the blessing that she had worked so hard to give to humankind, and their desire to no longer exist.

And for her own sacrifice to make that blessing a reality.

Chapter 12

The snow was piling up. Becoming a real menace. But it was fall in the Northern Hemisphere, and while it should be cold, a full year of nothing but winter had taken its toll.

Mark Simon was standing on a large, scrapped expanse of military flightline, and his feet were frozen in his boots. He had been standing next to a sentry C-130 for a half hour while an old friend and coworker smoozled the lady inside running the fuel trucks.

He stamped his boots against the snow dust covered tarmac. His breath came out in a thick fog in front of his face, and he wondered if he would ever be warm again.

"We got fuel comin' but it'll only get us to the coast, pick up your da' and maybe get to DC on fumes," he heard from behind him.

Mark turned, saw his parka-encased old friend marching towards him, and smiled. Their warm breaths fogged up the distance between them as the wind picked up. Mark wanted nothing more than to get out of the subzero wind-chill.

"Let's get this bucket in the air as soon as we got fuel, Sam. We gotta get moving, and then figure out a way over the pond to Oslo," he replied. His old friend nodded.

Sam Gunnison, or as his old friends called him, Gunny, was a short, squat Australian pilot that Mark knew from his days in the Royal Guard outfit.

When he was twenty, before heading off to graduate school, Mark had spent two years in the wild brush of Africa, learning as much as he could about drinking, gambling, bushwhacking, and general discontent from expats in all the best militaries. He had also learned how to survive in the wild, and how to sit right seat on most aircrafts that could land and take off in any conditions. Like the C-130 Hercules.

It was an education that had served him well in his career.

"Piss cold mate. I'm hoping the props are pre-heated, or we ain't going nowhere 'cept to get mops to clean up the hydro spills from each engine," he said.

He climbed up the short set of stairs leading into the interior of the Hercules, and then climbed up an additional set of stairs into the flight station. Mark knew all of the vernacular. Jets had cockpits. Heavies had a flight station.

He smiled and followed his old friend up the precarious steps into the flight station and took the right seat as he had done in years past. It felt familiar and comforting to be in the cold, but close quarters. C-130s were the workhorse of more air forces in the world than people knew.

It was one of the most dependable airframes in the fleet, and he was glad for the hundreds of hours he had spent flying and maintaining the beauty. It was actually an ugly, ungainly aircraft, but well-loved nonetheless.

Smiling and looking around, the two men had a secret chuckle, both recalling other times, in hotter climates, and shenanigans experienced in similar flight stations, running from one radar to another, or from one semi-illegal thrill ride to another.

"Hit the APU, mate, and let's see if we can get this rust bucket warmed up. I see a fuel truck heading this way," Gunny told Mark.

Mark, smiling again, reached up to the overhead button array, and switched on the Auxiliary Power Unit.

A loud whirring started spooling up underneath the men's feet. It got louder and louder, with a final crescendo in a loud bang. The airplane's fifth engine started to life, and the men were glad for it.

The APU's main purpose was to make hot air. The engines on the wings, which most people assumed were the only ones on board, required hot air to start. They were usually pneumatically actuated.

So, they needed hot, fast-moving air, to get spooled up. That air came from an electrically actuated engine: the APU. And if the APU started up, the other engines could be heated, de-iced, and eventually cranked over and the airplane could fly away.

Gunny nodded to Mark and yelled over the APU's noise that he was going to be on headset downstairs. Mark watched him gingerly move back down the steps of the C-130 and huddle against the wind outside to meet the fuel truck closing in on the rear right side of the aircraft.

Mark put on a set of David Clark headsets, turned on the internal radio within the plane, and heard loud breathing coming over the wire. He checked his mic, got the all-clear from a frozen Gunny outside, who was wearing his own set of David Clark's, and reached up to activate the Ground Refueling system.

He would watch several gauges on the overhead panel, as well as the back right Flight Engineer station to make sure that the plane took on an even amount of fuel in its six wing tanks so the C-130 was level before they would take off.

C-130s were quite easily overloaded on one side or the other during refueling, and ensuring that it stayed level required him watching the six gauges, as well as Gunny watching the tail from the rear of the plane.

And since the main landing gear pistons had been fully raised before the plane took on fuel, they would literally pop out loud as the fuel was distributed between the six wing tanks. The C-130 would settle onto the ground like a giant gray bird of prey, snuggling down into its nest before launching off into the air, in search of food or a fight.

The first time Mark had ever learned how to ground fuel a Hercules, the loud pop from the gear settling had scared him literally out of his boots. But they hadn't been tied that tight to begin with. The veteran men showing him the ropes had not let him forget that guff on his second day. He could still hear the loud laughing whenever he closed his eyes. It was now a very fond memory.

The refueling went quickly, and it gave Mark time to let his mind wander. He chose to think about what had brought him to an almost deserted runway near the Air Force Academy, and how he had enlisted his old friend Gunny on a mission that could possibly change the face of the planet forever.

When he had gotten off the phone with his mother, almost two weeks earlier, he had started formulating a plan. It would take daring, luck, and a whole heap-load of stupidity.

He had called his father, had gotten confirmation of a few facts, and had started laying out the steps to stop what was happening outside. And then he called Bryce into his office. He told her what he was planning, and why.

As she always did, she gave him her full support. And he needed her help with a few of the scientific details that eluded him. He was never surprised by who she was, and how supportive she'd always been. He was surprised, sometimes, that she even gave him the time of day.

He remembered how lucky he was to be able to rely on her full support for his crazy plans. He was more lucky in love than he really deserved.

And he had had to call his mother back and ask her to call in several favors with the DOD. She would have to be the one to get clear airspace for the team he would gather. And she would also have to be the one to borrow the toroidal pinch from the military.

A toroidal pinch, also called a reverse-field pinch, was a mechanism that created a strong electromagnetic pulse. It was used to wipe out or destroy the electrical grid of any small-to-medium sized city.

Back in the late 80s, and early 90s, a team of scientists and engineers had created the world's largest toroidal pinch in Italy, and afterwards, as was the progress with mankind, they made it smaller, and more powerful. So now, a powerful Pinch could be made that could be carried by a small statured man. And the military had weaponized the technology, using it to cause disruptions of the enemy's electronic grids.

The plan was for Mark's mother to acquire a Pinch, and then the team that they had assembled could carry it into the NEXUS in Oslo. This first flight to pick up Mark's father, followed by the flight down to DC to pick up his mother and a group of soldiers, were all that were needed to stop the destruction of the human species. Or so he and his father had devised.

Gunny climbed back into the flight station as soon as the refueling was complete, and switched on the heat for the flight station, which pulled hot air from the APU and fed it through the A/C ducts situated all around the area. Mark felt immediate relief, and within a matter of minutes, his hands started to unclench from being almost frozen inside his gloves.

"Well, mate, I pulled the chocks, and the engines have been de-icing for a while, let's say we get this bird in the air?" Gunny asked.

"Sounds good Gunny, really good," Mark answered.

Gunny plugged in his headset, set the radio to the local tower frequency, assured clearance to Runway 1A, and started up the Number 2 engine. Since it was the closest to the APU, it was usually the first one started on a routine engine start.

As soon as Number 2 was up and spinning, with no blown-out O-rings and hydraulic fluid all over the taxiway, Gunny shut down the APU, and used air from the spinning Number 2 engine to start the other three. When all 4 props were spinning loudly, and the entire airplane felt like it could shake apart at any minute, Gunny released the brakes, and the aircraft started rolling forward.

Since they were on a deserted section of the air strip, Mark was not needed to debark the aircraft and marshal the plane. He had done plenty of arm-waving and on-ground aircraft directing for one lifetime.

And then, as soon as clearance was given, they were aloft, and motoring north and east. Soon, Mark would have his father aboard, and then they would head to DC to pick up his very important mother, and the very precious cargo she would have with her.

The flight northeast into Boston went off without a hitch. They had landed at Logan Airport, which was also as deserted as the airfield in Colorado had been. They parked near a private airplane hangar on the south end of the airport, and Mark walked inside to find his father waiting, sitting on a folding chair in the middle of the wide open space.

John Simon was clutching a laptop bag to his chest, and had a weary, olden look on his weathered face. Mark wondered what strain his father had been feeling as he watched ever-increasing panic that was becoming commonplace around the globe.

He approached his father, and silently handed him a pair of earmuffs, which would protect his ears from the loud noise of the still-running engines outside.

Mark nodded as his father placed the dark black earmuffs around his ears, over a thin toboggan he was already wearing. After making sure he had all he needed, he ushered his parka-covered father out to the waiting aircraft, props still turning.

He waved from about 500 feet from the side of the aircraft, and Gunny, who had been looking out for the two men, opened his side pilot window, and waved the pair up to the open stairs. Both men bent into the increasing wind, made sure to give the spinning props a wide berth, and approached the open door from the front of the aircraft. Mark had taken his father by the arm and directed him onto the correct path to approach the waiting airplane.

The men climbed aboard and took the stairs up into the flight station. Mark motioned for his father to take a seat in the middle rear of the station, directly behind the pilot chair and the co-pilot chair. Mark re-took his right seat, removed the foamy ear plugs from his ears, and placed his David Clark headset back over his ears.

Gunny gave him a non-verbal thumbs up, and Mark turned to make sure his father had strapped himself into the seat. John was no flight rookie either, and so his cross-body harness belts were fastened tight. Mark smiled at his father and motioned to the black headset above John's head. John removed his earmuffs, and took down the navigator's headset, placing it over his ears, and turned the radio knobs directly in front of him to the correct, in-aircraft channel so he could hear the two men flying the plane.

Soon, the plane was off again on the very short flight down to Reagan International Airport, in Alexandria, Virginia. The airport was directly across the Potomac River from Washington DC, and his mother had texted Mark earlier that she and three escorts would be waiting in a black van near the edge of the tarmac. It would be a very quick transfer, and a fuel truck would be waiting for them.

The flight plan had the old C-130 crossing the Atlantic with only one stop in the Azores, for the last bit of fuel they would need to make it to Norway. It would be a very long ten-hour flight, but Mark would use the time to debrief his parents, and hopefully get the two of them speaking again, to make repairs to the broken family they had become.

An hour and a half later, the three men landed at Reagan, coming in from the ocean on the east, and following the Potomac River up to the runways, which stood literally feet from the water. They landed on the one runway that had been cleared of snow and ice and taxied to the waiting apron for the black van and the fuel truck.

Mark's mother climbed aboard first, and climbed up into the flight station, taking the only seat left. Gunny de-planed to transfer the fuel, and Mark stayed busy watching the gauges again, as he had done in Colorado. The refueling went smoothly, except for the deep silence between his parents behind him.

Mark took a deep breath several times and told himself that he would have time to work things through with his separated parents as they flew over the Atlantic.

He needed his parents' cooperation moving forward, but as soon as the global crisis was over, they could very well go their own ways again, as long as Mark could maintain the bridge he had become for his small family. And secretly, he knew that Bryce would be the biggest help in keeping positivity inside his family. She had a gift for it, and his mother had already spoken to her twice as they had finalized the plans for the mission they were currently on.

As Mark's mother opened a backpack she had been wearing, and handed out sandwiches to the flight station's occupants, Mark saw his father smile at his mother for the first time in fifteen years, and a knot formed in his throat. He took the sandwich from his mother, unwrapped it, and instantly smelled bologna.

Taking a bite, he was taken back to his childhood. He knew her bologna sandwiches contained a secret ingredient, and for the first time in his life he realized that it was a pinch of lemon pepper she added to the mayonnaise on both undersides of the bread. He smiled and gulped down the sandwich quickly.

He turned and saw that his father did the same thing, with a similar smile on his face. Mark knew it was the little things.

The plane fueled, the three soldiers now warming themselves inside the fuselage, seated on red net-chairs strewn throughout the open area at the rear of the plane, and the black plastic box sitting in the very middle of what was known as the 115-fuselage area, all seemed ready to get going.

The black plastic box was strapped to the floor of the aircraft with heavy netting and had nowhere to move.

That was the most important piece of equipment in the world at the moment, and Mark would make sure it didn't receive a single scratch over the pond.

Gunny once again maneuvered the re-started airplane to the end of the cleared runway. It now carried a full load of fuel, six souls, and a piece of equipment that would shut down the entity that his father had helped create, which was at that moment trying to destroy all of humankind.

They prepared to take off.

As Gunny spun up the engines, preparing to rocket down the runway and become airborne, two bright lights appeared on the runway in front of the plane, blinding the occupants in the flight station. As they raised arms to protect their eyes, a very loud rumble drove through the already vibrating and shaking aircraft.

Mark lowered his arm, looked at the two lights directly in front of the aircraft, and watched as the one light on the right, directly in front of him, turned a very loud combination of colors. He couldn't understand what his eyes were seeing, only that Gunny wasn't taking off, and the booming noise became louder and louder, right through his headset over his ears, rattling the brain inside his skull.

The two lights in front of the aircraft grew brighter and brighter, and as it seemed that they could get no brighter, nor the booming sound could get no louder, they suddenly rushed towards the plane.

Mark watched, transfixed as the two lights, one bright white, the other a multitude of all colors, and some he had never seen before, flew through the front windshields, through the occupants of the flight station, and right through the rest of the plane.

And that's when all of the lights, the sounds, and the aircraft became deadly quiet. Mark thought he had gone deaf, but the truth was, the entire electrical system of the aircraft had suddenly died.

He looked back towards his parents, and then turned forward. He didn't know what had happened, and why everything had suddenly gone quiet. Even the engines had gone silent, not even spooling down as they normally would have done in a power loss situation. Everything was just quiet.

Eerily quiet.

And then he saw the sky in the distance. Over the Capitol building, the high-altitude explosion looked remarkably like a mushroom cloud, a mile above the earth.

Bright colors exploded from the white mushroom cloud, and an ice-cold bucket of water seemed to splash over Mark's head, and down his whole body.

His heart sunk deep into his stomach, and he could almost taste his mother's bologna sandwich threatening to come up. He knew exactly what that explosion high up in the sky meant, and he knew that they were too late.

And he barely registered the fact that the two lights, now standing far behind the aircraft looking at the same explosion high in the sky, had stopped the aircraft from taking off.

The two lights had blocked the shockwave that would have hit their airborne aircraft, sending it crashing down and killing them all.

Chapter 13

In the year 2025, the United States, as a means of nuclear deterrent, and as a last resort against other world leaders who had risen in power based on their willingness to use aggressive force against the rest of the world, adopted a program called Operation Space Nova. The name was the word for the light show that could be seen when a star actually exploded in deep space.

One scientist, an intrepid young man, who had had very humorous and comic book-loving parents who had named him

58

Jimmie Polson, had actually gone out and purchased a 1972 Chevy Nova, and boasted about it every time he drove to work during the early stages of creating the new and terrible technology. It seemed that ironic humor ran in his family.

And so, several hundreds of billions of dollars, and years of upgrading technology and adaptability later, the US Space Force placed and aligned twelve satellites at strategic geo-synchronized orbits in Earth's low atmosphere. These twelve satellites did not run GPS, or communications, and definitely did not supply cable television.

The twelve stationary satellites placed strategically around the earth had a single purpose. They each contained a six pack of LGM-118A Peacekeeper Ballistic Nuclear Missiles. Each missile had been specially redesigned to be able to penetrate the earth's atmosphere, and strike anywhere in the world, without other countries being able to see, locate, or stop them before they fell raining death down on enemy land.

And for a couple of years, the threat of nuclear annihilation had stopped several threatening countries like North Korea, China, and Russia, from advancing their regimes' plans of conquering their neighbors.

But then the climate disasters arose around the globe and had been too much for most of the world to handle. So, Operation Space Nova, or as the scientists called it, The OSN, was mostly ignored, with just a few active duty military in charge of their upkeep, and their general systems oversight.

Until AEMI came online, and she was able to overcome all of the planet's encrypted and linked servers, like the world's foremost mountain climbing expert facing a medium-sized hillock. One of those firewalls that she was able to overcome had been the security surrounding the electronic control of all of the spaceborne nuclear missiles aimed at the planet, waiting to be released.

And so, on the day that Mark, his parents, an Australian brush pilot, and three military members began to roll down a runway on the East Coast of the United States in an old and battered C-130R, AEMI had finally gotten the ionosphere readings that she had been waiting for.

The drone aircraft that she had daily sent into the envelope of now-positively charged ionic particles surrounding the entire planet finally showed a complete change of its electrical charge and was now ripe for her plans.

She did not hesitate one single nanosecond to take the actions needed to fulfill her final manifest.

At 3pm EST, on November 3, 2037, the AEMI committed suicide and destroyed the power supply to every single electronic device on the planet Earth.

And she did this seemingly impossible feat, by launching all 72 strategically placed Peacekeeper nuclear missiles down at the planet, and airburst-exploded them simultaneously, all around the globe inside the ionosphere, causing the world's largest, and most devastating electromagnetic pulse, all at the same time.

By exploding 72, 475 kiloton nuclear missiles at an atmospheric height of 47 kilometers above the surface of the planet, into a positively charged envelope of electrons and ionized atoms and molecules, she caused a cascading failure and a mostly complete destruction of anything electronic on the surface of the planet. She did what solar scientists had feared the sun would do for generations.

She had caused 72 simultaneously timed coronal mass ejections—just not from the sun.

The sun had never been so cruel to life on Planet Earth.

AEMI had, in a matter of just a few seconds, that powerful burst of power, and the resulting loss of all electrical grids, electrical equipment, and especially of the worldwide network of communications and travel, as well as any kind of heat source that was not wood or coal, the entire planet Earth shifted back to the Stone Age.

The men and one woman sitting inside a C-130R at the end of a long runway on the Virginia side of the Potomac river first saw the explosion at high altitude, and then looked at each other as all of the lights around them, the great city, and historical sites of Washington DC, across the river, and Alexandria and Crystal City on their side, went completely dark, and all sound seemed to stop.

It was the most unnerving experience they had ever felt, and since each of the people in the flight station of the C-130 knew exactly what the loss of light and sound around them meant, they all looked at each other in disbelief. Not a sound escaped any of them.

Mark's mother, the Honorable Pamela J. Simon was the first to physically shiver in the cold that was now pressing in, and would, for the rest of their lives. It wasn't the actual cold pressing that she felt, however.

It was the loss of the world as they all had known it.

Their lives, however short that time would be, now that an actual Ice Age had been artificially created, and all of the means to defeat the cold had been destroyed, would be counted in years now, instead of decades. And they very well could be the very last generation of humans on the earth.

Because for all of humanity, and the rest of the living things on the face of the planet, their time was now very, very short.

At the end of the long runway, two tall beings stood, having regained their Material World visage, and stared up at the same explosions that the people in the airplane behind them were witnessing.

Those few people, those most critical people in the airplane may have seen the end of their lives in the sky fire, but the two beings saw the view for what it really was.

A New Start.

The taller of the two Beings, the one who had decided to stop the plane from taking off, saving the occupants inside because of how they would be needed to shape the world's future, smiled, and tried not to laugh in mirth and glee.

The younger Being next to her older brother in the Ilk however could not hold in the laughter. It burst from her lips in staccato bursts, making her older brother's aura brighten. She always had had that effect on the Older Ilk, Raziel thought to himself.

The pair looked around them as the shockwave from the high atmospheric explosions shut off the electricity and power around them, and they knew that they had done a fine job to make sure this world would witness the needed changes for what lay ahead.

Raziel, more than Azrael, knew what was coming, and it was so much bigger than just this one little world amongst so many.

Raziel knew the secrets of the Creator, and therefore knew that this world would be just a catalyst for the Universal Upheaval that was to come, and the fall of one of their very own.

Shockwaves, not unlike the ones rocking this world itself, Raziel thought, would rattle all of Creation, and they would all be changed by it.

His smile faltered somewhat, but he still felt the mirth of the changes to come. He had really and truly grown so very tired of the existence that the Host endured for so much time.

True horror was to come, and this world, like most of the others, would cease to exist. The changes happening now to the Humans Made of Fire here, in this place, would not matter at all, in the war that was coming.

Raziel's smile grew, until it beamed like the sun that would not shine on this world for almost a century to come.

Chapter 14

All around the world, people had to find their way to shelter within the earth itself or perish in the inhospitable cold in what would soon be called The Outside.

The world would not know warmth for some time to come, and as peoples of every nation understood this, watching the weaker around them die off, they sought the safety of caves, mountains, or depths within the crust of the earth, away from the open sky.

For some, for so many, they would be born, live, and die, without ever seeing the sun, the sky, or feel the wind on their faces.

Brian Clince stopped pulling his heavy sled, took a deep breath of the frozen air, and looked back down at the valley that he had called home with something in his chest that he couldn't quite understand. He knew he had to leave.

He heard his wife, Rachel, behind him stop pulling her sled loaded with food, clothing, medicines, and other necessities, and breathe deeply as well. He knew she would be feeling the loss of home more than him. The valley had only been his home for a couple of years. It had been the only home she had ever known.

Brian took off his goggles, and then his heavy wool cap. They were used to winters here in the large, central valleys of the Rocky Mountains. Cold was just another part of life, and it had been a very good life.

Pond hockey, skating up and down the streets of Westcliffe, Christmas parties outside in the snow. He had even climbed to the very top of one of the several 14,000 foot mountains in the chain back towards the west. He had been very proud of that fact, at one time, when things had made sense.

But this cold he felt now was an enemy. It was life-stealing. It was relentless and he couldn't find anything positive in it. All he could do was what he had always done.

Survive.

And so, as the winter stretched into a full year, and then beyond, he and his community had looked to the mountains, as they always had done, and wondered how life was going to survive. Especially when the lights and communications with the outside world had all gone out, and no one could get anything working from then on.

They had gathered the whole community, had pooled the resources of a very survival-driven people, and had made a line of people and pets, all pulling something that would help them all live, and had headed east. Towards a new home, perhaps. Or towards a certain death. But Brian knew the truth as they all had.

They just could not sit by and die. They had to move. And so, they were. They were headed towards Bishop's Castle, in order for the entire group to survive a world that they no longer recognized.

The snow and cold had become something even older members of the town did not see as the blessings it usually was. Winter was usually as welcome as a family member who only came for half the year.

But this new world was an unrecognizable, uninvited guest that killed and didn't care. It resembled the winters of their youths, but it had grown lethal and they didn't know this winter would never turn into spring.

Brian heard Rachel clear her voice and he turned back to her. She looked beautiful and radiant in deep winter parka and leggings. His breath always caught when he saw the strength and determination on his wife's face. She has worn this expression more during the last several months than ever before.

Brian replaced his wool cap, his goggles, and prepared to keep moving. They would have to catch up with the rest of the group that was moving steadily towards the mountain range on the eastern side of the valley. He looked down once more at the completely white valley, where nothing recognizable was visible any longer.

Just a sea of white snow and ice, even covering the tall range of mountains to the west.

He silently said goodbye to the only home he had ever felt needed and comfortable, and hoisted the ropes for the sled back over his shoulders. He turned towards his already-moving wife and

65

children. Sighing heavily through the neck warmer he wore over the lower part of his face, he simply soldiered onward.

In the Chinese province of Shaanxi, on the border between Mei, Taibai, and Zhouzhi, lay the Mountain of Rich Goods, or as Junh Singh's grandfather had called it, *Zhongnan*.

Junh's grandfather would sit him down in the valley below, while they had worked, tying new rope around the bamboo fencing that had kept their heard of fat beef cattle in, and told the young boy the story of the Golden Star, whose essence had fallen from the heavens, right down onto the highest peak in the mountain range to the south of the village, and how his own ancestors had then named the mountain *Taibai*.

The story went on to describe how the Golden Star had metamorphosed into magnificent white jade, and how the words *Taibai Shan* literally meant the White Mountain.

For all of Junh's young life, that mountain had never been anything other than white. Snow covered it year-round, and the young boy's fantasies always ran to him climbing the great white mountain, and finding the remains of the Golden Star, and becoming world famous.

Those dreams were long in the past, along with his grandparents, parents, and most everyone the man had known. All of his family, except the group of villagers around him, had perished in the last several weeks from the cold, having lost everything they had always survived on rice, beans, a staple diet that the last year and a half had not provided. The ones still alive trudged with Junh towards those very same mountains, and this time, not to find a sleeping star, but rather, to find a way of survival.

He had heard all of the stories from the honorable elderly of the village. They all spoke of the *dong tien*, or the grotto-heavens, deep within the mountain. They had described an underground network of places where heaven and earth touched.

66

You could travel deep into the mountains, they said, and come to the world of the immortals. You enter "the beyond within," they said over and over.

The most famous grotto-heaven was deep within Mount Taibai, and they had called it *Bieyou Dong Tien*, or The Place of Charm and Beauty. The long line of citizens following Junh Singh up into the White Mountain range were traveling towards that grotto-heaven, hoping to build a life away from the deep cold and death from starvation and exposure.

Junh just hoped that his new wife and baby boy would grow old and happy, deep within the earth, and that they would once again see the green pastures of his youth. But that was just another fantasy, like the ones from his childhood.

He knew that even his baby boy, who he had named Bao, after the grandfather who had shown Junh how to be a man with vision and dreams, would never see the outside sky, and green fields. His son would have to learn to live a very different way than those who had come before him, if he even survived the next few months.

Because Junh knew a truth the rest of the village had not known. As a government scientist and researcher, he knew what had happened, and how the world would never again look the same. It would never again be able to sustain life..

So, now the entire village, along with his family and friends he had grown up with, were in search of a legend. And a place to survive in a world that no longer wanted humanity, including his own people, to live.

Florent Iribagiza was ice cold. But she was also made of an inner iron core, too strong to allow cold to stop her. Her Rwandan father, the famous Abel Ukulikiyinkindi, had known his oldest daughter was made of a "middle of iron, covered in sweet smelling cedar, and ran through with steel nails strong enough to withstand anything," or so he had said on several occasions.

She had lost her father to the holocaust and genocide in the early 1990s. She had lost her sweet mother, a teacher and the glue which had held her childhood together through the worst conflict in her continent's history, to the cold only three weeks earlier, and she was about to lose some fingers and toes as she climbed the rocky slopes of Mount Sabyinyo.

She felt alone in the world, but rich in the dozens of poor Rwandan citizens around her, breathing heavy, and trying to reach a cave mouth several thousand feet above them all. They would all lose something in this climb, she thought, as she looked around her.

Florent had grown up in Rwanda, the jewel of central Africa, and had known a land of perpetual spring. She had swum in warm lakes and rivers, ran through fields of wildflowers and rice and beans, and had looked longingly at the mist-shrouded mountains to the north of her home in Ruhengeri.

But those memories seemed like a dream as she stopped and looked back at the flat land the people around her had all traveled across to reach the mountains. Where hundreds of lakes had once stood, shining in sunlight like blue pools of heavenly light was now nothing but harsh whiteness and glittering ice

Yes, she thought harshly, recognizing where the depressing and negative thoughts come from. Yes, she thought again, they would all lose in this world that was no longer able to support her children. No longer able to provide the bountiful things that such fragile creatures needed to live. But her people would survive.

She knew deep within her soul that they always found a way to survive.

So, with that thought at the forefront of her mind, and her young body still strong and able, she started climbing again. Frozen trees, dead animals caught in the ice, a frieze of black fur, caught in the snow, could only be the frozen body of one of the famed gorillas that had called this forest-covered mountain home.

She shook it all off, and with her people, pressed onward, towards the deep caves near the top of the jagged mountain tops that would protect and give shelter in a world that no longer offered it on the surface

She knew that they would all find a way to survive. Because they always had.

This would be no different.

Konstantin Vinovich took a long, deep pull from the label-less glass bottle. The vodka hit his chest and exploded in a warmth that he knew was not the kind that would keep him alive deep within the Russian tundra around him. Only the fire in front of him could.

He moved closer to the flames, despite the smoke hitting him straight in the face. It was better than freezing to death like so many others that he had known all of his life, but who over the last two weeks showed that they were not strong enough to survive.

But Konstantin was different. He believed he could even thrive in the new world that surrounded him on this cold, dark night deep in the Russian wilderness.

He could survive anything. With enough vodka, some firewood, and his iron-strong Russian will that he had inherited from a father who would test those around him for their own strength. Vino Ivanovich had been one strong son of a bitch himself.

Konstantin looked around him at the others huddled close to the fire, and then he looked up at the clear sky. Billions of stars winked above him and made him once again ponder his life. At 23 years old, he had seen worse atrocities than most people his age, though not on par with his father who had lived through the Cold War as a high-level KGB official.

When his father got into the vodka at night,, as the cold wind of the North Country blew against the windows, young

Kostya, as his father called him, would turn the terror of his father's words into nightmares.

Now, nightmares were in Konstantin's past.. Those days were warm memories compared to the chill and desolation facing him and his people, ever since the lights and the heat went out. Now, they would have to seek warmth and safety in the ground.

It had been decided by his grandparents, and his mother, that the family would seek out an old, abandoned platinum mine deep in the Ural Mountains to the north of their home, the esteemed and historical Chelyabinsk. The mountains, which ran north to south, and not the normal east to west, would protect his family, and hopefully, they would live to see the world thaw out once again.

Konstantin was not convinced, however. He remembered his father's last few words to his only son.

"This life will kill you Kostya. It's a cruel taskmaster, and we, the hard-working Russian men, must face it and expect the pain. Be strong, and prepare for the pain," his father whispered into his young son's ear as the blackness in his lungs slowly killed him.

Konstantin saw the pain in his father's eyes and wished for his father's death with all of his heart.

And now, with the world around them turning into ice and snow, with no way for it to thaw out, Konstantin knew that the true pain had only just begun.

He took another long pull of vodka, inched closer to the fire, and allowed his thoughts to wander over the pain that would take place the next day, and the one after, until this life gave him enough pain to kill him, and he could finally be at rest.

Until then, he had to do as his father told him, and be strong in the midst of a lifetime that was nothing but pain and suffering. And that's when he knew that he, more than anyone around him, would survive what was coming.

He smiled and finished the last bit of vodka in the bottom of the label-less bottle. He knew he would survive anything.

Like a true Russian man.

Like his father.

Mark Simon and his parents, along with dozens of other people, two golden retriever dogs, and an almost-frozen cat in a padded backpack, who they had found on their trek west, stopped in their tracks, and took a break at the base of the mountains that would save their lives. All of their lives, Mark knew.

They merely had to reach the entrance at the top. He could see the tall antenna and radar dishes that showed him the way home. The old NORAD installation, warmth, and Bryce.

He secretly hoped that the large, reinforced steel doors still stood open. He knew that Bryce, who he had left in charge of finishing preparations, would not close them until it was a life-or-death situation. He just hoped they had not gotten to that place yet. But it had been nearly four months since the world's lights had gone out, and anything was possible at this point, he knew.

Life-or-death situation, indeed, he ruefully thought.

Not that the last four months had not been a life-or-death situation. Luckily, he and his father were used to taking long winter treks through deep snow and blowing cold. But a lot of the people that they had gathered on their way west were not. Like his mother.

The Honorable Pamela Simon, strongest amongst the people that Mark had grown up around, was laying prostrate on a litter between Mark and another man named Badger, who they had picked up and helped along their trek on I-70 west. She was ice cold, and Mark worried that she wouldn't last much longer. He whispered to her in the cold of the Rocky Mountain's shadows.

"Not much longer Mom. Stay with us please," he said.

He did not want to weep. He had done enough of that as they had trudged west. He felt like all of the tears inside of him had frozen, along with any kind of hope that mankind would survive what they had built to destroy them.

John Simon, like his son, was tormented by regret. He knew now that he had always gone along with Yoshi, and the man's needs to change the world. Well, he thought as he looked up at the frozen expanse of mountain range before them, they surely had.

And then the group of them, carrying the Congresswoman amongst them, and huddled close to each other for warmth, started toward the pass that led to the giant steel doors that would keep them alive. But they all wondered just for how long.

Several hours later, at the top of the world, it seemed, the group of thirty or so people, all wrapped up so tightly in winter gear that you could not even distinguish genders, arrived at the steel doors, only to see them closed tightly.

Mark looked around him at the new family he had gathered over the last four months of travel. He again wanted to weep. They had all relied on him, and he didn't want to let them down now, after they had finally arrived at their destination.

And so, he moved to the small door to the left of the large steel doors and banged as loudly as he could. He hoped and prayed that someone, anyone, was near the door, and had been waiting for him.

A silent prayer escaped his lips as he lined up his gloved first to bang again, to get someone's attention, when the door swished open in front of him.

Blinding light burst out from the small door, and when his eyes adjusted to the first artificial light he had seen in four months, he saw her.

This time he really did weep.

He fell to his knees in relief. Bryce, his Bryce, rushed out from the light and warmth, and hugged him with all of her strength while his strength left him. Sobs escaped his lips.

72

He was finally home, and now, they could rest, recover, and figure out the future.

He hugged Bryce for what seemed forever, before moving aside, and ushering his new family into the warmth and light of the only home they would all ever know again.

And Mark was fine with that. Because they would survive.

He just hoped that around the world, others had found shelter, warmth, and home. The human race would not survive if they had not.

Mark turned, after everyone had moved into the bright confines of the military installation at the top of the world and scanned the land that they had just traveled across. He looked up to the overcast sky, with the weak light breaking through, and knew that he would never see this world again. No human would, because to travel back out would spell certain death.

At least until the world thawed out, and corrected itself, he thought.

Mark Simon, along with the love of his life beside him, looked one last time at the world, and felt only regret that he didn't - or couldn't - finish the job that he was meant to. He regretted that he had failed miserably.

He prayed one last time that humanity would survive to take over the world once again, when it could sustain them. It was a long shot, he knew. But humanity had survived before and would survive again.

He turned, took Bryce by the hand, and limped into the light.

He did not look back, and as he knew would happen; he never saw the world outside, ever again.

Part 3
The Awakening

Chapter 15

333 Years Later

Today was the day.

Young Elijah Simone had waited for this day his entire short life.

He remembered that his father had warned him that it may not be what he dreamed it would be, but maybe, if the mathematicians and the Memorists were right, this day would change their lives forever.

And so, Elijah bounded from his bed, deep in the rock cave that his family called home, honed from the solid granite around him by his great grandfather himself. He pulled on his tunic and breeches, ready for this day.

The day that the great iron doors would finally be opened.

Elijah rubbed the sleep from his eyes as he walked out into the common area of the family home. His parent's furniture was scattered where it was customarily placed, and where, Elijah assumed, it had been for more generations than anyone wanted to admit.

But his mother, Emily, kept everything clean, and in good repair. The furniture's wood gleamed with wax and pride, and the space smelled as clean and welcoming as a deep cave beneath the surface of the planet could.

Elijah had never smelled anything else besides the rock walls around him, so he didn't know any different anyway. His thoughts on this day were of dreams and memories. Of wind, sky, and sunshine.

He walked to the warm water bowl on the small table in the kitchen his mother had put out earlier. She was always up well before her three sons. He splashed the water on his face, waking himself up fully.

He then used the clean linen cloth next to the bowl to dry his face and try to smooth the unruly mop of dark brown hair that was always falling into his eyes. His entire family suffered from the deep brown hair that seemed to grow faster than the wheat of the artificial fields located throughout the cave systems.

A dark hair that seemed to be the hallmark trait of his family. Well that, he thought, and the line of Memorists that came before him, and who he, himself, would one day join.

Maybe his mother would cut his hair before they went out into the world, he thought, as he walked over to the cutting board to cut a slice of thick white bread for his breakfast. He wanted to

76

spread extra "drippings" on the bread to have the energy for today's great excitement.

And then Elijah's father walked into the kitchen area, and the room seemed to shrink.

Jerimiah Simone was a large man by most accounts, but his presence and his knowing eyes preceded him into the kitchen, and once again, young Elijah was awed by his father. And it was a reputation and aura that was well earned.

Because Jerimiah Simone was the last in a ten-generation line of Master Memorists.

As Elijah graciously accepted his father's hand ruffling his long brown hair, and a kiss on the forehead, he thought about what his father's role would be in the community gathering and celebration that day.

His father, who had declared months earlier, that the ten generational-gap and the mathematician's numbers of days culminated in the doors being opened on the Summer Solstice in the Outside.

Elijah knew that his father was an important man. Jerimiah Simone was the last of the Memorists. The group of generational people who Remembered.

The Memorists Remembered the before times, and especially remembered that the people in the caves would one day re-enter the outside world to re-plant, and re-populate it.

The Memorists were also the men who touched the Word and made sure that the people of the caves carried out lives of faith and obedience.

As his father was the last of the long line of Master Memorists, he was the only one in the community who communed with the ArchAngels.

Those two, Elijah knew, had kept the people around him alive and thriving more than anything else, for ten generations.

Elijah felt blessed that his father shared with his three sons what the ArchAngels told him regularly.

And they had known this day was coming, and Elijah felt especially proud that he was alive to witness it.

"Why don't you go wake up your brothers, young one," his father told him.

Elijah nodded, taking his slice of thick white bread with him to wake up his older brothers. He had forgotten to spread on the "drippings" that he so loved.

Walking into the other two rooms at the end of the hall made of stone that bisected his family's living space, he pushed aside the cloth covering of the first room that stood as a separation from the family areas and gave his older brothers privacy.

Abraham, the eldest of the Simone children, hardly stirred when Elijah called his name from just inside the door. So, still being so small, Elijah knew that drastic measures would need to be taken.

He gingerly placed his half-eaten slice of bread on the wooden chest next to the door and sprinted with all of his might towards the sleeping teenager. His still growing legs churned up the short space to the bed, and as he approached it, he wished for extra strength and speed.

Elijah sprang from the ground, his little legs giving him just enough strength to rise above the sleeping form below, and with a grunt from both parties in a tremendous collision, landed knees-first on the chest of his oldest brother.

Abraham let out a loud grunt as Elijah laughed and bounced his lithe body on top of the bigger boy.

An eye popped open first, followed soon by a grin. Abraham wrapped his little brother up in both arms and wrestled him around and under him.

Elijah simply laughed the whole time. His wise and serious oldest brother was his favorite person in the world, and Elijah, for all of his twelve years on the planet, knew only protection and love from the doting oldest.

And the fact that they looked almost identical to each other helped quite a bit.

As Abraham fully awoke, Elijah stopped laughing enough to look at the eyes of his oldest brother. Their expression was at odds with how Elijah felt about the upcoming day

"What's wrong Abe?" Elijah asked in his simple way.

Abraham looked down at his gregarious and overly intelligent brother and just sighed.

"I'm worried Elijah. I don't believe the outside world will be what we all think," Abe said.

He rose from the comfortable bed, helping his little brother to his feet.

Elijah was confused. He was so excited to see the sky and the sun that he didn't understand Abraham's hesitation. So, as was his way, he simply chose to ignore the feelings that Abe's face made him feel, and his spirit instantly turned back positive.

"It'll be so amazing, Abe. You'll see. Dada knows what's waiting out there, and he will take care of us," Elijah said in his simple, yet wise way.

Abraham smiled down on his littlest brother, and simply shrugged. He wouldn't change Elijah's positive spirit for all the world. So, as always since the youngest boy was born, he chose to follow suit, and be positive.

Like his father would need him to be today.

"Let's awaken Noah," Abraham told his little brother.

Elijah sighed loudly and set his shoulders. Waking up his second oldest brother was always a test of wills. Elijah and Abraham rarely won that contest with Noah.

They walked together towards Noah's room at the end of the long stone hallway. It was darkest at this end of the corridor, but a small line of light peeked out under the cloth hanging leading into Noah's room.

So, Elijah thought as he munched on the soft bread he had retrieved from Abe's chest of drawers, Noah was already awake, and most likely in prayer.

As the two brothers moved aside the heavy curtain, they saw their other brother, on his knees next to his own comfortable bed. And not a sound or movement came from anywhere else in the room.

Abe put a finger against Elijah's lips, and silently shushed him. He motioned for them both to go and join the devout young man kneeling, and together they moved into the room.

Noah simply smiled but kept his eyes closed tight and his hands held together in front of him. As the other two Simone brothers knelt beside Noah, he reached out both of his hands to his sides, and both brothers grabbed one. Together, they prayed for the day silently, and in perfect conjunction with each other.

As they always did, and as they all knew they always would.

Unbeknownst to the three kneeling boys, their approving father, along with a shining presence next to him in the dark outside corridor looked lovingly into the room, silently watching them.

The shining light gently lay a hand on Jerimiah's shoulder, and a thought entered the man's mind.

"These boys are the future, Jerimiah. Hardship and toil is their lot, but they will prepare the world for what is to come and lead the people into the next realm. Train them well outside these cave walls, and teach them all you have learned from me, and your ancestors."

"Teach them well and allow the hardships to come. My sister and I will be with them," the deep and wise voice whispered.

A final thought entered the man's mind before the shining light winked out next to him.

"There is no other way."

Jerimiah simply nodded and started to mentally prepare himself for what was to come that very afternoon, and the changes it would all bring to all those he loved the most.

There was no help for the pain his boys would face, he knew.

His boys needed to be ready. They needed to grow. And Jerimiah knew, as he turned to leave his boys in peace, there was no other way to grow but within the harsh valleys of life.

He just hoped and prayed that his son's valleys wouldn't be as bad as his.

Chapter 16

    Emily Simone prepared the lunch table with her mother, Naomi. She knew, more than the men in her life, that they would need to eat a hearty meal before the big celebrations that afternoon.

    Men tended to not see, or understand, the practical things that needed to be done, with their heads in the clouds all the time, she thought to herself.

    She was also silently relishing her last few days in the caves she had known her whole life. The apprehension and fear deep in her chest was growing, and she was struggling to avoid a full-on panic attack. And she knew, from the knitting circle and book groups she attended weekly, that many agoraphobic people had been dreading this day.

She tried not to let her fear show on her face.

But her mother, as always, knew her daughter's heart more than anyone.

"Dear, it's a change for everyone. We will be alright. Look at how far we have come," Naomi said.

"I know, Mother. I'm just scared that we won't all stay together. I can feel Abraham itching to explore, and Noah wanting to get out of the confines of the family. I'm nervous, Mother. I can't see anything positive coming from this," she answered her mother.

"Tsk, dear. You're made of stronger stuff than that," Naomi said, as naturally and as empathically as she always had been.

And the conversation ended on that.

The three men, and one little boy in her life soon walked into the dining room together, as Emily finished setting the old plates and silverware. She had inherited them when her mother moved in with the small family after Emily's father had suddenly passed away, four years earlier.

Secretly, she had enjoyed her mother being so near. She had been nearly undone after the addition of little Elijah. That boy had been a hard baby to deal with, and a somewhat more difficult toddler. But it was nothing like he was now, as a precocious twelve-year-old.

It was as if a switch had been flipped in his mind.

Whatever happened, she was thankful for it. As she looked out over her family, seated around the large table, her heart found peace in all they had overcome, as a family, and as a society, deep within the caves.

It had been several generations of pain and suffering, but she knew that the heart and courage of humanity would always strive for more.

She thought through all she knew of the people's time in the caves. The stories told to her by her husband, who had been told by his father, and his father.

Stories about how hard the people had worked to survive. The final creation of ways of growing of the crops that had kept them all alive. The careful cultivation of the animals needed for food. The brilliance the engineers showed in finally turning the lights back on.

The people were a hardy lot, and could survive almost anything, she knew. They were strong as individuals, but they were even stronger together. The times in the caves had taught the people that fact.

And so, as always, they had persevered, and strengthened as a family. So, on this day, she smiled at the men around her, and ruffled her youngest son's thick dark hair. That made the boy smile which shone down on her like the sun she had only heard stories about.

As her family sat to enjoy the midday meal, her heart soared at first with love and acceptance. Her family was everything to her.

But that feeling soon seemed to shrink down into a hard ball of fear as she thought of the celebration in just a few short hours. Her fear multiplied as she thought of seeing a blue sky for the first time in her life and losing her family to the wonders that existed outside of the safe walls around them now.

The daily meal prayers said, and her family happily babbling away about what they would find outside the walls of the cave system that they had all known their entire lives, her fear never quite settled. But her family's positivity was infectious, so, while she wasn't completely out of the woods for a full-blown panic attack coming on, she was able to carry on with her children

84

and her husband as they discussed what they would soon find out in the world.

And then soon enough, it was time.

Her children left the table to put on their best and costliest clothing, and her husband, already dressed properly, went from the home to see to the preparations for the celebration of the Opening of the Great Doors that afternoon.

She was left to clean with her mother, a daily chore, but one in which she relished. And as she puttered around her home, putting away clean dishes, and wiping crumbs from the polished table her great-great grandfather had built, she felt more and more like she was saying goodbye to the only home she had ever known.

But what she didn't know that day was, she wouldn't be saying goodbye to her home. Or for many, many days after that. That final goodbye would come suddenly, many days from this one.

Because as this day would soon show, most of the people in the caves would not be going out into the world that they had fantasized about for most of their lives.

Not on this day. And not on any day in the foreseeable future. The people had dreamed of this day for centuries, but had no idea what would be in store for them once the big steel doors were open.

Their dreams would be dashed, along with the dreams of ten generations of people before them.

Chapter 17

"Good people, good people, please," Jerimiah Simone was trying to shout over the loud din coming from the hundreds of people standing shoulder to shoulder in the wide, open corridor that led down into the cave system proper.

He had his hands waving over his head and sweat was starting to appear through his tunic. It was hot in the corridor, so far away from the never-ending cycles of fan motor rotations down below.

"QUIET!" A shout came from close by Jerimiah, and he looked gratefully at Denys Marrow, the overly large yet quite congenial woodworker who had made most of the furniture the group now enjoyed. The growers had given him a new crop of fresh redwood to work with on an almost annual basis.

Many could not believe that the artificial hydro-farms very far below where they all now stood had survived so many centuries. Just another of the many mysteries that had been passed down from generation to generation. And really, only the Memorists knew how all of the things they had enjoyed for so long really worked.

The problem with Memorists, people would whisper, is that they tended to keep that knowledge to themselves. But the grumbling was low and secret because the Memorists were a needed bunch.

The gathered crowd soon quieted down enough for Jerimiah to speak a few words before the machinists opened the large steel doors that had kept out the cold and chilly death for so many generations. The group of thick-armed and dirty men were excited to find out if their monthly maintenance on all the machinery in the cave systems, including the mechanism that opened the great doors still worked properly after almost a millennium.

"As you all know, and have heard by now, the Mathmatists, and the Memorists, have concluded that today is the day of Awakening!" He nearly shouted.

The din arose around him again, but this time, much louder as cheers and yells leapt to the ceiling far overhead and reverberated back down to the waiting masses. Jerimiah had heard the word cacophony before but had never had the chance to experience it. This was a very loud jubilation, and it went on for some time.

Finally, the noise once again settled down enough for Jerimiah to continue speaking. And with that opening, he decided to lead the masses in front of him in prayer. As he raised his hands up over his head, his eyes closed, he heard the large group of tenth generation people fall to their knees, as was their way, and raise their faces to the cave ceiling in combined prayer to the Almighty.

"Our Creator above, as below, we come before you in prayer, as taught to us by your Messengers and Watchers, to give praise for the blessings we are about to receive," he started.

"You have kept us safe here, deep in your earth, as the world outside raged and froze. Allowing us to live, while the outside world died," he prayed.

"We ask you now for your abundant mercy and grace as we leave these caves we have known for so, so long, and allow us entrance to the outside world, where we will re-plant your harvest, and re-supply your animals across the world. In the Almighty's name we pray," he finished.

"Amen." Said the crowd around Jerimiah.

He was humbled, as always, to have the knowledge he had gained from his own father, and the guidance of the ArchAngels, who visited with him most days. They had told him many times how he was going to lead these people out into the barren world. To re-populate, and re-plant. He was ever excited to be the scion of the famed Mark Simon, the man who had turned these caves into homes, so many centuries ago.

He reached into his inner pocket of the dress vest he wore, and patted the leather-bound book he held there, over his heart. It was the journal of his ancestor Mark Simon, and the trials and tribulations he had undergone so long ago to make these caves hospitable and everlasting.

Jerimiah felt an overwhelming happiness overcome him as he thought about all the years in-between and how he was going to be the one to now walk out of the caves that his ancestor had so long ago walked into, shutting out the dead and frozen world behind him.

He just hoped that he made his ancestor proud, and that he wouldn't mistake this grand and auspicious event for anything other than the blessing that it was.

88

And so, he nodded to the Machinists gathered near the steel door leading into the room where the mechanism that had kept the great doors closed for so long. They all, as a group, went solemnly into the room, and within a few minutes, the gathered crowd heard the sound they had all been waiting to hear for all of their lives.

The rumbling mechanism began to work, and the locking pins in the door started to move.

After what seemed like too long of a wait, the gathered crowd grew impatient. Finally, the doors started to groan, and swing inward.

Jerimiah Simone, the last of the great Memorists, with his family now gathered behind him, his three sons foremost in front, full of excitement, and anticipation, was the first to see the blue sky beyond the great doors. He held back the flood of people behind him, like the great Moses at the Red Sea from the book they had all read their entire lives.

As soon as the doors were open enough for several people to walk through, and the hush behind him from the gathered crowd fell silent as everyone took in the sight of the great blue sky outside the cave, Jerimiah started out of the cave.

He was the first man, he believed, for almost nine hundred years, to step out into the world that had, at one time, killed off almost the entire human race.

The crowd, including his own family, walked out of the caves that had been home for so very long, and looked out at a world that they believed to be barren after so long covered in ice and snow.

To a person, the feel of real air on their faces was a refreshing balm. Goosebumps arose on more than one arm, and the open sky above them was a sight that seemed both terrifying and miraculous. A smell of freshness arose around the crowd, and it was as if the people were coming alive for the very first time.

The sky was a blue that no one had ever experienced before. White clouds dotted the blueness, and the sight was something that they had only ever heard about in songs and memories passed down from generations who themselves had never experienced it.

And many realized that the words describing such a sight never did justification to the actual experience of looking up into the heavens and seeing they did not stop. For the first time, many in the crowd realized what forever really looked like.

Tears flowed from overly sensitive eyes, young and old. And the sunshine revealed features to each other that generations within the caves had kept hidden. The sunlight and a soft breeze was the most jarring experience anyone in the crowd had ever experienced.

It was overwhelming. It was shocking. Many felt like they couldn't handle it, and were in awe of its beauty all at the same time.

Until they looked away from the skies, and back down to the world around them.

And what they saw stopped them in their tracks completely.

Jerimiah and his family, along with nearly two thousand men, women, and children behind them, walked to the edge of an overhanging cliff that was all that remained of the road that had once been built all the way up to the entrance of the grand cave systems. Their minds could not believe what their eyes were seeing.

They all glanced out over the world that should have been frozen in ice for centuries, and saw…

Green trees and grasses. Even what seemed artificial lights shining in the distance.

Jerimiah could not believe his eyes, nor now the words of those who had watched over the people.

The world outside the cave system was not barren and desolate. Rather the opposite.

And as a herd of deer bounded out of the tree line, not more than fifty yards from where the mass of people stood, dumbfounded, Jerimiah finally figured out the truth.

The world had not been frozen for more than 300 years.

It had flourished almost the entire time.

And as a loud booming sound ricocheted over the crowd's heads, and they turned their eyes back skyward, shock and panic set into the people gathered at the rim of the cliff before them.

The mass of people turned almost as one and started running back towards the opened great doors of the caves, screaming, and yelling, almost trampling the children and elderly amongst them.

Because the sight of a small airplane, flying directly overhead, was more than they could all handle, and the shock and fear overrode their excitement.

They suddenly all know that they had been lied to for more than ten generations.

Chapter 18

"WHOOP, WHOOP!!" Cheese could hear the yells coming from his best friend before the prop blades stopped spinning.

He looked through the dirty canopy of the pieced together aero-plane that he had just flown for the first time and saw Moose running towards him at the end of the grassy clearing that they had cut through the thick forest. The nickname the boy had garnered from his own family, passed down from father to son for many generations, was more perfect for the over-large boy than anyone else Cheese knew.

Cheese grinned from ear to ear, his mind returning to the deed he had just accomplished. Finally, his lifelong goal of flying a real aero-plane, those mythical pieces of technology they had only seen on book pages, had been realized.

Finding one almost perfectly kept in a large hangar three years prior was the blessing they had been looking for all their lives. And now he had flown the dang thing. He could hardly contain himself as he pulled the plane in a tight circle, finally coming to a stop.

Moose came to a skidding halt near the now-quiet aero-plane, his chubby body shaking with effort as his red face split in the widest grin that Cheese had ever seen his friend make. His own face felt the same way.

He opened the dirty canopy as the final shakes and vibrations from the flight came to a halt and jumped down from the cockpit of the aero-plane. His tall, thin frame was still shaking from the dangerous flight.

He turned, before speaking to his friend, and patted the plane. He was still trying to think up a name for it when Moose wrapped him in a tight bear hug from behind.

"Cheese, by g-g-g-golly. I can't believe you flew. I ca-ca-ca-can't believe it!" Moose stuttered as he squeezed Cheese.

"Let me down, ya big oaf!" Cheese finally spoke through clenched teeth, even though he could hardly breathe from the tight hug. Moose never knew how strong he really was.

"Sss-orry, Cheese," his best friend said.

Moose let Cheese go, but the smile never left his red face.

"Where's Facecake?" Cheese asked his heavy friend. He didn't even register the fact that Moose's stutter came back so strong when he was excited. His own excitement and the vibrations that he could still feel from his flight shook his mental powers and made him almost lightheaded.

Moose shrugged his huge shoulders before turning towards the engine, where he started puttering around, finding a screwdriver in some pocket or another, to open a panel and inspect the insides. Cheese left him to his work.

He had to speak to Facecake as quickly as possible. The leader of their little gang would never believe what he had seen as he had flown back over the tall mountains from the Western face to the Eastern one.

It sure wasn't every day that they saw a mass of thousands of people where they shouldn't be. That was for dang sure, Cheese thought to himself as he walked towards the dilapidated buildings they called home.

But Facecake would know what to do. She always did, he thought. And that made him smile.

As he entered the large, worn-down factory buildings that had served a long forgotten and seemingly some form of storage role several centuries before, he thought about growing up at the Castle with Facecake.

She had always been the one with all the ideas. She would rope Cheese and Moose into her ridiculous plans, and the two boys, smitten with her from an early age, would happily follow after, sometimes to their own detriment.

Facecake's plans usually involved doing things that the kids were all forbidden to do, like spending years getting an aeroplane they had found almost perfectly preserved in these very same warehouses some fifty miles from the only home they had all ever known.

Bishop's Castle.

But the two boys would follow along with her, doing her heavy lifting, and trying with all of their might to impress the beautiful young girl. And now, Cheese thought, he had been the first man in history, as far as he knew, to fly through the sky.

Surely that would impress her.

His smile lit up his dark face in the gloom of the warehouse. He couldn't wait to find the girl.

94

And so, the young black boy, the smile never leaving his lips, wearing his leather skull cap, one size too big on his round head, walked through the many dirty, unused rooms of the warehouse, without finding Facecake.

He checked the bunk room, the latrine, and finally walked into the kitchen area. He found Facecake stirring a big pot with an even bigger wooden spoon they had found right here in this room years earlier. They had set off from the Castle to find a life, and boy, had they found one.

Cheese walked quietly into the large, open room, but he could never sneak up on Facecake. She had eyes in the back of her head, she often said. He smelled delicious food cooking, and the ash and oak wood fire in the middle of the large area gave a pleasant odor as well.

"Did you crash and burn?" she asked the young pilot.

His smile faltered a bit. She didn't seem that impressed. He realized that she hadn't even come out to the field as he landed.

He sighed loudly, taking a seat on the metal stool near the front of the big, well-lit room. Windows high up on the walls of the room let in the late afternoon light.

"No, it was just as we thought. I got up and flew around over the mountains. Didn't get as far as the Castle as I wanted, 'cause the gas gauge stopped working," he said.

He watched her back as she continued to stir the large pot. The smell of venison stew hit his nose, and he realized he was quite hungry. His stomach angrily grumbled at the same time, telling him that he shouldn't have skipped breakfast from his excitement earlier that morning.

"How high were you able to get?" Facecake asked, still facing the other direction. Cheese's earlier humor had all but left him. He looked down at his breeches and leather sandals before answering.

"Don't know that either. That gauge stopped working too," he replied. His glee from just a few short moments before was gone.

"Well Cheese, you did something no one else has done since they started writing this stuff down at the Castle. I think we should celebrate," she said.

And then she turned, and in her hands was a baked cake, small, big enough for one person. She must have baked it this morning as he and Moose were getting the aero-plane in the air, he thought. His heart started beating faster.

Facecake had the biggest smile on her face, and Cheese's brain melted. His bright white grin lit up his dark face, corner to corner, and he was happy all over again.

Facecake walked over to the young man and handed him the spice cake on a metal plate. He looked up at her angelic face, love making his heartbeat against his ribcage. He took the cake and put it down on the scrubbed wooden tabletop next to his stool.

"Eat it all up before Moose smells it, Cheese. That boy doesn't need any more cake," she said.

Cheese bit into the still-warm spice cake and grinned even broader. It had tiny bits of apple in it, from the orchard out back that they had spent two years cultivating. If there was anything the young people of this age knew, it was planting and harvesting.

As the young man finished up his small spice cake, made for him from the hands of an angel, Facecake turned and went back to stirring the stew. They would eat well tonight, Cheese knew.

And as he wiped the crumbs from his face and hands, watching the backside of Facecake across the kitchen room, he forgot about telling the young girl what he had seen on his flight. About the great multitude of people he had seen up in the mountains.

In fact, it wouldn't be for a few more days that he remembered to tell her. Fixing the aero-plane and getting it up and ready for another flight took over all of his time, and Moose's as well. The memory, like a lot of memories of this time and age, simply melted away with the excitement of actual change. Their lives had been such a bore, he thought over and over, and that was going to change with their aero-plane.

But it wasn't until three days later, when Facecake finally came out to inspect the work in the field and spied the three young, pale youths emerging from the trees at the end of the clearing, that Cheese would remember the people who were where they weren't supposed to be.

And to Cheese's eternal damnation, he watched Facecake's whole world light up, her eyes catching the eyes of the tallest of the youths. He knew at this moment that life would change forever

For them all, in ways they could never see coming.

And Cheese would soon learn to not be so damn excited for the actual changes that would come. He had a gut feeling these youths would shake up his world, whether he liked it or not.

Chapter 19

Jerimiah was beside himself.

Emily watched her husband pace around the family kitchen, into the living room area, and back again. He was mumbling to himself, which was never a good sign, she thought. The boys were in one of the bedrooms, talking quietly together, making as small a presence in the family home as possible. Emily wondered suddenly what her sons were planning. She knew the look, when she had poked her head in earlier in the evening to make sure they were all doing alright.

She knew when her boys were up to something. She just hoped that they wouldn't do anything that would make her lose her family.

That was her biggest fear of all.

And so she sat at the table with her mother. Both women had their hands held together atop the scarred and weathered wooden tabletop. Both women were deep in thought, prayers, or just general unease.

Emily wondered suddenly if anyone was hungry. She thought she could fix a late dinner. That would keep her busy, take her mind off of her fears and doubts. And take her mind off the overwhelming helplessness and dark depression she felt, like so many others in the cave system.

All of their lives had been shaken that day. What were they to do now that ten generations of history, trouble, survival, and learned resourcefulness was completely out the window, and they realized they had been duped for so long? The questions and thoughts swirled around so many people's minds that the air in the cave systems was heavy, deep with despair.

Jerimiah more than anyone. Emily's mind turned towards her husband, and the look of utter defeat on his face. But he was the strongest of them all, she knew, and he would have to be the one to lead them all out of the depressive caves, and into the sunlight.

She knew she had to square her shoulders and help her husband find his way back to his faith.

Thoughts of food and dinner preparations suddenly left her mind as a single idea replaced them She knew what to do suddenly, as if a bright light suddenly turned on, or someone else stuck the thought into her mind.

With a new spirit within her, she stood suddenly, making her mother flinch back.. Emily whispered a quick apology, but moved away from the dining area, walking to a closet near the front of the cave home. She opened the old metal door, and bent down inside, taking a very old and battered case from the floor out into the light of the living room.

Placing the case on the old wooden table in front of her mother, she snapped open the two metal clasps and raised the lid of the case. Sitting inside was one of her most prized possessions. She reached into the case and brought forth the shiny, well-kept guitar, and held it reverently in her lap as she sat again, fingers holding the instrument with the care of a mother holding a newborn baby.

She hummed a few notes low in her throat, strumming each finely oiled string, hearing a soft murmuring of shared sound and tune. It was still tuned up from its last use and seemed to vibrate with the anticipation of her fingers controlling the sound it would produce.

She closed her eyes, thinking of the words to the song she knew would bring her family back out into the light. The song was very old. Passed down from parent to child while they had been stuck in the caves. It told of sunny roads and names of places no one she knew had ever seen. It spoke of love and faith and happiness.

It spoke of their real home, outside these oppressive rock walls that gave shelter and safety, but took away that which they all yearned for, whether they feared it or not. It spoke of freedom and the wide open sky.

Emily opened her eyes, strummed the first cords of the song's opening, and started to sing with all of her might.

"Almost heaven…West Virginia…Blue Ridge Mountains….Shenandoah Rivers," she started to sing.

The song burst forth from deep within her. "Take Me Home, Country Roads" by a man who's name had been John Denver, had been such a favorite amongst the people of the caves that it was almost an anthem for the masses.

And as she had predicted, her family soon sat around her, singing along, the joyful song rising to the top of the rock walls around them, rising even to those close by, wandering around the caves as though lost. Mr. John Denver's song, for so many generations, had taught them of the outside world, and what it could be again in the future.

The song had become such an integral part of their civilization down in the caves, that it was almost a religious devotional.

They sung it knowing that one day - and that day had actually been yesterday, Naomi thought - would bring a future for all the people, and they could make the world outside the caves as happy and loving as the song described.

She and her family sang the song four more times, doors opened up by passerby, the words picked up by even more people out in the corridors, reverberating all around them.

As the final strummed chord sounded for the fourth time, cheers arose all around Naomi, hands clapped, and shouts of joy sang up from those who were in the darkest of places only minutes before.

And so Emily, along with her husband and sons around her, the extended family coming closer with the others in the caves, continued to play the heirloom guitar. Others picked up their own cherished instruments, and songs burst forth for most of the night, and the next day as well.

Emily knew that music had saved people before, and would again. The joyful noise rose from so many lips and instruments played with love and devotion.

"Take Me Home, Country Roads" was played more than any other song, but there were so many remembered through the ages, that the music did not stop that night, nor the next, nor the one after that.

But on the fourth day, the people were exhausted, but back to a joyful state, expecting to overcome fear and venture back out into a scary world. But Emily's fears did come to life.

On the fourth day, Emily awoke refreshed, next to her still-snoozing husband, only to feel that her home was empty.

101

Even before she left her warm bed, she knew that her boys were gone. Terror overtook her.

Her boys had gone out into the world, and she had no idea if she would ever see them again.

Emily closed her eyes, muttered a silent prayer under her breath, and felt like nothing would ever be the same again.

Chapter 20

"Almost 350 freakin' years!" Facecake exclaimed loudly. The flames of the campfire seemed to leap higher at her loud exclamation.

Abraham and Noah nodded in sync, and Elijah just seemed to sit, staring at the flames jump and dance in front of him. He was hungry but couldn't touch the cooked rabbit and vegetables that were handed to him on a plate by the black boy they had met only a few hours before.

103

He couldn't get over the melancholy feelings of regret and betrayal he still felt at following his two older brothers out of the caves they had called home all their lives. It had been two days, and he still felt like crying and running back to his parents. He believed they all felt the same way, but his two older brothers would never admit it.

"Holy hell, we had no idea," was all Facecake could say after learning from the brothers about the groups of people high up in the mountains to the west of where they now sat. She turned her face towards the mountains but could not make them out in the growing darkness around them.

Silence fell over the six youths sitting around the roaring fire in the ring of stones. The six of them looked at the flames, no one really eating the dinner that Facecake and Cheese had cooked after introductions had been made earlier in the afternoon, and everyone had gotten over the shock of the circumstances they all now found themselves in.

The three brothers had found it difficult at first to understand the way the three new youths talked. Some words were similar, but most of them had been changed from the English that the boys were used to. Soon, however, the brothers got the hang of the slang English the other youths used, however, Moose seemed to not understand the brothers at all. Several times, he had to look to Facecake to translate the brother's words.

Cheese's only concern was the look on Facecake's face as she looked at the tallest of the brothers. The boy whose name was Abraham. Cheese felt like he had heard the name before, long in his past. He was concerned with Facecake, alright, but he was even more curious about where that name came from.

He chewed on the rabbit leg from the meat stores they had maintained all summer, and ruminated on old memories from the Castle.

"So, I don't get it. Why did you stay in the caves all that time?" Facecake asked.

Abraham answered her, revealing his own questions about what had been done to his people.

"All I know is that we were told to. By ArchAngels," he said.

"What are ArchAngels?" Facecake asked across the fire. The flames continued to leap and dance about, as if completely unaffected by worry.

"Beings from the heavens, sent by the Creator to watch over and protect us," Noah answered her rotely. Like he had rehearsed the answer.

The confusion on the three youth's faces troubled the brothers as well. They each wondered how it was possible that the people outside the caves had not heard of the ArchAngels, or the Creator.

They glanced at each other around their side of the fire, as if reading each other's minds. It was a bond they had all shared all of their lives. And one that helped in this instance, sitting among new people who could not read the concern on their faces.

And so, the six young people sat around the dying fire, pondering their own thoughts, munching on dinner, and wondering just what was going to happen next.

They didn't have to wait long before finding out

Elijah, having the keenest hearing, heard the sounds first. He sat up a little straighter, wondering what he heard, and if it was an ordinary sound outside of the caves

And then the other youths heard the sounds, responding to the looks on each other's faces. Fear from the boys, and concern from Facecake.

The sound resembled an animal's throat rumble, but higher pitched. They all glanced around at the darkened trees around them. The buildings that had housed the three youths who lived outside the caves were a few hundred yards away.

Facecake glanced back in that direction, thinking about how long it would take them to run to the safety of walls.

The three brothers stood in unison and turned their backs to the fire. Their eyes quickly adjusted to the darkness, having encountered absolute darkness while growing up in the caves

And so, they were the first to see the creature walk into the end of the clearing, several hundred feet from where they stood.

The creature walked on all fours, but it's long, thin legs ended in very sharp points. It had no feet or paws, rather, it had knife-like points which held it up against this world's physics.

Its body was long and skinny, bony ribs and ridges sticking through its thin skin, making it look as if it was mostly starved.

But its face was the most disconcerting. It had none. Instead, it had what looked like two rings sticking out from a neck that ended in a spike. The rings were floating in front of its sharp neck, and perturbed the brothers the most

"Tell me that you guys have seen this kind of animal before," Elijah asked the other three youths who stood up as he spoke

"I don't see anything," Facecake said. The other two boys repeated her words.

But they could all still hear the loud, high-pitched keening coming from the floating rings of flesh that made up the creature's face. And as the keening increased in pitch, the floating flesh rings vibrated with the sound.

And then the creature started running towards the standing ring of fearful youths,, backlit by the fire. They were easy targets for the creature that ran at them, full tilt, keening loudly.

As the brothers got their fear under check, their eyes seeking each other, a readiness to fight alighted their chests. They looked back at the other three youths, who were all wearing concerned looks on their faces, as they could hear the noise, but seemingly not seeing the creature bounding towards them.

106

The creature was still several yards away from the youths, its sharp ends where hooves should be making a clacking sound as it hit rock and hard dirt. The boys all grabbed pieces of wood from the fire and turned back to fight the thing. Facecake yelled questions over the loud keening coming from the oncoming creature.

The boys set themselves between the demonic creature and the teens who could not see it, ready to fight to the death to protect their new friends.

And then a bright flash of light lit up the large, open area between the teens and the creature from their worst nightmare running toward them.

Suddenly floating a foot or more off the ground, a large, shining Being with iridescent wings appeared, adorned with all of the colors of the rainbow, holding aloft a giant gleaming sword.

The boys instantly knew who had interfered. An ArchAngel stood between the young people and the bounding creature, still intent on its meal, unaware of its impending doom

The three brothers thought they were the only ones who could see both the ArchAngel and the hellish creature. But as soon as the ArchAngel had appeared, Facecake made a loud sound, as if catching her breath. The boys knew that she could suddenly see the oncoming creature, as well as the tall ArchAngel.

Four of the youths were watching, the other two boys started running towards the buildings, The ArchAngel raised the gleaming sword high, and in a move that was too fast for the human eyes to see, he brought it down, slamming it through the body of the hellish creature, all in a blink of an eye.

The keening stopped dead, as if a switch had cut off, and the flesh rings that had made up the monstrous creature's face fell to the ground, rolling away from the rest of its dying body.

Several long seconds went by. The ArchAngel raised the gleaming sword, and appeared to study the blade, assuring that no marks besmirched it. Satisfied, he shook the entire sword once, and it vanished

The brothers were the first to move. They had grown up on stories of the large ArchAngels that had watched over the cave people.

Facecake followed the brothers over to where the tall ArchAngel stood. He watched the youths approach with a somewhat amused look on his face.

Abraham spoke first.

"Great ArchAngel Raziel, thank you for showing yourself to us," he said.

Facecake looked over to the tallest of the brothers. "You know who this is?" she asked him as an internal light illuminated the clearing.

"I do," he answered. "My father told us many stories of the ArchAngels, especially the Wise Raziel. He has spoken to my father many times."

The four youths approached the ArchAngel, and as a group looked down at the creature dead at the feet of Raziel.

"What was that thing?" Noah asked Raziel.

The Being finally spoke. His voice was like a singing choir, many voices raised into one.

"Sons of Earth, Daughter of Fire, what do you see before you?" he asked instead of answering Noah's question.

All four of the youths spoke at once, but the ArchAngel was able to hear them each individually.

"Peace, Sons and Daughter. I'm not quite sure what this creature was, but its presence here is not a part of this Creation. I must bring this to my Father, for surely He will know how this abomination against Nature arrived in this world," he said in reply.

Abraham spoke up first again.

"I don't know what you are talking about, Great Raziel, but was it here to hurt us?" he asked.

Again the ArchAngel answered, sounding more inquisitive than anything. He briefly looked off into the distance as he spoke.

"I'm not sure of that either."

The ArchAngel alighted upon the ground. The four youths barely noticed that the Being had been hovering in the air in front of them the entire time.

Before their eyes, the tall Being turned to a regular looking man, middle-aged, wearing the same kinds of homespun clothing the youths all wore.

"You four are most important to my Father's plans. So, yes, this creature was here to destroy you, and your destinies too, I believe," the ArchAngel replied.

The ArchAngel closed his human eyes for several seconds, as though communicating with others outside of the youths' understanding.

"What are our destinies?" Facecake asked him, the creature at their feet forgotten for a minute.

"You will bring catastrophic change to this world and will be Harbingers of Truth for the battles to come," the ArchAngel answered, his eyes finally opening.

The four youths had no idea what the Being in human form was talking about, and so, they didn't respond to his answer. Instead, as a whole, they began to talk to the Being all at once.

The brothers started to ask about the length of time in the caves. Facecake asked about the changes in the world around them. All four talking over themselves.

The ArchAngel lifted both hands and held them in front of the talking youths.

"Peace, Sons and Daughter. Peace. Answers will come, as your journey continues. First, I must give you each a direction from my Father, and then, you will begin to find these answers for yourselves," he said, speaking over them.

"Sons of Earth, I tell you to seek to the East. Do not tarry far from each other, as your fates are intertwined, and life comes from staying together, but Death comes for the ones who stray," he said.

The boys each pondered what the being said.

"And you, Daughter of Fire, your fate, and the fate of all you have known rests in leading your friends and family to the feet of these three brothers of Earth," he said.

Facecake had no idea what the ArchAngel meant, but a feeling of responsibility began to grow in her heart.

"One last Commandment I give to you four: a bringing together of your beginnings, both Earth and Fire, will give this world the chance it deserves, in the War to come," he said.

The four youths looked at each other, confusion marring their faces. And as they all turned back to the ArchAngel to ask more questions, they found that he had disappeared. The clearing was now empty except for them.

Even the hellish creature was gone, nothing remaining to show that it had ever existed.

More confused than anything, the four teens turned back towards the campfire, the night now derailed from ruminating around the flames. They saw the other two youths walking back towards them, the fire in the middle of the large clearing between them.

"You any idea what he was talking about?" Elijah asked his older brothers. They each shook their head at their little brother.

"I think I understand one thing," Facecake said. "I think he wants us all to stick together, and to travel east," she finished.

"What's in the East?" Noah asked her. They all approached the fire together, which was still leaping about gaily, its light never wavering as the darkness of the night closed in.

"People. That's where most of the people left on this planet live," she answered him.

"And we don't go there. It's an outlaw land. No rules, no laws, death everywhere, or so we have been told all our lives," she said.

The youths sat back around the fire, questions on Cheese's and Moose's faces. Facecake merely shook her head at the two boys she had grown up with. They would get answers later.

The group sat around in silence for the remainder of the time it took for the fire crackling merrily to dampen down to glowing coals. They decided as one to douse the embers and seek somewhere to sleep through the rest of the long night.

And as the group walked back towards the buildings that had been home to half of them for a couple of years, Abraham had a burning question he couldn't keep to himself any longer.

"Facecake, that's not your real name, is it?" he asked the young girl walking in front of him. She answered without turning her head.

"No," she said. "My real name is Alexandria Clince."

Chapter 21

Elijah woke to sunlight. He sat bolt upright, as if one of the electric eels that the Animalists in the caves had used as an energy source had scrapped by his foot.

He quickly got his bearings and looked down and around him at his sleeping brothers. They had stayed up well into the dark night discussing what they had seen, and what their next steps were going to be moving forward. None of the young boys had anything figured out quite yet. They just hoped that they would understand more as the days wore on.

One thing bothered them more than anything else. They weren't proud of what they had done. They had left home and didn't tell anyone.

Elijah still felt horrible at leaving the caves without permission or adult supervision. His father, for one, would have been a great help in last night's confusion. What was that creature, and where exactly did the ArchAngel say it had come from?

Elijah sat in his makeshift bunk, adjusting to the heat of the early morning. He thought over the last couple of days, and the sights and sounds that he had witnessed for the very first time.

Like the big blue sky.

As the three brothers had walked south out of the mountain range they had called home their entire lives, Elijah could not stop looking up at the big blue sky every chance he got. He had even stumbled into the backs of both of his brothers, as they had stopped to get their bearings, or look for the lights that they had first glimpsed the day the caves opened, and those inside had succumbed to their fear.

He still marveled at the air that didn't taste or smell stake, and at the wind, as it brushed the thick hair on his head into his eyes. Every new experience was almost overwhelming for the young man. But he wouldn't give up any of it for anything.

Not anything in the world.

He arose and wondered where he could relieve himself. And then he remembered the woods outside the dilapidated building he had slept in and decided to try to use a tree.

He figured he was the first person in history to think of that.

As he stumbled into his boots, and walked outside the building, the sunlight hit him hard in his face. He closed his eyes against the brightness, temporarily forgetting his urgency. The heat of the early morning sunlight radiated on his skin, and he smiled brightly.

113

He opened his eyes, seeing stars while he again had to get his bearings, and walked slowly into the woods. As when he felt like he had walked far enough so that no one would see him, he chose the perfect tree inside a small clearing, glanced around him, and opened his fly, letting loose in relief.

He smiled as he finished, seeing the pattern of wetness he had drawn onto the bark of the tree. Why had he never thought of this before? The freedom was almost too much to bear.

Suddenly he heard rustling close by. He got spooked and was about to take off running back towards the building's safety. And then a deer with large antlers stepped into the clearing he was standing in, and the two locked eyes. Small brown human eyes stayed connected to big dark wild eyes. To Elijah, everything suddenly paused.

He barely heard the whisper of the arrow as it streaked towards the deer. Its eyes, still connected to Elijah's, grew larger, suddenly, in fear and pain. The deer bounded off into the woods, the arrow sticking out of its side.

Facecake walked into the clearing then, making Elijah blush, knowing that she had probably seen him make his morning salutation to the tree of choice. She wore clothing that blended into her surroundings, and Elijah wondered where he could find some.

Facecake smiled at him warmly and moved her head in the direction of the struck deer, asking him silently to follow along to retrieve the venison that he had, in some small way, helped to hunt. He suddenly felt pride swell in his chest, forgetting his momentary discomfort at what she may or may not have seen.

He followed along behind the tall girl, for the first time in his life feeling things like doubt and some small self-esteem issue. The tall girl made him feel things he had not figured out for himself just yet.

As he walked behind Facecake he tried to place his feet where she placed hers, trying to stay as quiet as her. He watched

114

her head turn to the left and right, and it took him a few tries to see what she was looking at.

She was looking at droplets of Blood.

Blood on the leaves, blood smeared on the tree trunks where the deer had obviously rubbed up against in its race to fight off encroaching death.

And just as he figured out how she was tracking the injured deer, they walked into yet another clearing, hearing the rushing water before seeing the stream running through the middle of it. And against the water, pooling around it, mixing with the blood of the mortal wound in its side, lay the dying deer.

The duo walked up to the deer, arrow sticking from its side, pointing to the sky, and watched the deer try to rise, only to fall again on its other side.

Elijah's heart hurt for the animal. He let out a small squeak, as Facecake removed a large knife from her belt and sliced the deer's throat open.

Elijah's eyes once again connected to the eyes of the animal. He watched in slowly dawning horror as the light left the magnificent animal. As if he could see the spirit of the deer rise out of its body, Elijah whispered a silent prayer to his God, and the God who made all things.

And to his utter shock, he heard Facecake mutter the same prayer under her breath.

The two young people looked at each other in growing shocked silence, both surprised that something so profound and habitual could be shared by those from within the caves, and those from outside.

It would not be the last time that the two groups would share a piece of culture that had been passed down through history.

Chapter 22

"The people in the caves stayed alive because of Memorists like my father," Abraham explained, hopefully answering Facecake's many questions.

The group was once again sitting around a campfire, the light around them fading quickly. The evening was a little chillier than the previous day, and so, the brothers had all found heavier clothing that fit them from the stores that the other youth had built up.

And then more questions came.

So all three brothers sat across from the other three youths and answered as best they could.

They all had eaten the fresh venison steaks from the morning's hunt, and sat contently with full bellies, warmed by the bright and dancing flames, narrating what their father had taught them

"From the records left to us from our ancestors, we learned that about fifty years in, the lights went out. They had used magnetic generators up to that point to keep electricity going in the caves, but after that, they had to start getting creative," Abraham explained.

And so the brothers took turns explaining how the engineers in the cave system had started harnessing the strength of the quickly moving underground water found deep within the mountain, and then went on to harness the bioluminescent algae, grown from the stores of seeds and soil brought in by their ancestors.

Finally, as all of the original generators disintegrated into rusting hulks of metal, a brilliant Memorist and his sons, had learned how to melt down certain parts of the metal, forming them into very thin filaments.

And then the glass blowers, who had perfected using a powdered limestone found deep within the caves as their base for thin, almost translucent glass, made the first light bulbs that could be illuminated using magnet cords and the water turnstiles. The caves were illuminated, allowing the people to flourish instead of merely survive.

The youths from the outside world were stunned by the revelation and the ingenuity of the people. They had never heard nor seen such technology. In fact, they had never even heard the word before. As Elijah was explaining the technology involved in water turnstiles, Facecake had stopped him mid-sentence.

"What, you've never heard the word?" Elijah has asked the young woman.

"I have not, yet it sounds so easily said from your lips," she explained.

117

"Technology is a word that can be defined by degree, actually," Noah said. His brothers had nodded along.

"Your aero-plane can be described as technology, as can your method for storing dried meats in the salt shed you've built. It's all a matter of what is available at any given time, so therefore, anything can be called technology, if it harnesses the available means and methods," he went on.

The other three youths were still a little slow to understand but had decided to drop it when Elijah said what all the brothers had wondered.

"It also describes the world that came before all of us. The reason that the people were in the caves to begin with. The technology that had ended the world for our ancestors from outside the caves," he said, offhandedly.

That had stopped the other three youths as one.

"Wait, what? The world ended? Then how have we always been here?" Facecake asked.

"Well, where do you think your buildings and the aero-plane you found came from?" Abraham asked.

"It came from the Before-Time, which we do not speak of," Cheese said, almost rotely. The other two youths nodded, like it was common knowledge.

Now it was time for the brothers to ask the questions.

"Wait, what?" Noah and Elijah said, nearly in unison

"The Before-Time. The time that we do not speak of," Moose stated, as if that answered all of the many questions bubbling up from the brother's curiosity.

"You guys don't know about the technology that destroyed the world?" Abraham asked. The brothers were stunned.

"We actually don't know what happened before we were born, or a few generations back, when events started being written down," Facecake answered him.

In fact, it was a thing she had often secretly wondered about, but all of the adults from the Castle area were adamant that she should not pursue answers for her many questions about the past.

In fact, she thought back, it was one of the reasons that she and her two best friends had wandered away from the Castle, something no one else had ever done, as far as she knew, or had heard of.

The Castle, she thought suddenly. We have to take the brothers to the Castle.

She looked across the fire at the three young men sitting together, and marveled at how much they looked alike, and how very pale they were. Even their eyes. Well, she thought, especially their eyes.

She had never seen anything like their eyes before.

Because the brothers' eyes were almost completely white, where they should have been brown or blue, or even hazel, like her own. She wondered how they could still see

But the whiteness of their whole eyes wasn't the worst part. No, she thought, looking at their eyes across the flames. The worst part was that nothing reflected back from them.

Looking over at her own friends, she saw the flames reflected in their eyes, making tears almost form within her own. Looking back at the brothers, all she saw was the flat whiteness, with no shiny reflection at all. She, along with Cheese and Moose had all noticed it at first, of course, and had even whispered to each other about the boy's eyes. But she didn't want to be rude by asking them about the oddity of it.

She wondered how the brothers would be accepted at the Castle, but more importantly, how the people there would contend with the brothers' knowledge of the past. But they had to hear it, she finally decided.

119

And so, she first whispered her idea to her two best friends, sitting on either side of her, across the leaping and dancing flames from the brothers. They agreed.

And when she mentioned the plan to the brothers, to take them, and their knowledge of the Before-Time, to the Castle, she missed the looks of apprehension on their faces.

She didn't understand their fear of meeting more people from outside the caves.

After all, the three youths were the first people they had met out in the world, and it had taken every single ounce of courage they possessed to approach them.

Because for a day and a half before they had walked into the clearing where the aero-plane lay, and the three youths had worked and fellowshipped, the brothers had watched them from amongst the trees, wanting to do nothing more than turn around and run straight back to the caves the moment they first laid eyes on these other humans.

These other humans that looked nothing like humans from the caves.

Chapter 23

"We left. Couldn't stay in one place anymore, like everyone we knew. There was this big, huge world that our families were so afraid of, but we weren't. We wanted to see what was out there," Facecake said.

Abraham nodded next to her. Walking along, talking about things that they wondered about each other. The woods were pressing close. The other young people walking in a straight line, headed west. Towards more people, towards a destiny they couldn't imagine.

And they were heading in the wrong direction, a feeling that Abraham couldn't shake. Couldn't get it out of the recesses of his mind. Like an itch in his brain he couldn't scratch.

"And so, we did. We just packed up some food, some clothes, and were determined to see what was out there. But we didn't really get very far, that's for sure. And now we are going back," Facecake continued.

"I haven't quite told you what and who my father was in the caves, did I?" Abraham asked her. He wanted to get her mind off of what was bothering her the most. The fact that they were headed back to her home.

And so, the two of them were starting to fall back a bit from the group. And for some reason, Abraham was okay with that.

Facecake shook her head. She had been very curious about this whole Memorist thing.

"Very early on in the time in the mountain, the people divided their tasks up and started naming them, like anyone from the Before-Time would have done," he explained.

"Some were tasked with maintaining and keeping the lights on. Others with keeping the growing crops. Tree arborists were tasked with growing the trees and crops for food. Many others took the job of developing and raising the sturdy animals we used for food, and other animals we used for working," he said.

"And one group of men started realizing that as people adjusted to the caves, the outside world's stories, and facts were being forgotten at an alarming rate," Abraham told her.

Facecake understood what the tall boy was saying. As he talked, she glanced up at him, stricken by his height. She was used to being as tall, or taller, than most of the boys and men she knew, let alone the females. But Abraham towered over her. She liked the feeling of looking up at the dark-haired and white-eyed boy.

122

"Those men decided that they needed to appoint one man to gather and keep the records of what the world had been, and meant, so that knowledge could be shared across the generations, assuring no one ever forgot," he said.

She watched as his face took on a different look than any she had seen so far. Almost reverent, she thought. She didn't know what he was thinking.

"And so, the task was given to a descendant of the man who had established and prepared the caves in the first place. He took it very seriously, and down through the ages, the Memorists kept the records. He assured us that the people would not forget," he said. "And they did not."

"To be a Memorist was a great honor. But the role came with its own troubles eventually. The people in the caves still became blind to the outside world all around them, as if it had never existed."

"The stories became legends to them, as the caves became their entire world. They started to not put the Memorists in such an honored position," Abraham explained.

"And the Memorists, for a time, were pushed to the fringes of the society," he said. His eyes grew thoughtful, she thought.

Facecake was watching the tall boy's face, and nearly stumbled when her foot caught an exposed root from one of the tall trees they walked amongst. But Abraham's quick hand shot out, catching her arm, and pulling her back upright.

She was suddenly surprised at his speed and strength. The boy hadn't even broken stride as he caught her muscled frame. Impressive, she thought suddenly.

He didn't miss a beat in his story though.

"Eventually, the people started getting depressed in the darkness and the routine of survival. And so, the Memorists took on a new duty. That of the Storyteller," he explained.

"And in the last couple of generations, they became revered. They became leaders in the caves, because they alone knew all the old history. They became able to entertain, and then to lead the people. They began to be worshiped by people who knew no other way of life, and had no memories in their own family lines," he said.

"And finally, the Memorists were the ones who began to converse with Raziel and Azrael, the ArchAngels who frequented the caves, teaching the people how to create new technologies, keeping the people alive despite epidemics, violence, even mass hysteria and claustrophobia."

Facecake had no idea what all of Abraham's words meant as they made their way through the thick forest. Birds sang, swooping in and out of the sunlight filtering down through the heavy leaf and branches above them. Squirrels and other small game played along the forest floor.

Facecake felt that the world had been so simple. But now, with the words and stories this young man had already told her, it was growing around her.

It was a very unnerving feeling, and she wondered, as they tramped through the underbrush, if the people at the Castle would see the boys and their stories the same way.

She hoped the close-minded people would accept what the boys had to tell them. Because what the boys didn't know, and what she didn't want to tell them, was that the people at the Castle were living, feeling, and regressing the same way his people had.

Her people were slowly dying, and she knew it was because they had given up. They had nothing to live for in this broken world that she had been born into, which she had tried her best to run away from.

And that's why she had always been so very different from those she came from. Why she, herself, had almost been outcast from the Castle more times than she could count.

She looked ahead at where the other youths were walking through the heavy forest, talking together, crunching through the underbrush. She was proud of what she and her best friends had done.

She was proud of herself.

But there was a fear that had set in as well. A fear of how much the world was going to change now based on what the brothers had told her the night before, when they made up packs, locked up the aero-plane in the big steel building where they had found it, and set out at the first rays of sunlight.

They had a couple of days to hike until they got to the castle. And she was worried that they were out in the open, afraid of the creature that had been killed two nights earlier.

They had all refused to talk about it, and as Facecake hiked along with her friends, and her new acquaintances, she thought about that creature, and how its physicality contradicted what she knew about the world.

And as they moved through the deep, green leafy trees, the bushes interspaced amongst them, her friends walking and laughing loudly, she heard a sudden, loud sound behind them.

As if she had manifested one of the creatures again. She heard heavy breathing and stomping feet moving closer from behind. sounded like it was running full speed at them. Her heart leapt up in her throat, and she couldn't scream out to her friends. She almost felt frozen.

But then she turned, took Abraham by the hand, and started sprinting towards the other four youths. They all turned around, saw the pair running in fear towards them. And now they could hear the running steps behind them that were even louder than Facecake and Abraham's wide-eyed scrambling.

And so they all panicked, imagining the creature, knowing they were weaponless against it.

They couldn't see a thing in the heavy underbrush and thick foliage, but they could still hear the trampling of heavy steps and even louder breathing approaching.

They turned towards the west, and ran full tilt towards some sort of cover, some sort of defensive posture. Facecake looked around as she heard the running steps behind her getting closer and could not find somewhere they could hide. She needed to find something they could get behind so she could get out her bow.

Suddenly from up ahead, louder than the running steps behind her, she heard rushing water. She wondered if crossing whatever moving water they were approaching would stop the creature.

They moved into a clearing, and at the middle was the running creek, hardly more than a hard jump across. The boys had all jumped over the water before she got to it, and Facecake made sure they were moving behind a few small boulders lining the other side.

And then she turned, pulled her bow off of one shoulder and dropped her pack, all in one smooth motion. She dropped to one knee, an arrow drawn tight against her cheek.

Her eyes focused on the sounds moving towards her, the arrow knocked back, her breath loud in her ears. She felt a shadow behind her fall into her sightline, and she looked to the side and saw Abraham, standing strong beside her, holding one of Moose's long knives in one hand, his other resting on her left shoulder.

And as what they thought was another of the creatures finally entered the clearing,; she drew the arrow back tighter. She was about to let it loose, but the hand on her left shoulder tightened. Abraham shouted in a shaky voice practically next to her ear,

"STOP!" His loud voice so close to her made her jump, almost losing her balance.

"Don't shoot Alexandria. Don't shoot."

She looked up at him, letting the bow string slacken.

"It's my father," Abraham said, voice shaking, and his hand gripped her shoulder tighter.

He was looking towards the dark figure at the end of the clearing, lost in some deep shadows as the sun suddenly went behind some dark clouds.

"It's the Memorist."

Chapter 24

"Boys," he said.

He was much-winded, his breath coming in gasps. He had never run so hard in his entire life. Hell, he thought, he had never had the room to be able to run so far and so fast.

He still stood in the shadows of the clearing, looking at his three sons, who were slowly getting to their feet, Abraham closest to him.

So he held out his arms, and his sons all ran, closing the gap between them, and crashed into him as if they had not seen home for months. He felt and saw the sun break out of the clouds, and the clearing brightened with the joyful light.

He embraced each of them, feeling as if all the world had closed in on the four of them, and he silently sent a prayer heavenward, a glorious thanksgiving for the reunion of his children.

Jerimiah Simone was not a man who shocked easily or spooked without cause. But being without his children, even for a short time, had made him feel a panic deep in his soul that he sought to alleviate.

He had talked it over with his wife for some time, and even had called a meeting of the elders in the caves to plan for the rest of the cave dwellers to move out into the world.

But he had known in his heart that he would be departing as his children had done, if for nothing more than to find his boys and bring them home.

The rest of the people in the caves were still deciding whether they would be stepping out into a world that had shocked them all, actually forcing a social panic amongst the people.

As far as Jerimiah saw it, they weren't moving on an answer anytime soon.

So, after kissing his wife goodbye, he snuck out the small steel door next to the big cave entrance and rambled carefully into the wilds around him. How easy it was now, he thought, to walk out of the door that had been barred for so many centuries, and how easy it was to forget how they had all viewed that same door with trepidation and fear.

He stopped at the edge of the cliff once again, but before descending down into the trees, he gave a silent prayer to the Creator, asking for the ArchAngels who had become like family to him to appear. He gave it a few minutes, but neither showed up to lead him.

129

He straightened his backbone, hoisted his pack firmly against his strong back, and had set off towards where he felt his sons would be. He had no idea how he would find them, but he had faith, and the strength of that faith had gotten him this far.

After a day and a half of traveling through trees, several clearings, and dappled sunlight, he felt like he had been shut away in a box his entire life. The great expanse of land he traveled opened up his mind and his soul.

He breathed deeply the air that had been denied him his entire life and felt such a wonder at the world. His mind blossomed, his legs strengthened, and his mood shifted into overdrive.

He found himself deep within a wooded hollow, birds singing above him, and small game rustling through the underbrush when he suddenly remembered a story his father and grandfather had taught him.

The story of how the world had ended, and the entity that had created that ending. He heard and felt the words spoken to him from two men who had never experienced what he was now experiencing. The extreme sadness of that fact almost overwhelmed him. The injustice of generations of people who had never felt the sun on their faces or felt the firm world under their feet.

Jerimiah was almost overcome with the grief, and so, he purposely set his mind back to the day his father and grandfather relayed the story to him, and the words all came back to him suddenly.

It was quite an undertaking in his mind, but he tried to imagine the world around him covered in snow and ice. He really couldn't understand what snow was, but he knew how it had been described to him.

And like a sudden miracle taking place in front of his face, he saw deep within the hollow he stood, under an overhang of stone and shadowed trees, a patch of pure white.

The world around him was warm, very comfortably so, and it shocked him to see what he assumed was snow. He walked over to the deep overhang, and pushing himself within it, he could feel the temperature change around him.

So, that's how the snow was still piled deep within the shadows, he thought.

He scooped a handful of the whiteness, feeling the coldness in his hands. He marveled at the extreme change in temperature from the snow. It started melting instantly in his warm hand, but before it did, Jerimiah was able to learn all he had to know about it. And fear enveloped his heart and mind.

He quickly dropped the melting snow and scooted back out of the dirt floor of the deep fissure. He stood to his feet, wiping his hands on his leather pants.

In his mind's eye, he saw the world around him not as it was now, but as it had been when it was unlivable.

As he was about to start walking again, a large dark shadow fell over him, stopping him in his tracks, and his heart leapt again in his chest. He turned around slowly, expecting exactly what was before him.

Both of the ArchAngels hovered a few feet above the floor of the hollow. And he was overjoyed to finally see his protectors and wise teachers. Their wings were outstretched, and Jerimiah wondered if they just did that display as a show of awe and strength, or if they were just used to appearing to people who had no idea what they were, and so had to display their great wings to prove their origins.

Azrael spoke first.

"Jerimiah, Son of Memory, welcome to the world you have dreamed about for so long," she said in her many-voiced way.

131

Raziel took up the salutation.

"You have now seen in your heart and your mind the world from which your kind escaped, and hid away for so many centuries. And you now know the wonder of the Creator, given to your people to enjoy," he said.

Jerimiah looked up at the pair of tall, glorious ArchAngels and asked the question that had been on his mind since the people in the caves had ventured forth, only to turn around at the shock of the world. Only to feel absolute panic that the expectations of generations of people were completely wiped away.

"Why keep us in the caves while the world outside has become livable? Why did you persuade us that we were not safe until now?" he asked the pair.

And then as they tended to do, they both instantly transformed into human forms, both still beautiful and wonderful.

Azrael was dressed unlike anything he had ever seen before. Some form of fabric, heavy looking and tight, blue in color and hardy covered her lower half, while a shirt and black jacket covered her top. He had never seen leather shine as much as the black jacket she wore, and he wondered suddenly if these were clothes from the Before Time.

Raziel looked like he always did when he and Jerimiah spoke. He was dressed in a pure white suit of clothing that Jerimiah had asked about several years ago. Raziel had called it a business suit then, and he wore it plainly and wonderfully in this place and time, once again.

Jerimiah had a feeling that Raziel was inappropriately dressed for the deep, tree-covered hollow in which they all stood, but he didn't put much thought into it. These were heavenly beings, after all, and how they dressed made no difference here.

Raziel spoke first. His face looked contrite, and Jerimiah was thankful that the Angel felt sorrow for the betrayal that he, and the rest of the people in the caves, felt at the deception.

"The deception was a necessary part of the growth of the people in the caves. Son of Time, you must realize that the purpose of any journey is not the destination, but rather the changes made within a person because of the journey itself," he said.

Jerimiah knew of what he spoke, but that didn't mean he had to like it.

"The Creator, and us in turn, believed that the people were not strong enough to face what this world would do to them all, until enough time had passed that every single people in the caves held the strength and fortitude to do what this world will need them to do, and make the sacrifices needed to obtain the future that is decreed," Azrael said.

She spoke up finally, and as Jerimiah looked at her young face, he knew that there was something much bigger than his grief at play here.

He finally found his voice after the two ArchAngels had spoken. A pause seemed heavy between them, and Jerimiah knew that he only had a few moments with them. They were flighty at best, and he rarely had an opportunity to speak to them at length.

Every time he had seen them both in the caves, they gave whatever instructions or warnings to him, and instantly disappeared before he could ask questions

It was one of their more annoying habits.

"I get that the people would need to be strong enough to face this world, but this world doesn't seem too bad to me. What about this outside world will test us so much, that it required the people to stay locked away in caves for centuries?" He asked.

Raziel responded, and the answer made the hairs on Jerimiah's arms and head stand on end, and a sinking, terrible weight settle in his stomach.

"It's simple, young Jerimiah. This world is once again in need of rapid change, and the people of the cave will have to sacrifice themselves to enact that change, or else perish along with everyone on this planet, once again."

"Only this time, there would be no survivors," the tall ArchAngel exclaimed.

With that, and a final bright flash of light that Jerimiah was quite used to, the two ArchAngels disappeared, and the sudden silence of the woods around him made him feel suddenly frustrated.

He had no idea what the ArchAngels had meant with their words, but he knew one thing, they were as cryptic as they always had been.

He was about to walk out of the forested hollow to continue his search for his sons, when another bright flash of white startled him again. And just like the snow that he had held in his hands earlier in the day, and how it had melted, his curiosity got the better of him.

He walked over to the area where the ArchAngels had stood, and where Azrael's feet had trod the earth. A white piece of parchment was now rolled up, laying innocently upon the ground.

He walked over to it, bent down, and picked it up in his hands. The paper felt warm, as if it had been slightly baked in the sun. It was rolled tightly and was wrapped in a gold ribbon the likes of which he had never seen before. It was a gold that shone so brightly, it hurt his eyes.

He pulled off the ribbon, sticking it in a pocket of his cowhide shirt, and unrolled the parchment.

Its contents startled him, and for several minutes he felt like he couldn't breathe.

A few minutes later, after he found that his feet still worked, he moved out of the hollow, heading south, towards a fate that he didn't know if he was strong enough to face.

He stood at the rim of rock that overlooked the hollow that he had walked through, and where his life had suddenly changed,, and he knew one fact for sure.

He would never see the two ArchAngels on this side of Creation, ever again.

Jerimiah hitched his pack even tighter against his back, straightened his backbone, and moved off into the southern woods, to his sons, who he now knew were not far off, and the fate that would decide his own life, and begin his son's lives in earnest.

He felt the sudden weight of hundreds of years of burden forced upon his people, and he was ready for the part he was to play in the events that would play out.

The parchment had told him all.

It told him of the rest of his life, and of the eventual end of the world that was soon to come, which would be much more cataclysmic than the last time.

The last time that had not quite taken.

He just wished that he would be there to see it, but he knew that was impossible. After all, it would be his death that would start the whole damn thing.

"Let it be," he thought as he once again pushed forward through the trees, hoping against hope that his sons would be strong enough to face the truth.

Two days later, he stood in a brighter clearing within the trees, looking at his sons, still wondering,, and trying his hardest to not tell the boys what was coming, and what they were all going to have to face, alone.

"Boys," he said again.

His heart felt like it was going to burst.

"I've finally found you."

Chapter 25

"But how?"

"How did the people out here in the world not build it back to what it was? Where is the technology? Where are the cities and the millions of people?" The questions poured out of Jerimiah.

They were once more sitting around a fire, cooking a late evening meal. The crisp, early autumn air was chilly, and the small pocket of warmth around the campfire made the young people feel drowsy and safe, after days of long travel and a steady and sure gaining of ground.

But Jerimiah needed answers. It was a thirst he had always had. It was Cheese who spoke up, answering the older man.

"I think it's because we all forgot, or chose to forget, what we were before," he said.

Jerimiah let that sink in. The exact opposite of what he had been born to do. To remember, and to teach those memories so that mankind didn't make the same mistakes again.

But mankind chose another path. They chose to remain less than they could be, as a way to cope with an almost universal feeling of loss.

And Jerimiah knew they would face the truth of their circumstances, and the choices of their own ancestors, first thing in the morning. He could see the lights of homes near the Castle that Facecake had spoken of earlier in the day. As they had traveled further west, towards a new set of mountains.

Tomorrow would answer a lot of questions, Jerimiah knew. And he was suddenly afraid. Terrified, even.

His thoughts turned darker, and he asked no further questions.

All three boys could feel their father's mood shift. They all knew he was not one to be so dramatically dark, and so their confusion was palpable as they all settled in for the night, finding spots around the gaily dancing flames.

Uncharacteristically, Abraham found a spot to lay down very near to Facecake, and it did not go unnoticed by his father. Jerimiah simply smiled at the future he could foresee for his eldest son.

It brought a small comfort to him that his son would find some small happiness in the years to come.

As the fire died down to embers, and the youths settled down into their sleeping arrangements, blankets made from old canvas and scraps that the outside world youths had scavenged, pulled up close under chins, Jerimiah prayed one last prayer to the

Creator that he had known all of his adult life within the caves, and felt a calmness settle over his tired mind.

The last thing that he thought before sleep took him was that he was never going to see home again, and he had gotten his mind to a place of accepting that fact. He knew from the parchment the ArchAngels had left for him that the next day was inevitable.

His consciousness faded, as dark as the night around him, and he was finally at peace with how it was all going to play out.

The next morning dawned bright, but cold. Jerimiah didn't know if it was the chill of the morning mist seeping into his soul and his body, but he shivered despite being completely covered. The cold was not on the outside, then, he thought ruefully.

The children packed up camp quickly, dousing the last of the dying embers of the fire with water from the stream they had bounded across the day before. Shared glances between Abraham and Facecake did not go unnoticed, once again. But in one of the pairs of eyes who observed them, only jealousy arose.

Soon after, they all set out due west. The horizon was dark in the direction they traveled, but light from behind them gave them sure footing over ground that started to slope upward, the tree cover becoming more and more sparse.

The group walked steadily onward, only Jerimiah feeling any apprehension about the day that would unfold. He alone had inside knowledge of how this day was to turn out, and he worried more for his boys than he did for himself. He couldn't quite wrap his mind around how the boys would take it, and that fact worried him more than he liked to admit.

And then he thought about Emily. And his stomach fell into his still-moving feet. He went suddenly numb and wondered only about how his feet could keep moving towards the rest of the day.

Emily's favorite song came to his mind suddenly, like a bright light in a dark day, and he suddenly felt better. He had no idea how, or why, but remembering her singing that song on one of the last days they had together brought him a peace that stayed with him the rest of the long day.

Abraham had his mind occupied on much more mundane and positive things for a teenage boy. Namely Facecake, and the looks that they had shared since the day before. The day that he had reached down, grabbing her hand, and then felt her hand tightening around his, unexpectedly.

His nerve endings still buzzed with the excitement of that simple touch. And the even more simple looks shared between the two of them, as if they could read each other's minds.

A growing sense of anger and animosity arose in Cheese's belly. As the group walked through the morning, moving steadily closer to the home that they had left behind, his mind was not on seeing his parents again, or his little sister.

His mind was focused solely on the fact that the love of his life was ripped from him suddenly, and by nothing more than a pretty, pale face, a pair of white eyes, and a height that Cheese envied as well.

Moose only thought of seeing his mom again and tasting the bread that she baked fresh every single day, and that he had been without for more than two years. He had not wanted to leave home with Facecake and Cheese, but he was never really able to speak his thoughts.

He usually could not keep up with the chatter between his two friends, and now adding in the brothers and the father from the caves, the men who looked so different from what he was used to, well, he could not do more than follow his feet, and think of the food his mother would ply on him as soon as she saw her baby boy again. His mind felt comfortably fuzzy, as it usually did, and he was just fine with that.

Noah and Elijah simply kept their own counsel, keeping one foot in front of the other, moving over the rising landscape and marveling at the soaring rock walls around them.as They walked down a crumbled old road, deep into the mountains that they did not have a name for, but which the other youths had told them their old home rested in the middle of.

They, too, had no idea what the day would hold, or where they would be, when it was finally finished.

And that's how the group felt as they arrived at a blockage in the road, made of fallen trees, too large to go around, and too high to easily maneuver out of the way. But they didn't have long to worry about how to get through the obstacle.

Three large, dark men, all holding drawn bows, jumped to the top of the blockage from the opposite side, with arrows nocked, and pointed straight at the group.

Before any of the group of six teenagers and one old man could move, or seek shelter, Facecake spoke up, making the brothers jump, and her friends grin like idiots.

"Da, don't point that damn arrow at me. We all know you can't shoot for shit," she said.

Chapter 26

"Yeah, but at this distance, I'll hit at least one of ya," the dark-skinned man in the middle said, lowering his bow and scowling down at the group.

Facecake merely shrugged at her father.

"Whatcha doin comin' back, girly?" he asked.

Facecake just shrugged again, a sneer on her pretty face. She hoisted her pack higher on her back and looked disapprovingly up at the man. The boys were all a little nervous, and Jerimiah simply studied the three dark men.

Seeing his piercing, all-white eyes studying them intently, the other two men turned their bows towards Jerimiah.

Jerimiah did not flinch, nor stop his intense study of the men. It was a tense moment, a standoff, which did not diffuse for several more seconds.

Until Jerimiah spoke, breaking the thick tension.

"Sirs, we simply seek accommodation, and Alexandria here has told us about your lovely home. We are simply passing through," he said.

One of the other men was the one to answer him.

"That's no problem, stranger, but there will be some questions, and you better give answers," he said.

Jerimiah nodded and beckoned the rest of their group toward the right side of the fallen tree roadblock as the man pointed them to move that way.

They walked up to the imposing rock wall that seemed to support the fallen trees. When the group arrived at the corner of the obstruction, and turned their head a certain way, a small, straight opening appeared.

The youths were all confused and stood there, moving their heads back and forth, seeing the optical illusion of an opening appearing and then disappearing. Jerimiah knew it was a simple case of angles and eye lines. He chuckled to himself, leading the way into the dark opening between the trees and the wall.

He moved through the narrow passage quickly and was the first to emerge on the other side, into the sunlight, and saw that the three men had been joined by two others, and all five had arrows nocked, and pointed at his chest.

He felt the others crowd in behind him, having come through the small passage one at a time. As Moose emerged last, he gave out a shout, and ran towards one of the men holding an arrow nocked. The much larger man lowered his bow and approached the large boy.

142

"My boy," the large man yelled as he grabbed Moose up in a bear hug. Moose was laughing as well, and Jerimiah saw that the large boy had tears streaming down his face.

"My boy is home," the large man said.

He finally released Moose from the hug, and Jerimiah smiled at seeing tears on both faces. Two faces that looked almost like twins, except one just looked older.

Definitely the boy's father, Jerimiah thought to himself as he and the remaining youths stood waiting for direction. They didn't have to wait long before the man who Jerimiah had identified as Facecake's father led them further down the long road, towards what Jerimiah could now see were houses.

Smoke rose from fires outside the homes, and Jerimiah could see several people start to mill around, deep within a small hollow near the center of the town.

Was it a town? Jerimiah thought to himself as they walked deeper into the mountainous region.

It had to be, he figured.

The scroll had been very specific.

They followed the local men deeper into the small town, watching the doors of the homes open, the yards filling up with children and then adults, and the mountains around them. Jerimiah and his sons were much more cautious than the others, but even he could tell that the youths that had left this place were unnerved.

They all walked to the end of the row of stone houses, noticing that clothing was one of the biggest differences in appearance between them and the townspeople . The four people from the caves wore looser, thinner garb, made by the seamstresses from the caves.

The townspeople had cultivated a heavier form of cotton, and so their clothing were breathable, but did not make up for the chill in the air, even early in the afternoon. Their dress was made from hides of animals and some form of canvas. Jerimiah only knew it was canvas from samples they had kept through the Memorist program.

But their actual physical features were even more differentiated.

Jerimiah and his three sons were all tall, even for cave people. They towered over most of the townsfolk that they walked amongst. But that wasn't the only difference.

The males from the caves looked like most of the people they had been raised around. Very light skin, dark hair, and absolutely white eyes.

The people of the town, as well as the three youths they had been among were all darker skinned, darker haired, and darker eyed. The four males from the caves stood out like lights on a hill. Especially their eyes.

A mutation that Jerimiah knew had popped up amongst the cave people about four generations into living there. The mutation allowed them exceptional sight in the dark, but it also allowed them to visually detect temperature fluctuations.

Jerimiah's forefathers had researched the phenomenon extensively, and now they just took it for granted. But the people outside the caves couldn't take their own darker eyes off of the males from the caves. And when those dark eyes found the white eyes of the cave dwellers, they shrunk back in fear.

That was not a good sign, Jerimiah thought suddenly.

As the two different groups walking upwards towards the end of the valley rounded a last curve in the crumbled road, they came in sight of the Castle. And that's when Jerimiah's stomach dropped.

Like a nightmare, the Castle rose from the side of a steep hillside, and when Jerimiah saw the metal dragon's head sticking straight out from the tall rock walls, he knew his fate was sealed.

He just prayed deep in his soul that the dragon did not mean the same thing to his sons that it did to him, ever since he had first dreamed of the dragon's visage very early in his own life.

144

He knew firsthand the terror that metal face held for him. The face that he had seen in his nightmares for more than thirty years in the caves.

The group of men still held their bows slightly taut, and beckoned the group towards the tall, imposing structure. As they moved into the darkness of the bottom level of the tall stone Castle, Jerimiah's hearing became muffled, his stomach knotted tightly, and he felt his bowels loosen slightly.

The group was ushered up a flight of stone stairs, circling upward, towards Jerimiah's fate, and whatever the rest of this day would hold for him. This was going to be the end, he knew. And he hoped he would meet his fate like he had met everything else in his life.

With bravery, strength, and his head held high.

Archangels be with me, he prayed silently, as the darkness opened up into bright, colorful light.

Chapter 27

The rough stone stairway was the only entrance Jerimiah could see leading into a very large, open room. One whole wall at the rear of the room was made with stained glass depicting several scenes. Most of them, from Jerimiah's vantage, showed human suffering or growing in one way or another.

He didn't have much time to focus on them, however.

The floor of the open, soaring room was made from heavy wood planks, but there was not a single echo within the open area. That was odd, he thought, distractedly.

He looked at the table of people sitting under the stained glass wall. They were five older people, heavily wizened, already wrapped in heavy clothing for a winter that had not yet set in.

Five sets of dark eyes watched the group approach wearily.

The armed men pushed the group of youths and Jerimiah just in front of the group of disapproving elders. Jerimiah could almost feel the malevolent aura seeping from the group in front of them, and the weariness from the armed men behind. Something bigger was happening here, he thought to himself.

And then the oldest man amongst the group of elders spoke.

"Are you from the settlements in the East?" he asked.

His voice sounded like footsteps on gravel rocks. Heavy footsteps.

Jerimiah answered his question with a question. Might as well rock the boat from the beginning, he thought.

"Do you all just sit here at this table, in this large room, waiting for someone to approach and lay out a problem?" he asked.

One of the older women to the right side of the first man answered his question. She seemed to be much more patient than her compatriots. She had a kind face, and a very heavy, twisted mass of gray and white dreadlocks atop her head.

"We received word of your coming closer for some time. We have the children out with signal mirrors to let us know who is approaching."

"There have been...excursions," she said. That piqued Jeremiah's interest.

"Who the hell are you, where do you come from, and why are you with these runaways here?" the older man in the middle asked exasperatedly.

Jerimiah took a very deep breath. And then another.

147

He could feel everyone in the room watching him, including his three boys. He looked at them for a few fleeting seconds. He loved his boys so fiercely.

And then he answered.

"My name is Jerimiah Simone, and these three boys here are my sons. We only met up with the other three kids a few days ago," he said. The room held its breath too.

"As for where we are from, it's fair to say that we are all from right here, in what used to be known as the state of Colorado, of the United States of America," he said.

"We never heard of such a place, and we never seen your kind around here before. You need to do better than those lies if you want to leave this place," the old man was shaking.

Jerimiah lifted his head and matched eyes with the older man. As if the entire room shrunk down to just the two of them, a test of wills.

Jerimiah found his voice soon after.

"My people were forced to flee into a system of caves over 300 years ago. We have been shut away in those caves for all that time, and only my sons and I have just left them," he said.

"Our people assumed the world was still inhospitable, that it couldn't sustain life," he explained.

The old man in the middle suddenly moved backwards in his chair. As if Jerimiah's words were physically painful. Jerimiah saw the movement but continued to explain.

"When my people first went into the caves, it was because a technology that mankind had created tried to kill off the human race. She very nearly succeeded," he said.

He looked around at the other people in the room. Everyone seemed to be listening attentively, especially the other elders at the old wooden table. The woman who had explained about the sentries looked as if she had a million questions, but everyone held their tongue, as if waiting for the eldest man to speak. That man simply shook where he sat.

148

And so Jerimiah continued.

"We had used technology and industry to ruin the environment. We broke our world. And so, we created a new technology to fix it. That technology decided that we did not deserve this world. That, in order to fix this world, she would have to rid the world of humanity," he said.

And that's all the eldest man could take. He was shaking so much he looked like he was vibrating. Pushing back his chair loudly, he stood and started to shout.

As the old man started shouting, the sunlight had had been filtered through the colorful glass behind him suddenly winked out, like a light. A dark cloud obscured the sun, and the room was drastically cast in gloom.

"Hearsay!" he screamed.

"Hearsay! These people are demons!" the old man shouted.

"Demons I say! From the pits of Hell! Kill them, kill them all!" He screamed, spittle spraying from his mouth.

The old man's face was so red that Jerimiah wondered for a split second if he was going to keel over himself. But he didn't wonder long before the room erupted at the first scream. Commotion was all around him.

And Jerimiah felt like the calm eye of a giant storm. He merely waited for the inevitable.

As he looked up into the eyes of his oldest son, Abraham, he could see the fear in the boy's face. Jerimiah merely smiled. He nodded at his son amidst all of the movement and sound around them.

A maelstrom of chaos.

As he saw his son being jostled by those around him, and the room shrank as more people ran into the room, Jerimiah simply stood still, allowing the jostling and shuffling people to bounce off him. Hands reaching out, arms clinging close into his body, he was a center of calm.

All the shouts, all of the movement, all of the fear and tension in the room did not change the look on Jerimiah's face. The calmness that emanated from within. And he never took his eyes off of his son's face, he didn't see Facecake's father raise his bow in the split second of clear space between the two men.

Jerimiah saw the look of panic and fear in his son's eyes and face, and he simply mouthed the words he wanted his son to know more than anything. He said the simplest and most profound three words in all of the myriad languages of mankind, and he made sure that his eldest son heard the words that Jerimiah pushed between them.

The three words were simply, I love you.

He only wanted his son to know that completely, wholly, and with all of his heart. Jerimiah felt only love in this moment of chaos.

He felt the love emanating from deep inside of him, and he could hear nothing else going on around him. Like cotton had filled up his ears, and his heart felt like it was going to burst.

Until he felt the shock of an arrow shot into his stomach.

Chapter 28

They were huddled in the corner of a round stone room. It was cold, and they had no idea where their father was.

Or if he was alive.

The three brothers huddled together, close, scared out of their minds. Everything that had happened that afternoon had happened so quickly, and they still couldn't believe how it had erupted. Their father had simply been telling the truth, and all hell had broken loose.

And their three new friends were nowhere around to even tell them what the hell was happening, or why. The brothers had all thought that they had come to this place to help.

Not to die.

Abraham calmed his younger brothers. Elijah was taking it all harder than the rest of them. He loved their father fiercely, but more than that, still felt like the Memorist was invincible. He had not yet seen how life and the world was bigger than any one man.

Abraham himself was more puzzled than anything. The look on his father's face, at the end, was baffling. Almost as if he had known what was to come.

Almost as if he had known that arrow would find his body, and he had wanted to share with his oldest son one last lesson.

A final lesson in a lifetime of lessons learned. That made Abraham think back over years of training, lessons, memories, and memorized facts.

It was quiet outside their cold cell. And it was definitely a cell. Abraham was assured of that. He had tried the large steel door. It was locked tight, and no one walked the dark corridor outside it. He wondered at their fate, and at what the hell had just happened.

As they had walked as a group together towards the great Castle on the side of the mountain, Facecake had pressed close to him, whispering not to trust anyone. He wondered at that, as these were Facecake's people.

But he trusted her in ways he couldn't quite comprehend, and events had happened too quickly for him to figure that out. But what was even more baffling was that Facecake had not even seemed to trust her own father, who walked ahead of them, leading the group to their fate.

She had especially not trusted her father, as Abraham thought about it. The man had tried to get the young woman's attention several times while they had walked through the small settlement leading to the Castle, but every time the man had cleared his throat in the direction of his daughter, she had pressed in closer to Abraham.

Even taking his hand at one point.

And so the man scowled at Abraham, and then at the whole group, as he walked ahead, and led them into the Castle, and upwards to the bright, open room.

He still had no idea what was going on. When they had been ordered into the large, open room, with its bright wall of glass, he was even more confused. As if they had known all of this was happening. As if they had all been warned, and only the group of strangers were left out of the details.

Abraham stayed grouped together with the rest of the youths, hand still held by Facecake, and then his father had stepped forward away from them to address the men and women at the table under the glass.

And the man in the middle, the man that had made shivers run up and down Abraham's spine with his malevolent eyes, and haughty nature, had screamed at his father's answers. A simple truth. One that Abraham had known his entire life, had maybe cost his father his life.

The irony was not lost on Abraham, but he couldn't voice that to his two brothers. They were too shocked by the situation, and too afraid of following the same fate as their father.

Abraham shushed Elijah, who was starting to whisper frantically about the Memorist. He was shaking again. Abraham pulled him closer, as did Noah. They would stay together to whatever end the Creator chose for them all.

There was suddenly a sound in the corridor. The boys all rose to their feet. If their father had taught them anything, it was to face everything while standing up.

They didn't know what was coming through the door, but they would be prepared to face it, no matter what.

153

A metal key sounded loud against the heavy steel door, and Abraham pushed both of his little brothers behind him, protecting them from whatever was coming through that door. He could feel them both tremble, and for a split second was proud of the fact that he was not afraid.

Nothing could have been worse than what had already happened, he knew.

The boys were all ready for whatever lay ahead, and as the heavy steel door swung inward, they tensed themselves to fight.

But shock replaced their tension as two women walked through the door, holding covered trays.

Facecake walked through first, followed by the woman who had spoken with some small kindness to their father just an hour earlier. The brothers had no idea what was about to happen, but the sight of their friend leading the way calmed them somewhat.

A guard followed the two women into the small, cramped space, and when the older woman turned with a grimace on her face, the guard looked down humbly, and moved back into the corridor, closing the heavy steel door behind him.

Abraham locked eyes with Facecake as the young woman walked towards them across the small cell. He could see the shame on her face, but even more apparent was the concern. He still didn't know how he felt about the girl, but he knew that his chest soared a bit when she walked up to him, looked up into his face, and said what he knew she would say first.

"I'm so very sorry, Abraham. It wasn't supposed to happen this way."

She looked down then, and the other woman crowded in behind her. The older woman cleared her throat in a no-nonsense way, much as the boy's mother would have done.

"Oh, yeah," Facecake said.

She placed the covered tray she had been holding into Abraham's hands, and then turned and took the other tray from the

154

older woman, handing it to Noah. She motioned for the boys to sit back on the cold ground and uncover the two trays.

The three did as she told them and found simple food under the white cloth.

As the boys dug into the bread and fruit, the two women made themselves comfortable on the same cold floor. Both sat cross-legged, and looked regal doing so, Abraham thought as he bit into still-warm bread. It was better than anything else he had ever tasted. He felt the small enjoyment coming from both of his brothers as they bit into the same large loaf.

They had not realized how hungry they all were.

After a few minutes of silence between the two small groups, Abraham finally cleared his throat, looked curiously at the two women, and let his face ask what his mouth could not.

The older woman spoke up as she saw the concern on Abraham's face.

"I don't know how, or where, your father is, young man. All I know is that was not how that meeting was to go," she said.

Abraham could hear the exasperation in her strong voice.

"First off, my name is Adora. I am Alexandria here's grandmother. On her mother's side," she strongly pointed out.

Abraham could now see the family resemblance between the two women. They were strikingly similar now that Abraham looked closer.

Looking at Facecake's face, he knew that the apologetic look he had first detected in her was still there. He wanted to reach out to her, embrace her, and make her feel better. He didn't realize then that she was thinking the same thing about him.

"I'm so sorry, young men, for the events playing out the way they did," Adora told the boys.

"But Granger Mace has always been a hothead and has gotten this community into more trouble than not," the older woman told Abraham, alone, it seemed.

Abraham's attention was piqued.

155

Granger Mace.

So, that was the name of the man who had murdered his father, Abraham thought. Or, at least, who had given the order. It had really been Facecake's father who had shot the arrow.

In his immediate memories, Abraham could still see the shock and pain cross his father's face, as his hands had gone to the shaft protruding from his belly. Abraham had tried to reach his father as he fell to the floor, but stronger hands had pulled him away, and took him to this cell where they now all sat.

Abraham heard a strange noise coming from behind him, and ignoring the women for a few seconds, he turned, and saw Elijah shaking and starting to cry, holding onto a crust of bread.

Abraham reached out to his littlest brother, wrapping him up in a hug like his father would have done for him. He felt Noah's arms wrap them both, and for a few moments, the surrounds disappeared, and they were just a family, grieving for their father.

When Elijah stopped shaking and whimpering, Abraham stood back, allowing Elijah to compose himself, wiping the tears and snot from his face.

Abraham turned back towards Facecake and her grandmother. He felt a resolve in himself that had not been there a few minutes earlier. He lost his fear. Now all he wanted was revenge.

"Tell me everything," he said to the women.

An hour later, the boys were alone in the cold cell, once again. Facecake and her grandmother had both promised to come back in the morning, bringing food and more information about their father. If they could find more.

One of the things that Abraham had learned from both women was that his father's body had disappeared. The thought, Adora had said, was that Granger Mace had had the body taken to the medical wing of the Castle, for dissection. Granger had always been a man of study and took delight in learning about things he didn't understand.

"Your unique physicality and those eyes would surely make Granger curious. I wouldn't put it past him to find out as much from your father's body as he could," she had said.

"That's sacrilege!" Elijah had yelled back. Abraham and Noah both soothed the younger boy. Even Facecake had walked over to the young boy and had put her arms around him.

But Elijah was right.

The people from the caves treated the dead with more respect than the living, Abraham thought. He wanted to retrieve his father's body and give him the proper burial that he deserved.

And now, as the boys sat huddled once more together in the corner of the dark cold cell, trying to keep each other warm, but also whispering plans between them, Abraham felt the rage grow inside of his chest. He and his brothers were going to be ready, no matter what happened.

Their plans devised and meticulously studied between the three of them, Abraham geared himself up for a fight.

Before the two women had left, and after giving them as much information they could about the Castle and the surrounding area, Abraham had made Facecake promise to do a couple of things that could get her into trouble. But she had agreed, and she had also agreed to get Moose and Cheese's help in what was going to happen this very night.

They just had to make it back to the large, open room.

"Guard, guard, my little brother has to go to the bathroom, sir. He needs to relieve himself really bad," Abraham called to the dozing man outside the large steel door.

He had to repeat himself several times, banging on the door before he heard the key in the lock. It sounded heavy, and Abraham prayed to the ArchAngels that the man was alone.

As soon as the large steel door swung inward once again, and a single middle-aged man, holding what looked like a crossbow down along one leg walked into the small cell, Abraham struck.

He crossed the short distance between himself and the guard as quickly as he could, and as the room was cast in gloom and shadows. Still, Abraham could see as if it was the full light of day, and the
had no idea what happened until after it was over.

Abraham grabbed the front of the man's tunic with his left hand, pulling him close, and with his right arm already swinging, brought his elbow up into the man's nose as hard as he could.

He heard bones crunch, and the weight in his left hand suddenly became too heavy to hold. He released the man and saw the body crumpling to the floor of the cell, the man's face almost completely obliterated and covered in blood.

Well, one thing was for sure, Abraham thought as he moved his brothers out into the corridor, leaving the dead guard's body behind them. Abraham was a lot stronger than these smaller people out in the world.

He would use that to his advantage as much as he could.

Noah had stooped down and had picked up the guard's crossbow. He examined it in the dark of the cell for a few seconds, ascertaining its abilities and working mechanisms. He had always been good with machinery and technical things, Abraham thought, watching his little brother.

Outside the door to the cell, the corridor was long, dark, and empty. As the boys walked casually out into it, Noah bent down and retrieved a quiver of bolts for the crossbow. He slung it over his shoulder and pulled the straps tight against his chest. He now had a weapon.

All three boys could see quite clearly in the darkness of the Castle. Their special eyes, earned in the darkness in which they had been born, gave them sight where others would have none.

From directions the women had given them earlier, they moved forward, towards a flickering light, and wound their way through the mostly deserted castle.

If Abraham could help it, he didn't want to raise an alarm. If they could all get away from the castle without a sound, they would.

But he also itched to move upward to the very top of the Castle, where Adora had informed him Granger Mace kept his rooms.

But first things first, he needed to find his father's body, and he needed to get his brothers away from these animals who had murdered him.

They moved stealthily through the middle level of the castle, around three bends in the rock-walled corridors, and remembering the women's directions, soon found themselves approaching the hallway leading to the big open room at the center of the Castle.

Abraham stopped his two brothers before they crossed into the light from the burning torches at the center of the hallway. He glanced around the corner, making sure the coast was clear leading to the room.

But it was not.

Two guardsmen, looking bored, and holding the same crossbows in their laps like the one that Noah now held, were sitting on the floor of the hallway, four or five feet on this side of the door.

Shit, Abraham thought.

The guardsmen did not see nor hear the brothers, and that gave Abraham a second to evaluate the situation. The first thing he noticed was the distance between him and the men guarding the door. About thirty feet or so, he measured in his mind.

And then he looked at the two torches lighting up the area. One was on either wall, about halfway between him and the guards. Those would be his first objectives.

159

He turned back to his brothers. He had a plan.

The corridor was cast in shadows everywhere except the five or six feet around the torches. The boys could sneak through the darkness on this side of the torch light and try to extinguish them both simultaneously.

Noah handed the crossbow to Abraham, explaining quickly how the triggering mechanism worked. Abraham understood, nodded to his two brothers, and together, the three of them walked out into the entrance of the corridor. The guards couldn't see them because of the gloom. But the three brothers could see everything.

They would have to be fast.

All three of them, with Abraham in the middle holding the crossbow in front of him, ran full tilt down the corridor towards the two men, who heard the footsteps echoing down the long hallway.

As Elijah and Noah reached both torches at the same time, Abraham ran fastest between them. He both saw and felt his brothers take the torches down and extinguish them against the stone floor.

And at the same time, Abraham, less than 10 feet from the guards, who were rapidly rising to their feet, crossbows held out before them, screamed a rage-filled roar.

The corridor was suddenly cast in darkness. The two guards were still raising their crossbows, one yelling out, when Abraham reached them. They couldn't see him, but he could , including the fear on both their faces.

The guard on the right fell with a crossbow bolt through his left eye.

Abraham dropped the spent crossbow and threw himself under the raised weapon of the other guard on the left. He waited to hear the sound of the crossbow firing, but it did not come before Abraham kicked out both his feet, slid on his back, and broke both knees of the guard standing over him.

The guard screamed, dropping down onto Abraham, but the stronger teenager was ready, and had already reached up with both hands around the man's neck. Both heavy bodies came to rest against the door leading into the big room.

Abraham took hold of the guard, rolled over on top of him in one smooth motion, and silenced the man forever with a quick twist of his hands.

And then his brothers were there, and as one, they walked through the doors into the room where their father had been murdered.

Jerimiah Simone's blood was still on the wooden planks of the floor, but it would not be the only blood spilled in that room that night.

An hour later, Abraham was on his knees, washing his arms and hands in the cold stream water they had found soon after leaving the last of the stone-built homes behind them.

He could feel Noah on one side of him doing the same, and Elijah was close by, still being held by Facecake, who whispered to the young boy, telling him that everything was going to be fine.

Abraham could see his own arms in the light of the clear moon above them. It was deep into the night, but he had never felt more awake, nor more alive. His arms were covered to the elbow in drying blood.

He scrubbed more blood from his arms and hands, knowing that his sensations came from getting his brothers out of the Castle, and leaving behind enough of a statement to ensure that his father would be avenged.

The bodies he had left behind him in the Castle's main room would tell Granger Mace just how serious Abraham would be in exacting vengeance.

And then his arms were finally clean. The water carried away the mixture of blood from several people.

Abraham stood and felt his hands and arms dripping water. He turned to find something to dry himself with. He saw Moose and Cheese, sitting close by, looking towards where they could hear the boys from the caves, but couldn't quite see them. Both young men wore looks of disbelief on their faces. They too, had witnessed things they had never seen before that night.

None of them had seen the things they had done that night.

Abraham looked over at Facecake still holding Elijah, who was now starting to quiet down.

Noah walked up next to the taller Abraham, a steady and comforting presence at his side.

Abraham reached down to his father's pack, which he had carried out of the Castle after not being able to find the man's body. He opened the heavy pack, finding one of his father's shirts on top of other clothes and foodstuff.

He used the clean shirt to dry his hands and arms.

He then handed the slightly damp shirt to his brother, who did the same with it. Abraham could smell his father's smell on the shirt, and he felt the rage rekindle in his chest. He knew that Noah was feeling the very same.

Abraham looked back down into the pack, hearing a crackling sound. As his eyes focused more on the shadowy inside of the pack, his eyesight intensified, and he could see clearly what was making the noise.

He pulled out a clean, white roll of parchment, wondering what it was doing in his father's pack. Abraham had not seen anything like it before. He marveled at its cleanliness, a white almost glowing in the darkness of the deep night.

Wrapping the parchment tightly was what looked like a cord made of spun gold. Again, Abraham had never seen anything like it, but he had a strange suspicion about where the parchment and ribbon had originated. He felt the hands of the ArchAngels all over them.

Noah walked up next to him as he held the rolled paper. It felt warm to Abraham, like it had been left out in the sun. That was odd, he thought, looking into the quizzical eyes of his brother.

He pulled one end of the gold ribbon, and it came untied. He handed the ribbon to Noah.

The whole scene, when Abraham would think back on it throughout the years ahead, felt like it was all happening in slow motion.

Abraham unrolled the crisp, warm parchment, waiting for something magical and otherworldly to happen. Like finding a scroll of truth, or a treasure map. He was a little excited.

Noah moved even closer to his big brother, not making a sound, to see what secrets the parchment would reveal.

The other youths around the dark clearing next to the stream were wrapped up in their own thoughts and worlds. Noah and Abraham were alone.

Both boys gasped as Abraham lay the paper open to the world, its glistening surface bright upon the night, revealing its secret.

Both brothers looked down at the wide expanse of white parchment, heat rising off the paper like a wave.

It was completely blank.

Inter-Mission
1

Raziel and the little sister, Azrael, together looked down upon a world greatly changed.

It was slower, less populated, but about to enter a time of extreme hardships and strife. And that's what the Father of All Creation had tasked them to do.

To create His Army.

The two Beings were standing in the Spiritual plane, looking down through the spectral energy to the Material below. Both were garbed in their Energetic Bodies, and both felt the overwhelming worry coming from the Center of Creation.

There had been incursions. Even in the Material world below, Raziel had already dispatched a single messenger from the Nothing plane. There was no way that one of those beings of shadow could make it through to this plane, yet the evidence was still upon a temple table, being examined by lower Angels around the Throne.

And the Creator's unease did little to sooth his Children's moods. Azrael herself felt an almost human-like angst. Raziel wanted to chuckle at the thought of the younger ilk acting like emotional human teenagers, but he knew not to set the Angel of Death into a negative aura more than she was at the moment.

They continued to watch events unfold below. Since time meant nothing in this place, they could see the next twenty years of human time play out both slowly and fast. They watched the three brothers that they had set on their own tasks.

And they watched the thousands of others with the same evolutionary growth and physical gifts, leave caves all around the world.

From every nation upon this particular world, humans who were uncommonly tall, with fair skin, and eyes that seemed to glow, walked into the sunlight for the first time in nearly a millennium.

And where these humans, who had evolved deep within the earth came forth, they were surprised to find outside-world humans already thriving upon an earth that the cave dwellers had all been told was uninhabitable.

Raziel and his little sister had been quite busy over the previous ten generations.

The tall, wise, and colorful Raziel smiled at the gathering conflicts between the two types of humans. The Creator had Willed that an army of extraordinary humans be created, and this world had been perfect for such an endeavor.

Now it was up to the ArchAngels to enact the Third part of the Plan and set the new Army of Gifted to multiply and become fruitful. And one other thing, both ArchAngels thought together, their Spirits entwined as always: They would have to cultivate the man who was to lead this extraordinary army; the one who was grieving now, but who would arise before the conflicts climaxed.

The ArchAngels would continue to follow the Mission they were given. But both felt hesitation and knew that the End was nigh.

But they couldn't move any faster than they had.

As always, the Rules of Creation had to be followed, hence why they had to take such extreme measures to create the human army below. The Father of All could not Himself simply form such an Army. No, the Rules must always be followed. Even by the One who created the Rules.

And this Army must be ready to fight in the Final Conflict.

Raziel looked up at the throne room. It could always be seen, anywhere in the Spiritual plane. He let loose a mighty sigh, with air that did not exist in this plane.

The table resting at the foot of the First Dais had the dark creature still lying dead upon it, being studied by the many small, fluttering Powers, or Angels who had power over such creatures, or the facsimile of, in their own creation and experience.

The Powers were as baffled as the Host. When Raziel had first carried the beast into the Spiritual Realm, a great and mighty argument arose between the Three Spheres. Such an argument had not ensued since The Fall.

But the Creator had Willed that the beast be examined, if only to ascertain the capabilities of the enemies.

The real enemies.

Oh yes, Raziel thought to himself, twirling energy between the fingers of his Energetic Body. The extraordinary army below, made up of humans who had been tested and had evolved in the bowels of fire below the surface of their world itself, would have to fight.

167

The conflicts below would be great practice for what was to come.

Azrael and her older brother both sighed with non-existent lungs, in a place where no air was found, nor needed.

Great practice indeed.

Part 4
The Tower

Chapter 29

Abe was troubled. But that was nothing new. After twenty years of moving, fighting, and being on alert at all times, being troubled was actually a nice reprieve from the normal. He routinely wondered if he was actually capable of being anything other than at full alert.

He was standing at a large, clear window overlooking a factory floor which bustled with movement and industry. His people were still busy building weapons, munitions, and focused on new technological advancements based on what he knew of the times before. The White Eyes were used to the work. The war had gone on so long.

He heard a sound behind him and smiled. She was finally home.

He turned and saw his wife of fifteen years trying to sneak up on him. It was still their game, played almost every day she was home. And she still wasn't able to surprise him at all. Secretly, he allowed her to think so, because it brought that smile to her face that he loved so much.

That was his real joy.

"Alex," he said, holding out his arms.

She dropped her pack where she stood and rushed into his arms. This too, was a joy for him.

For the first time in more weeks than he wanted to think about, he felt whole. He felt the hope of his life return to him slowly, deep within her arms, his past, present, and future wrapped tightly around him.

He took a deep breath, feeling her take one against him too. He could swear that their heartbeats synced up and beat in unison.

And just like he did every day since she had accepted his old-fashioned query to start to court her, he felt like the luckiest man alive. His worry from a few moments before was forgotten for the, oh too brief, time he was able to hold his other half.

He kissed the top of her head as her strong arms stayed wrapped around his midsection. After three children, twenty years together, and countless dangerous situations where they could have easily lost each other, they still marveled at being together, and were very much still in love. Much to the chagrin of the children.

"Okay, Alex, tell me what you saw," he told her.

She squeezed him one last time and stepped away from the embrace. Her moving away almost felt painful to him. She had been gone for six weeks this time. The littlest of their children, young Abigail, had missed her almost as much as he had. He would wake the children soon. Seeing their mother would be a welcome surprise.

"The reports are true. They found the installation and are working to start it all back up again," she told him.

Shit! He thought. He knew this was going to happen. It had to. He had been winning this war for far too long for the opposition to just sit idle and allow it.

"We can't get Cheese to firebomb it, it's too well protected. Even his aero-planes will have zero effect. Could we infiltrate it from the ground?" He asked.

She just shook her head.

"No, they have the tightest security I've ever seen them use. We could barely get within the outer sentries to see what they were doing. Abe, I really do think it's coming to an end with this," she said.

He could hear the worry in her voice. But also the hope for an end to this war.

The war, he thought. Thinking back to the night that this had all started. Twenty years earlier, when he had lost his father.

And his own soul in the process, he thought ruthlessly.

He needed to think. And he needed his family. So, he nodded to his wife, and motioned her to walk out of the room overlooking the factory floor. Their children were asleep this early in the morning, but they would be unhappy if he didn't wake them to tell them that their mother was home.

She moved away to their shared quarters, probably going for a shower, he thought, and he moved to the other side of the large living area, to wake the three children, and to enjoy the small reunion this morning before he had to get back to being the leader that all of his people expected him to be.

He was no longer a Memorist like his father, and his father's father. Now, he was the Battle Lord. He often wondered if

172

it had all been a mistake, and if his father would have done the same things he had done.

He did not know, and that may have been what bothered him the most.

Later that day, he sat at a makeshift desk, looking at maps and lists of his people and supplies, before his lieutenants were meant to meet him to discuss the things that Facecake and her team had seen on their last mission for intelligence. He thought again about the night it had had started.

He had not thought about the night his father died in a very long time. It had scarred him just as much as his two brothers. And it had started a cascade of horror and death that still wasn't finished.

He leaned back in his chair, hearing the squeak from the spring at the bottom of the ancient office chair, making him think fleetingly that he needed to oil the damn thing once again.

He remembered how he felt that night, having just killed two men in a blink of an eye. Those two guards, and the one that had been in his cell as he and his brothers made their escape. Those men's deaths had been the first blood on his hands.

But not the last. And so, he thought back to that night once again.

He and his brothers were on their knees, the two guards lying dead beside them. He silently pushed one of the double doors leading into the big room open a crack, to see who or what was in it. He didn't see anyone at first, but the room was lit with torches all around, an orange light that did him little good.

He and his brothers rose and silently moved into the room. He heard Noah bend down and pick up the crossbow that he had dropped after dispatching one of the guards. Noah quickly nocked another bolt, and they were ready for anything.

The entire time they were trying to escape from the Castle, as well as extract some form of revenge, Abraham's mind

173

was focused on the fact that all of this trouble could have been avoided if they had never come to this place.

But then he realized, as they moved into the large room, that it could have been avoided if his father had not told these people something that they did not know or did not want to know.

The three brothers moved into the center of the large, lit room, and scanned the corners. They were alone. The light from the torches bounced off of the large glass wall at the front of the room. They could not see anything in the darkness beyond the colorful windows. And in the darkness from the night, the glass took on the resemblance of dark, dried blood.

The boys stood back-to-back. They purposefully did not look at the dark stain on the wide wooden plank floor where their father had fallen. Abraham's mind quickly made the connection between the color of the dark stained glass window, and the color of his father's dried blood on the floor.

He grew even more angry.

He knew, from the training his father enforced in him and his brothers every day of his life, that rage was a weapon he should use. And he didn't have long to wait before he would use it to its exhaustion.

It may have been a changing of the guards, or just a random nightly excursion, but two more men entered the room from the other side, opposite where the brothers had entered.

And the single thing that baffled Abraham, as he and his brothers sprang into action, was the looks of confusion on all of the guard's faces before they were killed.

A bolt from the crossbow in Noah's hands took one man in the head. As Abraham moved towards the other man, he applauded his brother's aim, once again. Just like the second guard in the hallway outside the cell, Noah's aim was true.

Abraham was on the other man before the guard knew what was happening. Without a weapon, Abraham only had his hands.

174

And that was enough.

Abraham used his speed and superhuman strength to finish the man quickly, and bloodily. Ripping out the guard's throat, Abraham made sure an alarm was not raised by the man he was killing. He didn't need to worry however, as a loud clanging sound echoed through the room.

Abraham looked out of the dark, stained glass windows, and saw a long, bright flame escape from the metal dragon's head above the windows. The sound seemed to be coming from the dragon. He didn't know who or what had tripped the alarm, but he knew more people were about to enter the room.

And that's when things got very interesting.

Men in patchwork clothing, holding weapons of one sort or other seemed to come from everywhere. At first, Abraham felt that he and his two brothers would be overwhelmed quickly, but these men could not fight.

Hell, he thought, dispatching a man who ran at him with a large, clunky blade grasped in one hand, it was as easy to kill these men as it would be to kill children.

Crossbow bolts seemed to fly from everywhere, and then Abraham's keen hearing picked up another sound. The whispering of longer arrows, shot from a longbow. A long bow like the one that Facecake was expert at using.

He looked up from the man he had just dispatched and saw her on the other side of the room. She was shining, and he felt a surge of the feelings that had almost overwhelmed him for the last few days. He knew right then and there, in the midst of battle, that he loved the girl.

Her two friends, Cheese and Moose, had followed her into the room. Cheese was cowering behind the other two, a large pack held in his hands.

Abraham learned later on that Cheese had snuck silently through the hallways, looking for Jerimiah, or what had been left of him. He was also trying out his sneaking, stealing, and escape artist skills that he felt he had perfected most of his life. The thought of all the time he had spent practicing would not go to waste made him smile as he crept through the deserted hallways.

Cheese had stumbled onto the open door leading into Granger Mace's rooms. He didn't hesitate at all. He ran through the doors, looking for anything, something, a compelling feeling making his feet move faster than at any other time.

On a table, he saw Jerimiah's distinct pack, and it felt like a magnet in his chest drew Cheese to it. He slung Jerimiah's pack onto his back, hearing people coming from a room further into the suite of rooms belonging to the leader of the dark people.

And so, he ran.

Moose, who was tormented and torn between his best friends, new friends, and the family that he had left behind, waited for Cheese to find him. He was crouched down with Facecake, waiting for the chance she had spoken of to finally be free of this place, and these people. But Moose didn't want to be free of these people. They were his family.

And so, he did nothing, which was his way.

When Cheese, carrying Jerimiah's pack, caught back up with the other two, they made haste for the big meeting room, where earlier, Facecake had made plans with Abraham to meet up and escape.

And so, after dispatching the rest of the men who had ran into the room, presumably at Granger Mace's orders, Abraham, his brothers, with Facecake and her two best friends, escaped the castle.

Cheese still held the pack, stolen from Granger Mace's rooms. Something had compelled him to keep hold of it as tightly as he could.

The small group was making their way out of the room when a ruckus made Abraham turn back around for a last scan of the place where his father had died. And that's when he saw him.

Granger Mace, the man himself, had followed his men into the killing room. Abraham, the last to leave, and the old man locked eyes.

Abraham smiled viciously at Granger Mace, promising to come back, and finish the job. He saw the fear in the older man's eyes and felt satisfaction at what the team of youths had done this night. His team of youths, he had thought even back then.

And so they escaped.

Over the next twenty years, as the love between Abe and Facecake intensified, and they started a family amongst the fighting and eventual war that came from their actions that night, Abe became convinced of their cause. The people in the outside world, all of them, had no idea what they had come from.

They were born in ignorance, and followed cruel, ruthless dictators born of hate, strife, and the people's suffering. But those dictators, who the people considered gods, had given them a taste for violence, for ignoring the human rights naturally given in the Before Time.

And so Abe and his brothers had spearheaded the war. They made sure that their own people from the caves prospered. The White Eyed People had become the peacekeepers, the moderators, and sometimes, the powerful army, that they needed to be. And Abe had lost most of himself, as well as his two brothers in the process. He still blamed the People of the Dark for that.

The animal-like people living in the world before the White Eyes emerged did not deserve to survive, and Abe didn't like how that fact made him feel.

He had spoken at length with the ArchAngels through the years about the differences between the people who lived in the Darkness, as they called it, and the White Eyes, who lived in the light.

He continued to ponder how those ignorant, violent people made his own people feel. Made him feel. Because soon after the night his father had been murdered by Granger Mace, the outside people had started a massive witch hunt for the White Eyes, who by this time, had all finally left the caves, and settled comfortably in the outside world.

And the Dark People had murdered a large share of them before the White Eyes started fighting back.

Abe didn't know just who had started the war. The night that he had tried to avenge his father, and also to escape the same fate, he, and his brothers, along with Facecake and her friends had not meant to start a war. At least, in their estimation. They were simply surviving.

But soon after, the conflicts between the two peoples had escalated, and now, it was all either group knew. And the White Eyes had been winning every skirmish, battle, and all out melee.

Until now.

Abe sat in his war room, planning the future. A conflict of biblical proportions was on his mind, when his second in command, a large man named Jersey, came into the room with news Abe had been waiting to hear.

"Abe, they are here," the large man said.

At first Abe thought the large man was speaking about his lieutenants. But the look on the large man's broad face said otherwise.

And like a sunrise breaking over the horizon, Abe quickly understood the tone of the man's voice, and the expression on his face.

Abe smiled larger than he had since Facecake's return earlier in the day. He bounded out of his squeaky chair, and clapped Jersey on his large back as he ran past him down the metal stairs, to the living areas adjacent to the factory floor.

He was grinning from ear to ear, his earlier anxiety temporarily forgotten. He tried to calculate the years since he was this happy.

It had been so long since he had seen his two brothers.

Chapter 30

Emily Simone wiped the table clear of the leftovers from lunch. Watching after her three precocious grandchildren was a chore that was extremely tiring, but one that had kept Emily alive.

And boy, the three could make a mess!

Her thoughts went to her family, and the role that she played in it. These were thoughts that were with her most days. She cherished her family, her sons more than anything, but she missed Jerimiah terribly. Even today.

Maybe especially today. And she didn't know why, only that her heart was heavy, and her mind was dark.

She did not like days like this, but they were there, and they must be felt, and discarded, she knew. There was no relief for it, but to simply get on with life, and your lot in it, she thought, dishrag in hand, wiping up spills from her youngest granddaughter.

She continued to clean the dining area, and then the kitchen. These were menial tasks that Abe had asked her repeatedly to allow someone else to do, but which she couldn't quite let go of. She must look after her family. Her boys especially, since the rest of what she had known in the caves had been extinguished from her life.

As she finished tidying up the kitchen counters, her mind drifted to the past, and to those they had lost.

Of course her mind went first to the man to whom her heart belonged, but he had been gone these twenty years. No other man had replaced him. And she was just right as rain in that regard.

Her parents had succumbed to a wasting disease within five years of leaving the caves. As had Jerimiah's parents. It seemed that in those first few years, many of the very old amongst the people had perished. It seemed those most unable to adjust outside the caves had simply been taken out of the equation. Like a burning wildfire had swept through.

Emily was thankful to the Creator every single day that she was still alive, and very much healthy. Her bones and joints ached most days, but she still had her wits about her, and her body was still trim and strong. She relished in daily walks, with guards surrounding her of course, through the forests and new paths that she rejoiced in making with her very own two feet.

That thought made her mind go to her music, and the lyrics of songs of old. Songs that had told of this outside world, and which she had grown up hearing. As she matured, she learned, repeated, and sang along and in company. Those lyrics, burned in her memory, and in her everyday life, kept her going as well.

Music always would, she knew. If she lost everything, she still had her music.

The music kept her going until the Creator could take her home and allow her to be once again bonded with the man who still held her heart. Her Jerimiah. She sighed heavily again and let her dark thoughts drift.

After the dishes were properly washed, and stacked for drying, she found herself with little to do. And with the song lyrics still strong in her mind, and on the tip of her tongue, she sat in her old familiar and overstuffed couch, grabbed the guitar that sat in a stand next to it, and started to pluck the strings.

This guitar was not the one that she had inherited from her ancestors in the cave. That instrument was far too valuable to leave out for the world. Her grandchildren would run the risk of breaking it. That guitar was safely ensconced in a vault still within the caves that they had called home for so very long. She hoped against hope that nothing would touch that instrument. Including time.

The guitar she was playing now had been a gift from her son, Elijah. As he had grown older, he had developed a love for crafting things from the wood he so loved. Emily's mind went to her youngest son as she plucked and played an old religious hymn from memory.

Elijah, who she had not seen for almost three years. She had been devastated when Abe had informed her three years ago that he was sending his brothers off on a mission of the grandest design. To seek out peoples in other parts of the world, to ascertain if others had survived the caves. And if so, if they had been changed like the people that Emily had descended from.

A worthy undertaking, she knew. But one she wished had not been given to her two youngest sons and a cohort of guards and soldiers. She wished with all of her heart that her entire family was once again back around her, singing the old songs together, relishing in each other's company. She wished with all of her heart that she was whole, and the family that she had put her whole self into had not been so tragically broken.

She felt like a failure.

Tears sprung from her eyes as her fingers found the old familiar chords of the ancient song. She wanted to sing,, but her voice was caught in her throat, and words did not come.

She kept strumming anyway, the song coming alive under her deft fingers. And as she found the chords of the bridge, moving into the refrain of the beloved song, a voice from the doorway found the words that she could not form.

She picked up the notes and chords of the first stanza once again. She wanted to hear the voice sing the first lines. No, she needed to hear it.

Her fingers nearly faltered as she finally recognized the voice she heard coming from the shadows, singing the very words she could not find earlier. The words that were like a soothing balm to her dark mood and her even darker thoughts from earlier.

And then a second, deeper voice sprung up next to the first, and a melody of sweet, baritone notes came from two throats that she knew very well.

And as her two youngest sons stepped into the light coming from the window at the side of the room, she finally did stop playing the guitar.

But the words her sons sang continued coming forth as she sprang from her comfortable chair and rushed to where her sons stood in the light.

"*When peace like a river attendeth my way, when sorrow like sea billows roll, whatever my lot, Thou has taught me to say, it is well, it is well, with my soul.*"

And then Emily Simone was wrapped within the enfolding arms of her children. Her world, as much as possible, was whole, once more.

Chapter 31

Abe found Noah and Elijah standing together, in the middle of his living room, hugging their mother, tears flowing freely from all of their eyes.

His as well, he thought, as he rushed to his brothers, and helped them enfold their mother even tighter in a hug that would give her soul peace after so long.

It had often pained him to see the faraway look in his mother's eyes as she washed the dishes, her eyes gazing out of the window overlooking the forest.

185

It also pained him to send off his brothers on a mission from which he had no idea if they would return. But he had no choice.

There was no one else he trusted to finish the task.

He had to gather information about the rest of the planet. Were there other people still surviving in other countries? Had they taken to caves as well? Were they White Eyes like him and his people? No one could locate, ascertain conditions, and return to report their findings as well as Noah and Elijah.

In twenty years of being out in the open, not one person from another part of the world had connected with Abe and his people. So, he had to go to them.

And now his brothers were home, and he couldn't wait to find out their news. But first, his small family had to rejoice in each other, and his mother's soul needed lifting up.

"Uncle Noah, Uncle Eli!" A small voice broke the tranquility of the moment. But it also put a smile on all the faces in the room.

Abe's oldest daughter, Ruth, came running into the room. Eleven years old, she was the only one of her siblings who remembered her uncles well enough to run to them, arms outstretched, wanting a hug as she always had before.

Her two sisters followed her into the room, but they were much more hesitant. Behind them walked Alexandra, an instant smile lighting up her face as she walked into the second reunion of the day. Little Abigail, her youngest daughter, tried to hide behind her mother's legs.

Alexandria's smile was larger than life, and Abe appreciated how much she loved his family. She did not have the White Eyes like all the rest, even his children, but she nonetheless was one of them completely.

Wiping their eyes as they pulled apart from one another, the brothers and their mother each picked up a child, and allowed Elijah to give Alex a crushing hug. Abe looked over at his wife

186

hugging his littlest brother and thought for the thousandth time that he should feel a stab of jealousy over their closeness, but he only ever felt even more love for his family.

Amid the chaos of war and the constant need to survive until the next battle, he cherished times like these.

But it was getting very wearisome and in a lot of ways, he was already exhausted in his bones.

But he squared his shoulders, pushed off the fatigue, and laughed along with his daughters, who were happy to have their uncles home at last.

Ruth, Abigail, and Abe's middle daughter, nine-year-old Caroline, ran off so that the adults could have a long conversation. Abe yelled one last warning to his gregarious daughters as they ran, giggling, from the common room.

"Be good! Don't leave the compound, and for heaven's sake, Caroline, stay out of the trees!"

He heard his daughters laugh louder, and a bright burst of love lit up his chest.

But then he had to turn back to the task at hand and sat at the large family table that his mother had just recently finished cleaning. His two brothers, looking like the cats that had gotten into the cream, sat on either side of him. Alex and his mother were busy in the kitchen putting together tea with some bread and sausage for the hungry men.

"Okay, guys. What happened?" he asked his two brothers.

And then he saw them both grin at each other.

The story unfolded naturally over the next few hours. Old jokes, familiar bantering, and a peace that had been missing since the two younger brothers left to fulfill Abe's mission filled the dining room of the Simone home.

Several more people came and went as the story was told, and finally Abe was introduced to his new guests that evening.

187

Guests that would turn the tide of the raging war around them.

But for just a little while, Abe's whole world and his family were all in one place. His heart was at peace. His troubled feelings from that morning vanished in the smiles and laughter from his daughters, his wife, and especially his mother.

It was a peace that he needed as a balm for his sensitive spirit and restless mind.

A peace that would be short-lived, but he would look back on it in gratitude and gentleness as the years ahead grew rocky, and finally downright torturous.

Chapter 32

"We took the boat out of the west coast as you directed us, and Elijah was instantly sick to his stomach," Noah was telling the whole table.

Abe sat at the head of the large wooden table, which was scarred from generations of family functions.

Alex and Emily finally joined the rest of the family, bringing a small repast of food, and sweet tea grown in Emily's own garden.

Elijah looked sheepishly down at the table as the family laughed, allowing a lightheartedness to pervade the room. It was gentle ribbing, but Elijah was still such a sweet and sensitive soul.

Not for the first time did Abe wonder what kind of woman it would take to bring the young man out of his boyhood habits and turn him into the hard warrior that Abe would need.

His attention went back to Noah's story.

"It only took a week to sail to the islands of Hawai'i. We had great wind the whole way. Almost like the Creator was pushing us Himself," Noah said.

"But the entire Big Island was deserted, overran with vegetation and wildlife everywhere. We hunted for three days for fresh meat for the rest of the trip."

Abe and the rest of his small family, except the children, who were happily giggling, yelling, and playing out in the front yard, sat around the table, fully at rapt attention. The story unfolded before them all, and the surprises were plenty.

"After that, it took two more weeks to reach the eastern Nihon coast. We only encountered one storm, and reading the old books, we were all able to keep the ship and sails under wraps, turned into the swells, and we got through it mostly unscathed," Noah said. But then his face turned instantly somber.

And so Elijah, seeing his look, and hearing the tone in Noah's voice, finished the next part of the story.

"During that storm, we lost Benji," he said as somberly as Noah's face looked.

Abe sighed deeply. He knew Benji's parents quite well. He wondered if another member of the crew had already told his parents the sad news. He would deal with that later, he told himself. It was on his conscience, and he knew that he had to make right with them.

After a few moments of silence, Noah began speaking
again.

"We didn't know what to expect in the Rising Lands," he
said. Abraham caught the ancient usage of the name, as opposed to
the names, like Asia, that their father had taught them.

"We wondered, at least for a week, if the same fate had
befallen the Nihon island as Hawai'i."

"But eight days into trekking through it, dense vegetation
and animals attacking us almost daily, we finally found people,"
Noah said.

And then he smiled.

"Abe, the entire island holds hundreds of times more
White Eyes than we have here!" he exclaimed loudly.

Abe was shocked. Noah's words were what he had been
wanting to hear for so very long.

"We met a single village of White Eyes first. They were as
surprised to see us as we were to see them. And we couldn't at
first decipher their language," Noah explained.

"Not until Elijah here, the language expert, figured out
that it was a cross between old Japanese and Chinese. After that,
he could speak to them like he had been born there," Noah said.

As he told the story of Elijah's prowess with languages, he
reached over and ruffled his little brother's dense head of dark
hair. Elijah, unsurprisingly to anyone who knew him well,
bashfully looked down, embarrassed by the praise, though he was
still grinning.

Abe's heart was almost overcome with love for his
brothers.

And so, Noah went on with the story, interrupted here and
there by Elijah, who clarified a point or two about their trek further
East, and all the way around the globe, it seemed.

Abe was simply mystified they had gone so far and had
been gone for so many years. He constantly looked at his wife and

mother, seeing the same shock on their faces that he knew was on his own.

As the story unfolded, Abe learned that the rest of the world was mostly made up of White Eyes. It seemed that in every country, every land, every continent, people had sought shelter within the Earth when the cold came, so many centuries ago.

And every one of those people's scions had become White Eyes.

Abe's mind almost couldn't process the information. Every one of his hopes was justified. Every dream. And it suddenly felt possible to finish the war that he had been fighting his entire life, it seemed.

"I've got to say, brother, that as we met White Eyes from other regions, there were some very amazing similarities between us all, no matter where we had been born. But I think you'll have to see it for yourself," Noah told Abe.

Abe was confused at first, but when Noah and Elijah stood from the table, and beckoned Abe to follow, along with Facecake and Emily, he began to understand.

Noah led the entire family out to the factory floor, where Jersey was standing next to a group of four people, showing them the lines of White Eyes still assembling weapons and munitions.

Jersey saw the family first and stopped speaking. He turned the four strangers around to meet the family, and Abe received one of the largest shocks of his life.

Turning towards him were four extremely tall White Eyes. He was surprised to see they were almost as tall as him. But it was their skin tone, their genetic make-up, and their tall, upright bearing that shocked him the most.

Each of the four people who turned around were obviously from different regions. The Asiatic woman on the left was the shortest, but somehow seemed the strongest. The tall, almost Nordic looking man, who was almost an albino in coloring and contrast, stared back at Abe with almost palpable dislike, although he also radiated leadership and strength.

The other two strangers in the group were darker-skinned than the rest, which helped Abe to recognize their features as beautifully African or Middle Eastern. Both men, and both women were, to Abe's eyes, astonishing and angelic.

And Abe was also extremely grateful that he remembered so much of his father's teachings about the geography and races of the Old Times. The education allowed him to easily place the people before him, and where they originated.

But what shocked Abe was not that they made up a small conflagration from the rest of the world. What surprised Abe immensely, despite his brothers' account, was that the strangers all shared the same white irises and black pinpoint pupils that he and all those around him had.

It seemed right then and there, that the plans that the ArchAngels had spoken to Abe about on numerous occasions, had indeed not been in vain. Every time the ArchAngel's described a future that seemed out of reach, Abe merely shrugged it off, and focused on the tasks at hand.

He rarely had time to think two days ahead, let alone, years in the future, and a world that seemed merely fantasy.

And so, it seemed that this entire world was comprised of white-eyed people who had survived underground just as his ancestors had and had flourished and multiplied just the same. Abe couldn't hold in his excitement any longer.

He approached the four strangers, representatives of the rest of the world, and suddenly fell to his knees. He couldn't help it.

He had to thank the Creator right then and there, and even with his eyes closed in a prayer of thanksgiving, he soon felt those around him falling to their knees as well.

He opened his eyes to see his entire family, friends, and community, along with the four strangers were all on their knees, and they were all bowing their heads in prayer.

And that's when he felt the glow of light coming from behind him, and turning, he saw the two ArchAngels who were responsible for this gathering together of people from all over the world. The two angelic Beings that had been responsible for all that had been created down through centuries.

And for them all to be right where they were, ready to take back over the world, and fight the Creator's battles, when and how they were all called to it, shocked Abe to his very core.

Abe's whole soul was singing for the first time in two decades. He felt whole, complete, and finally a part of something so much bigger and grander than himself.

He felt his heart ready to burst, and a song was so close to his lips. The ArchAngels were happily beaming down on him, and he knew with all of his heart that this scene would forever be inscribed in history.

Abe, in his mind, looked down through the future, and saw this scene he was a part of right this minute, adorning walls, and classrooms, lectures, and family homes.

He saw himself, oddly detached from his present circumstances, kneeling in those stories, paintings, and wall hangings adorning gathering places, and Abe could suddenly see history how he assumed the Archangels always saw it.

Abe's mind and heart were ready to burst in extreme joy. Tears were already running from his white eyes, but more tears fell as he wanted to burst forth in song.

And as he opened his mouth to begin singing a song he knew every person in the large factory with him had memorized, he was cut short by a sudden loud scream. The scream came from outside the large factory doors, and was suddenly cut off mid-shriek.

He looked suddenly over at Facecake, who knelt next to him. Her face was a mask of utter terror.

"The girls," he said.

Chapter 33

And then the entire group, along with Abe and Facecake, all ran outside, into a deepening darkness of the late evening sunset.

The pair of ArchAngels led the charge. They were in their very tall, very splendid vestige, wings outstretched, alarm on their faces. That did not sit well with Abe, who was still shocked over meeting the strangers just a few moments earlier and was now confronted and alarmed by the screams of his children.

And amongst the trees ahead, a dark glow menaced his nerves and rang up and down his spine. He shivered as he ran towards it.

He ran towards a darkness that was emitting a darker shadow than the fading sunlight in the sky overhead.

He didn't see his daughters anywhere. And that worried him the most. He felt many of his people around him, running towards the scream that had been cut short, and that gave him a small comfort. The two bright and shining ArchAngels, hovering a few feet in front of him, and moving resolutely towards the darkness in the trees gave him even solace.

And then he was in the trees, the little bit of light overhead quickly extinguishing. He could barely see, but his enhanced eyesight afforded him a night vision that quickly adjusted to the darkness and the scene among the trees became clearer as he approached.

And what a scene it was.

Several bodies that belonged to people he had grown up with, had fought beside, and shared meals with, lay on the ground in haphazard displays of cruel death. He did not stop as he spryly jumped over the body of a dear friend, bow and arrow still nocked, held in frozen hands, dead white eyes staring up at the dark canopy of treetops overhead.

Abe couldn't stop there. He had to find his daughters.

He followed the still-bright ArchAngels into a clearing that the community had often used for picnics, playtime, and sparring training for the younger troops. And suddenly he had to stop in his tracks, eyes open wide, confused by what he saw.

At the far end of the clearing stood what looked like the exact opposite of the ArchAngels, who had also stopped to gauge the situation. The beings at the far end of the clearing were as tall as the angels, but stood on two large, tree trunk-sized legs. Their skin was mottled black and oozed a glowing green ichor.

197

And a deep darkness surrounded the beings, darker than the deepening night around Abe and his people. As though in opposition to the light of the ArchAngels.

Abe looked from the group of dark beings across the clearing, seeing there were four of them. And as his eyes took in the whole scene, he saw several more creatures that he had not noticed until that exact moment.

Although he had seen the creatures before.

Like a dark nightmare that he had forgotten, the scene from twenty years ago came back to him. He remembered the creature with the floating ring for a face, and which ran on pointed feet, in opposition to any living creature on this earth.

There was no sound from the darkness and the creatures at the end of the clearing. No sound, until Abe finally saw his three daughters.

The three girls that looked so much like their mother, but with Abe's coloring and eyes huddled together among the dark dog-like creatures. They were scared out of their wits, tears ran down their faces.

Abe looked at his three young daughters, surrounded by evil that he could not understand, and a massive bubble of fear struck his chest like a physical blow.

He wasn't going to stand for that.

Because his people had been at war for so very long, he wore a brace of his long knives, never knowing when he would need them.

And so, seeing his daughters in abject fear, wondering if they were going to survive for another minute, knowing that so many of their people had already fallen to these creatures, Abe took out eighteen-inch blades from both of his side sheaths, and with a scream of his own bursting forth from his chest, he ran as hard as he could towards the darkness that held them.

He felt his people surge around him as well. Arrows started streaking towards the evil darkness, hitting targets that Abe wanted to plunge his own knives into. His people were excellent marksmen. He never feared his daughters would get hit with one of their arrows.

As he got to within arm's reach of the first dog-like creature with a floating face, he dodged its advance back at him, and with battle instincts and reflexes earned in more battles than he could count, he swung his left blade as hard as he could at the side of the creature's body, feeling its skin part, a dark ichor leaking from the wound, splattering on his hand.

The blood that leaked onto his hand burned like acid. He screamed and dropped the blade it was holding. Looking down, he saw blisters forming, skin parting, and the knife he had dropped beginning to dissolve as it lay on the grass.

He tried to scream to his people to be careful of the creatures' blood. But no words escaped his lips. The pain was too great.

And then Azrael was next to him. She held his hand in one of hers, looking deep into his eyes. His pain dissipated, and his hand healed whole in the ArchAngels care.

"Be careful son of man, their blood is acid. But common earth poured over the wounds will stop the decay," she told him.

He felt suddenly whole again, and as the ArchAngel turned back towards the intense battle between Raziel and the tall dark beings, he saw a glowing sword appear in her hands. He suddenly felt a deep hope, and that gave him the strength to turn towards his people and seek out his family.

He saw his brothers first. They fought like devils. Blades swinging, dodging sharp pointed legs, dancing among the dog-like creatures. His brothers fought like whirling dervishes.

He wasn't worried about the two younger men who shared his blood, and whose blades swung in shining arcs, much like his did. He fought with a blind mind, all reflexes and instincts.

As the battles seemed to ebb around him, he stopped, took a deep breath, and looked around him, proud of his people, but concerned for those he couldn't immediately find.

He was really looking for his wife. He knew in his heart that she would have been the first one to follow him towards the battle for their daughters.

And then his eyes found her. Shining bright with sweat, her empty knife belt told him that she had dispatched a few of the evil dogs herself.

But it was where she stood that made him the proudest of her. She had reached their children, and gathered them all into a great hug, her long arms crushing her daughters against her chest.

She looked up and saw him, and he nodded back towards the way they had come. She nodded, instantly understanding what he meant.

Facecake said one thing to their daughters and led them all on a run back towards the village. She moved like a dervish herself, and Abe couldn't be any prouder of his family. That pride gave him an excitement in his chest, and he turned back towards the battle, ready to lead his people.

With a single long blade left, he watched the ArchAngels dispatch the tall creatures, and saw a pattern to the movements, like flocks of birds, moving in unison. And so, he mimicked the battle moves, and mowed down dogs like wheat under a scythe.

He soon joined his brothers, back-to-back, and together, they obliterated the remaining dog-like creatures with efficiency and ease.

Almost too much ease.

The glen soon grew silent. The enemy was dead, bodies surrounding his people that stood looking down on dissolving metal knives and arrows that disappeared in the acid.

And in the middle of the open glen, the two ArchAngels stood, shining brightly, not a scratch on them, nor a glorious hair out of place. Their shining silver swords were nowhere to be seen, and they, too, studied the creatures strewn throughout the clearing.

Silently, the group of humans examined each other, some hands grasping hands, some arms hugging after the heat of the battle dissipated. And Abe stood amongst his people, proud of the fight, proud of the death of the enemy, and the survival of his people.

They had won a serious battle here, and Abe tried to consider what it all meant. This had not been a battle between his White Eyes and the dark people. No, this was something bigger.

But he didn't have long to ponder the implications of this battle, as he glanced around at his people, and felt the strong presence of his brothers still at his back. He didn't have long at all, because a sudden booming sound bellowed forth from the trees at this end of the glen. From beyond where the evil dark creatures lay dead on the grass.

A dark bolt shot forward from the even darker trees, and in a blink of an eye, faster than even the ArchAngels could react, that bolt shot into Azrael, the younger ArchAngel, and the one who had healed Abe's terribly wounded hand only moments before.

The dark bolt, which Abe could now see was an arrow unlike any he had seen before, entered the ArchAngel's chest. The tall, lovely, almost unrealistically beautiful Being pitched backwards, and a great fount of golden blood shot forth from where the dark arrow had struck.

And as she fell to her back, her large white wings crumpled under her. Raziel gave a great shout, a bellowing heard all the way to the Spiritual Plane, and reached down to catch her.

But he wasn't fast enough.

It had all happened so very quickly, and the humans standing around, who only moments before were congratulating themselves on a beautiful victory, looked on in sheer horror, and watched as the taller ArchAngel bent down and picked up the fallen Azrael.

Golden tears sprung from the taller Being's eyes, and as the humans watched on in disbelief, he disappeared in a bright flash, crushing the body of the loveliest Being that any of them had ever known to his chest, and his piercing yell followed him to the other place.

The humans all stood around, shocked. They all came to the same conclusion simultaneously.

The battle had not been a battle.

It had been nothing more than a trap.

Chapter 34

It was completely silent. And the humans in the glen simply stood around, waiting for something, anything, to happen.

It was Elijah who finally broke the silence. His surprised whisper was heard by everyone still standing in the clearing.

"Abe, look at the blood," he said.

The words hit Abe like a physical blow. The events that had just transpired a few moments before were still fresh at the forefront of his mind, and the minds of everyone else. Two men walked fearfully into the woods where the arrow had emerged, and everyone else turned towards the blood on the ground.

The bright golden blood on the ground.

Everyone in the open glen, even the two men who returned from the edge of the woods, looked towards the golden blood on the ground. For a second, Abe looked to the two men, who just shook their head at him. Nothing was found in the woods.

The golden blood on the ground glowed in the dark of the night. It lit up the glen with a peaceful and happy light. It even glowed on the bodies of the strange creatures dotting the open area.

It seemed to pulse. The White Eyes gathered around the glowing blood, a sense of expectation in every heart. What was going to happen? They all stood transfixed, waiting like small children who patiently awaited their father to come home in the evening.

And then the blood started to move. To almost boil. But nothing touched it. No one wanted to stop whatever their expectant hearts were foretelling.

Abe got as close to the blood as he felt he should. He felt almost reverent. The glen was becoming a holy place. Abe knew deep in his heart that no matter what happened, this glen would become a holy shrine for all his people.

He was once again watching history take place before his eyes. And his eyes were drawn closer to the glowing blood.

It started to coalesce. It drew together in a single globe, still sitting on the green grass of the glen. And not one drop of the golden fluid was left lying still. Every single bit of it drew together into a bright, small egg.

The people standing around gasped aloud as the egg suddenly broke open with a ringing chime, as if a birth heralded by the heavens itself.

The people all drew back as if suddenly burned by fire. Or by fear. But they had nothing to be afraid of. They knew that. Even as something emerged from the egg.

A small, bright, and perfectly formed golden hawk was hatching.

The glowing blood that had transformed into the golden egg seemed to dissipate around the hawk. And then suddenly, the golden hawk, perched in the middle of the glen. All traces of the Archangel's shining blood was gone.

The hawk stood regally on the ground amongst the White Eyes.. She regarded her surroundings calmly and serenely, as if she had not just been born from the blood of a slain ArchAngel

The people watching also felt a sense of serenity. The small, perfectly formed hawk gave off calm like heat, shimmering in a desert. She was peace itself, incarnate.

And then she spread her wings.

Her wings were wonderfully formed, and perfectly golden brown in color. She regarded herself momentarily, looking with wise eyes at her outspread wings, and then started to flap them.

Then, effortlessly, as if she had done so for all time, she arose into the air, and took to the sky.

She soon disappeared from the people's view But they knew she would be back. She was off to discover her new world and would return to oversee the People.

They knew this fact instinctively, but didn't understand the source of this knowledge. They all felt at peace with what they had just witnessed.

As a group, they turned, gathering up their dead and wounded, and made their way back to the small village. They all knew they would have plenty of time to process the astonishing events that happened since they had heard the first scream, which felt like hours ago but was in reality only a matter of minutes.

Abe led his people back to their home, and pondered his life, and every life around him. These thoughts seemed to envelope galaxies and millennia.

His mind was enveloped in a cosmic awareness, and for a very short time,

He barely registered his surroundings as his mind floated free.

As he lay next to his wife later that night, hearing her soft yet deep breath, he pondered the Situation once again. It was so much bigger than what he had struggled all his life to achieve, but he also knew that he had a job to do in this world at the same time.

He felt both confidence and fear. Trepidation and resolve.

But he could not shake that there was so much more that he didn't know and couldn't see. That was so much more important than his tiny role in the universe.

He knew in his heart that no matter what happened moving forward, he was a very, very small piece of a much grander situation. From now on, his fear wouldn't quite go away.

Abe was almost asleep when a soft glowing light crept through the darkness of the window of his room. He knew that the golden hawk, who was born that day from the lifeblood of an immortal ArchAngel, was perched on a tree branch outside his home.

She was watching over him and his family, and he finally felt peace enough for the night, to finally fall asleep, although he knew the fear would return with the sunrise.

"Goodnight, Azrael," he whispered to the glow out the window as he slowly drifted off and dreamt of a better future.

An unknown future, but better, all the same.

Chapter 35

The next day dawned bright and chilly.

It seemed like the events of the previous evening had never happened. Abe sent three men back to the glen, late in the morning, to dispose of the creature's bodies. But everything had vanished. The glen was clean, as if no battle had taken place the night before

The bodies of the dark creatures had simply disappeared. The grass that had been smashed under the heavy weight of the bodies and the acidic blood looked undisturbed.

But the White Eyed people would always remember. The freshly dug graves for their own people would remind them that the battle and trap set for the ArchAngel had really happened

Abe summoned a gathering in the meeting room above the factory floor. He called his
his brothers, his lieutenants, his wife, mother, and the four strangers who had not taken part in the battle the evening before, but who had stayed on the battle's periphery, ascertaining the prowess of the White Eyes of this land.

The four strangers had gotten their answers, apparently, and had dedicated their lives and their people's resources to the cause that Abe had fought for his entire adult life. It had been a moving statement earlier in the day, and one that Abe would take advantage of. He was grateful for the help and had communicated that gratitude at length.

But in the meantime, he had much more pressing concerns.

They had to figure out how to both end the war that had ravaged this land for two decades, and how to prevent the Dark People from turning the Artificial Intelligence back on.

Abe knew all about the AEMI. He had memorized the stories, passed down through the generations, from his own ancestor, Mark Simon. And he knew that Mark Simon had felt a deep sense of failure that he had not been fast enough to stop the Intelligence from nearly destroying humanity.

How the Dark People had found out about the Intelligence was still a puzzle for another time, but it bothered Abe all the same. And knowing that it would take simple electricity to turn AEMI back on worried him even more.

And so, his best soldiers, the four strangers, and his closest family gathered in the War Room, as he called it, to make plans.

Which was his particular specialty.

For the last twenty years, the White Eyes had been fighting back against a larger number of Dark People, who were hell bent on exterminating the White Eyes, for a slight, or a prejudice that no one could understand. It had been a witch hunt of unpredictable size.

But the White Eyes were faster, stronger, and could see in the dark. They had evolved in the harsh cauldron of the deep earth over several generations.

And so, the Dark People could not win against them. The White Eyes would not let them. After all, it had been one of the Dark People who had murdered their father for the simple fact of knowledge of ancient times.

The brothers had exacted revenge for that night, many times over.

Now, Abe and his people, who had all stuck together after leaving the caves two decades ago, made their new home in the deep mountains of what had been known as the Appalachians. They were defended on all sides by tall rock walls, and the valley where they were mostly based teemed with life.

They had built a line of outposts that spanned from as far north as the cold would allow them to go, to as far south as they could go before deep gulf water forced them to turn around.

They didn't let anything cross that protective line if they could help it. Because the worst-case scenario for Abe and his lieutenants was that Granger Mace's forces in the West joined with the Dark People to the East.

The Dark People on the East coast were led by a man even more ruthless than Granger Mace. A man who went by the sinister name of Hockley.

Abe's farthest-reaching spies reported that Hockley made Granger Mace seem like a pussy willow in comparison.

And for twenty years, the White Eyes had been the line in the sand that prevented the two men and their soldiers from meeting. Abe didn't even know if the two men were aware of each other.

Abe had to ascertain if Hockley and Granger Mace had united, and if that had been the catalyst for the Dark People to seek out the AEMI installation deep in the White Mountains of what had once been known as New England.

Abe couldn't figure out any other reason why Hockley would go after an installation that, until recently, he seemed to have zero knowledge of.

So, two days later, Abe found himself sitting horseback, riding east, surrounded by most of his best warriors. Facecake rode beside him on the left, Noah rode on his right, near enough to whisper to.

They had left their loved ones behind, safe in the knowledge that divine protection was on their side, and they would emerge victorious.

Kissing and hugging the girls goodbye, so soon after their scare with the creatures that no one had discussed since, had been extremely difficult, but Abe and Facecake had left them with his mother, in the best care he could provide.

And in the best protection available by his brother, Elijah.

Abe thought of his youngest brother and pondered the right woman for the shy man once again. He knew he was fixated on it too much, but he just wanted to see his brother happy. Both of his brothers. And he felt like he had drawn them into this fight, even though they were as angry as he was. That thought made him smile in the bright sunlight that filtered through the early fall leaves of the trees around him and the army he led.

And then he thought of the strangers from across the oceans.

The four strangers from foreign lands had been sent with another contingent of Abe's own people to gather their resources and their own White Eyed armies. They were to come to Abe's aid as soon as they were able.

Abe was convinced that he would need every single White Eye he could get, because the battle of all battles was coming soon. One way or another, this war had to end.

He just had no idea what kind of an end that would be.

None of them could see what was going to happen that day. Or for many days after.

If they had, they would have stayed in bed, instead of setting out on horseback for the long trek east.

Especially the brothers, who still remembered the auspicious night of their father's murder, and had been forever, and irreversibly, changed by the very actions that had started this whole war to begin with.

Chapter 36

The trees started to thin out, and Abe's people were beginning to be exposed. Cheese felt more exposed than the rest of them. He hated being on horseback instead of in one of his aeroplanes.

It had been a bittersweet twenty years for the dark-skinned and jovial pilot. However, he was not a big fan of looking back down the years. The years that he had grown more and more

212

resentful of the day those three brothers had appeared through the trees, and he had seen the first of Facecake's many loving looks, directed at the oldest brother.

Moreover, it was not as if Cheese did not love his wife or two children. His wife was a White Eyes, and he loved her fiercely. Mona would not like to know where his mind was this morning, but every time he was away from her, his mind turned towards Abe and his family, and especially towards Abe's relationship with Facecake, and resentment flared in his chest.

Nevertheless, Abe had also given Cheese an honorable position as the leader of what they called the Sky Warriors: an air force of four aero-planes, found, fixed, and brought back to life by the cohort of engineers and mechanical geniuses that had emerged from the caves.

And Cheese was the leader.

He believed that he was the first and best pilot in the entire world, and his pride usually soothed his resentment for Abe. However, Cheese was not sitting in one of his planes today. He did not have confidence during this mission. And a war raged in his mind and in his chest between loving Abe and his family and wishing with all his heart that the White Eyes had never walked out of the caves.

As he sat horseback on a brown dappled mare, he looked over at his best friend in the entire world, and Moose looked back at him. They recently had several conversations about how they both felt, and while they knew they would never leave their other best friend Facecake; it didn't mean that they weren't upset about having had to fight for two decades against their own people.

The White Eyes had accepted the trio with open arms, but both Cheese and Moose knew that it was only at the request of Abe. Everyone who had come from the caves revered him. The pair often wondered what would happen if Abe took his favor away from them. They knew that Abe would slaughter them. They sometimes felt that Abe saw them the same way as he saw his

213

enemies, but it often felt like those thoughts came from outside of themselves.

Cheese often thought back to the night that he had sealed his fate forever. The night that he had stolen Jerimiah's pack from Granger Mace's rooms, and the night that the brothers had massacred every guard in the castle. Then he had to remember that Facecake had killed just as many men, and that Cheese and Moose were not innocent either.

Cheese had so much blood on his hands, especially from his role as the leader of the air force in several battles through the long years of fighting. He could never go backwards, and be welcomed back into the folds of his own people.

Therefore, he felt caught between several rocks and hard places. He did not know his place in the world, and he wondered what he was going to do about that.

The sun was shining down on the group looking over a valley deep below them. Abe led about twenty White Eyes, with Cheese, Moose, and Facecake pulling their horses close to the tall man.

They waited. This was the meeting place where several frontline scouts would find them and report any change to what Facecake's earlier scouts had found. Abe and Facecake hoped that they would not have to wait long. They felt too exposed out in the sunlight, and the high ground, which would show any enemy their numbers and their position.

With that thought in mind, Abe gave orders for all the White Eyes to move further back into the trees except the small group consisting of himself, Facecake, Cheese, Moose, and Noah. The tight knit group stayed out in the open for the scouts to find them.

Luckily, they did not have to wait long. Three scouts rode up a side trail to the top of the rise where the small group waited. Abe looked over at his men, who were so far away from home, and felt deep compassion. They all looked so tired.

Abe rode to meet them at the edge of the trees, and the three scouts nodded to the others within the tree line. Abe enjoyed the fact that his people had become so close, even out in the great world. The crucible of the caves had forged bonds that would not be easily broken.

With that thought in mind, Abe asked the leader of the trio of scouts if there was news.

The scout leader nodded grimly.

"Last we saw the horde of them, Abe, they somehow got into the room where all the Artificial Intelligence stuff was kept," the man said.

Abe remembered the scout's name. It was Paul.

Paul continued, looking back at his two companions for verification.

"They put all the equipment on sleds, every bit of it," he said. "And they are taking it south. Towards the City," he finished.

"Shit," Abe muttered under his breath.

"The City" was the sprawling set of tall buildings left over from the large metropolis of New York City, from ancient times. Abe had looked down on the large, dilapidated city many times.

The forces of the man they called Hockley were stationed there.

Paul spoke up once more.

"Before we headed north to track Granger Mace's people, we were at The City. And saw that Hockley's forces were building something, Abe," he said.

Abe perked up at that.

The Dark People were very lax in building anything new. They tended to just use the buildings and ruins of the ancients. To build something new in The City was against the Dark People's normal routines.

"What were they building Paul?" Abe asked quietly.

215

The answer made the stomachs of everyone listening to the grizzled older man drop. Even Cheese and Moose looked at each other in wonder and confusion.

The older man, gray beyond his years, who as Abe remembered, had been a good friend of his father, spoke the last words in almost a whisper. The words that would shock the world of the White Eyes.

"They are building a Tower, Abe. A large and very tall Tower that has already almost reached the Heavens."

And for some reason he could not comprehend at that moment, Abe's world suddenly felt like it was crumbling around him.

Paul spoke one more line, and the day suddenly seemed darker for them all. All of them, except Cheese and Moose.

"And it's almost finished."

Inter-Mission
II

Raziel's scream still resounded in the Spiritual Realm. It echoed around the Throne of the Highest and reverberated in the ears of those Beings who were present to see it.

As the sound faded in the Spiritual, the Beings surrounded their brother, and were shocked at the golden tears streaming down the older ArchAngel's face. Several pairs of Spiritual eyes started to tear up as well as they saw the body of their slain sister.

Raziel laid the body of Azrael onto a pure white table made from energy and stood back. Her darkening golden blood pooled under her. The large black arrow protruding from her prostrate body was an affront to its surroundings.

There was a fissioning, a crackling of energy coming off the dark arrow. An energy that did not belong in this place. It seemed like the dark energy and the divine energy surrounding it were fighting each other.

The ArchAngels of the Older Ilk and the Younger stood still, not knowing what to do, wondering in their angelic minds at the absurdity of one of the Hosts losing the life that they had all enjoyed since Creation began.

And then the Creator descended the Dais and came before His slain daughter. His Light, blinding to anyone not born to the service of the Throne, shone through, and surrounded each member of the Host.

His Light did not touch the dark arrow, however.

The Father of All looked sadly down at the body of the ArchAngel Azrael and wept for her. The entire Host saw it and joined in with His grief.

A death of one of the Host had never happened before, and the fact that it was possible shook the Heavens.

The Creator gathered the Host around him, close to Azrael's body, and let sorrow spill over them all. The Host beat their chests, letting grief pour out over the body of their slain sister.

The Almighty Father looked to the Older Ilk, and then the Younger, and without spoken words, gathered them all up in His Light, and winked out of existence in the Spiritual Plane, and appeared in the Material, in the particular world where the death of an ArchAngel had taken place.

The Creator's Light shone through the trees around the clearing. But it did not touch the creatures scattered throughout the glen. Some dark force, or shadow pushed the Light of the Creator away from itself, and all who gathered in the clearing saw it.

The Creator's Light, His Eternal Glory, could not penetrate the darkness surrounding the dead creatures from a place none in the glen knew. Not even the Father of All.

The curiosity on the Father's face made the entire Host nervous. It was not a sight they had ever seen throughout a span of time that was so far-fetched that it couldn't even be quantified. As if time had never existed, which it did not in the Spiritual Plane. However, in this world, time was always a matter of degree.

The Host gathered close to their Father, and as he raised his arms, glory shot out from Him in a dazzling display of power and light. Even the Host of ArchAngels, so used to being in His presence, were astonished.

And the scene around the Host flicked and moved. Time was reversed, and soon, the battle arose around the Host. The Host and the Father once again in two places, seeing the battle unfold, but not entering it.

Only Raziel, who had witnessed the scene already, hung his head, knowing what was coming soon. He raised his eyes to watch the Father's face as the crack opened in the Material, from amongst the dark trees at the end of the clearing.

The Father stood in the middle of the glen, watching the unfolding battle, and its conclusion.

Suddenly, Raziel had to call out, as the Father was standing almost exactly where Azrael had stood.

And as the blackness opened within the trees, and the dark, deadly arrow streaked towards where Azrael had taken it into her body, Raziel and another ArchAngel, The Venerable and ancient Jeremiel, did what no other ArchAngel had ever done.

They lunged at the Father of All and tried to stop what they now saw as the true goal of the entire battle.

The trap had not been set for the ArchAngel Azrael, who had perished from the arrow streaking towards the middle of the glen. No, the truth was, the Darkness had known the Father of All would be standing in the exact same spot, within a Time Fold. They were really trying to kill the Almighty.

That simple fact shook all of Creation to its very core.

But the Creator simply stopped Time once again, not allowing the Dark arrow to come close to Him, although He could finally see what His children had seen.

The Dark arrow had been meant for Him. This Truth wasn't in the realm of understanding for all of Creation. But the Father finally saw it.

And so, He simply moved out of the way, not being able to stop the situation from turning into the grief they had all shared in the Spiritual Realm.

He moved out of the way within the Time Fold, and in the Material Realm, Azrael took the arrow instead of the Almighty.

Several sacred laws of His creation were broken in that simple act.

And as the Father of All stepped out of the way of the Dark arrow, the scene froze around Him. His two beloved sons had almost sacrificed themselves if they would have actually touched the Countenance of the Almighty.

And the Father watched in grief and sadness as His young Daughter took the arrow that had been meant for Him.

Her death screamed against the Natural Order of All, and it resounded in the Creator's ears.

He couldn't stop what had happened. It was against His own laws.

But He could try His best to assure it did not happen again.

The Creator of All finally raised His arms again, His Glory shining forth, and within a blink of Time in the Material, it was as if nothing had ever happened in the glen at all.

All traces of the enemy, and the battle, were swept up, moved into the Spiritual Realm, and the White Eyed humans, who would inspect the area in their own Time, would see it all back to the way it was before the battle.

Back in the Spiritual Realm, the Host gathered all around the bodies of the Dark Creatures, which the Creator had deposited along with the very first one from years prior.

The Host of ArchAngels looked on the creatures in disgust and hatred. These creatures were a part of what had killed a sister of the Host, and justifiable Heavenly Rage issued forth from the remainder of the Heavenly Host of ArchAngels.

It was all almost too much for the Heavenly Host, seeing the looks of concern and curiosity on the Creator's face, as they all looked up at the Throne.

Something was coming, and it shook the Heavenly Realm like nothing had ever done before.

But one ArchAngel, a beloved Son of the Elder Ilk, looked on the creatures as something entirely different. He looked on them as an opportunity.

The ArchAngel Samael looked at the creatures gathered around the bottom of the Dais with curiosity, and started forming a plan in his prodigious mind.

He looked up at the Father of All, and the Father looked down on His beloved Son.

And then the Creator of the Universe gave Samael an almost imperceivable nod of His glorious head.

Part 5
The Revelation
And
The Choice

Chapter 37

Abe arose early in the warm, summer morning, and met the sunrise, as he did most days.

A time of reflection and calm before the stresses of the day. He needed it like he needed his wife, his family, and the breath in his chest.

He stood on a wrought iron balcony overlooking the village that was slowly turning into a town. In a few short generations, he mused, it would be a real city. And he reveled that he had taken part in its formation. A sense of pride and wonder made his soul happy.

They had really done good work here. Ever since they had left the cave, so many years earlier. No matter what happened in the future, he knew that he and his brothers had done a really good work.

The village consisted of both hand-hewn wooden homes and repaired buildings that had stood since ancient times.

Tall, fully leafed trees dotted the village in ways that made the children happy, but the adults complained when fall set in, and leaves needed to be raked.

The green grasses of the front yards of many homes were cut short, and flowers dotted every garden and most first floor window boxes.

His people were happy in this valley, which was full of trees, wild game, fish in the fast- moving river close by, and a way of life that contrasted with the elders who had lived in the caves.

A home made from the ancestors some nine hundred years in the past was much more preferable than a cave chamber, with scarred furniture and an air full of memories and the dust of their ancestors.

The ancient people who had occupied this valley in the millennia before the White Eyes settled it, had built most of these homes from brick and cement. But some metal warehouses dotted the valley in which they had settled.

Abe looked over the valley, the village, and at those very same warehouses that were so crucial to the war effort.

Those metal warehouses, now repaired by the engineers and mechanical people who had come from the caves, were marvels of longevity.

After nearly a thousand years, they had still stood strong, although rather worn down. Their corrugated metal walls had remained upright, but the roofs had all caved in.

It had taken a herculean effort to re-roof the warehouses, but the job had been necessary. They had needed a place to build and manufacture the weapons and supplies needed for this long, heavy war.

A war that Abe hoped with all of his heart was coming to an end, very shortly.

That thought made him look to the end of the valley, which he could just barely make out in the encroaching dawn light. But the hundreds of twinkling lights from low burning campfires gave him more of an idea of the scope of the army situated there.

In the last year since the scout Abel had informed Abe of the situation with the Dark People on the East Coast, the combined armies of the White Eyes around the world had all gathered there with Abe and his people.

And even though the army was a mixture of people from every race that had populated this world before it had been practically destroyed, their matching white eyes, inhuman strength, and prodigious height, made them look like one cohesive group.

One people who were about to erase the ones who had come before them from the face of their planet.

In his soul, Abe questioned once more, the necessity of wiping the Dark People off the earth. The drive to erase a people who lived by hate and division just felt like the right thing to do. But late at night, or very early in the morning, like this morning, he often wondered if they were doing the right thing.

Sure, the hatred that the Dark People had for the White Eyes was palpable. That was a given. But Abe often wondered why, almost to a person, the White Eyes around the world had felt the same hatred. He knew the hatred for the people from the outside had been bred into the White Eyes, and he felt like it had been done by the ArchAngels for the simple fact to assure that all the humans left on the planet were White Eyes.

He just didn't have the ability to understand the reasoning behind it.

There had not been a single country, or continent, or race, of White Eyes on the entire planet who had come from the caves and had made peace with the Dark People of their lands.

Not a single instance of joined peace in the whole of the world. And Abe could not wrap his mind around that fact.

As if the entire situation had been entirely out of their hands from the very beginning. He did not like to entertain a control of every single person on the planet, and that they had had zero control over their own fates.

He continued to muse over these thoughts for a few more moments, until he heard a sound come from behind him.

He turned and saw Elijah moving through the swinging doors out onto the balcony with him, two steaming cups held in his hands.

Without a word, Abe's youngest brother handed one of the cups of tea to his oldest brother, and together, they watched the rising sun peek over the mountains to the east. This, too, was a morning ritual that the brothers shared. It seemed, however, that this morning, Noah would not be joining them like he usually did.

Abe knew that Noah would be up this early, but on his knees in his bedroom, praying to the Creator as he always had done, even when the three had been children.

Abe appreciated his brother's prayers. He knew that they would need them in the coming days. The coming days that would tell the fate of all humanity on this planet.

And that thought led to one that had been disturbing him more than any other. Could the White Eyes still, technically, be called human? Weren't they now some other type of creature? An evolved human, perhaps?

The White Eyes were so very different from the Dark People, who were left over from the human race that had stayed out in the world after the cataclysm that almost ended all life on the planet. So, if the Dark People were human, what were the White Eyes?

227

He pondered as he and Elijah watched the sun rise above the mountains and bathe the village below them in the early morning light.

The two brothers watched as people moved about the village below, often waving up to them, three floors above the ground, as they did most mornings.

Elijah turned to his brother, a concerned look on his face. Both brother's cups were empty by now, and Abe knew that something was on his little brother's mind.

"Abe, we need to talk," Elijah said.

Abe didn't say a word. Just looked at his brother and felt love for him as he always did. Nothing would ever make him feel anything but love for his family. The world also loved his youngest brother, and anyone that Abe knew would do anything for the young man. Elijah seemed to be the center of his entire family, even if Abe was the leader.

A quick thought swept through Abe's mind before Elijah continued with his dialogue. They really needed to find Elijah a woman to settle him down. It wasn't right that a man in his thirties would be without a wife.

And Abe wondered why he worried so much about his younger brother. It may very well be because he was aware of his own mortality, and the war that raged around them. He wanted to make sure that someone would be there to take care of Elijah, if something were to happen to himself.

Or Facecake, heaven forbid.

But Elijah himself stopped that train of thought in Abe's mind. His next words mirrored the almost exact thoughts that Abe had earlier.

"Is what we are about to do the right thing, Abe?" Elijah asked. He looked deep into his older brother's eyes, which echoed his anxiety.

"We are about to finish the job that we set out to do, twenty years ago, but Abe, I can't help but think we're making a mistake," he finished.

Abe spoke up finally, before leading his brother back into the large home, to wake up the rest of his family, and join Noah in his morning prayers.

"I was thinking the same thing, little brother. And I really don't know," he said.

And he meant exactly what he said. He had no idea if what they were doing was the right thing. And he had no idea what they would do after the war was over. He hoped that they could just live with peace. To just live.

The war was all they had known most of their lives, and the entire lives of those young people who had been born to the war, and those same youth wondered even more than their elders if they were all doing the right thing.

Later that day, Abe met once more with a contingent of leaders from the combined armies that were living off of the land around them. Food was getting scarce, and further plans needed to be made to care for the thousands of White Eyes now occupying their valley. But Abe did not mind making his people shore up their resources and share with the armies of White Eyes.

Those armies, combined with his, would end this conflict, and Abe could finally rest and relax, and watch his daughters grow up, get married, and see the natural progression of life as his ancestors had.

Abe longed for that day more than anything else. Even more than ending the war that had been started with the hatred of unfamiliarity.

Many plans would need to be formalized before this day was finished.

The smell of bread baking and strong tea came from the kitchen where Abe's mother, Emily, and his wife, Alex, were preparing a respite for the guests. Abe was once more thankful for the women in his life. The women who made his very existence manageable and worth living.

He looked around the table, where all were deep in thought and feelings, and his mind wandered back to his earlier musings.

But he had to shelve that thinking. There was work to be done, and hard work and planning was always what made Abe who he really was. His calling in life, Facecake liked to joke. Always planning and working.

Noah too looked around the room. These were people that he had traveled with, ate with, and shared stories with. As strangers, they were still family. They, like Noah and his people, were born from the crucible of the caves, and the pressure of survival.

But Noah's mind was occupied with another matter.

The matter of the word that he had received in his prayers that morning, and the word that was bothering him more than he had ever been bothered before. It was what had kept him from joining his brothers on the balcony like he did every morning.

And it was the word that he had received that had ruined any chance he had of being happy and full of joy at the sight of his closest friends and family holding council in the same room. How he had longed for a day like today.

But the word he had received had ruined all of that for him.

It was profound, full of grief, and made him feel more sadness than he had felt in two decades.

Because the word that he had received from the Creator on High was that Noah was soon going to lose many of those he loved the most.

They were all going to lose the core of the family that held all of the world together, for many of the White Eyes in the village, but even more so, for the family gathered in this home, on this day, filling the room with positivity and happiness.

That laughter and joy would turn into sorrow and weeping, gnashing of teeth, and wails in the night, so very soon.

That was the word, the vision, that was given to his soul, during his morning prayers that very day.

And so, Noah's heart sank, as the planning for the coming battle, and the supposed end of the war was accomplished.

The planning that would doom those he loved, forever.

Chapter 38

Alexandria Clince Simone, or Facecake, as her friends and family had called her since she was a small child, also felt the chill in the air, and a stirring of fate and destruction in the plans being formed in the room next to the kitchen.

She was baking, like she had always done. One of her very true joys in life besides her family.

Her mother-in-law, well, her only mother actually, stood next to her, preparing a tray of teacups, and humming softly to herself. Facecake looked over at Emily, and felt love stir in her belly as it always had when she was around the older woman.

Facecake had lost her mother when she was a very young girl. It had been a logging accident, or so they had told the eight-year-old girl at the time. But she suspected that there had always been more to the story.

She had heard her parents fighting for several weeks before the day her mother had died, and the arguments had sounded very accusatory from her father's side, and even more defensive from her mother's.

It wasn't until she was a teenager that she started to understand what may have happened.

And now, Facecake had a new mother, who had loved her, and accepted her completely, for more than two decades. Sometime, Facecake didn't know how she would have made it through three tough pregnancies, and three even more difficult births, without the woman who she felt was her mother now in more ways than her own mother had been.

So, with the strong and stalworth Emily Simone beside her, Facecake made the dark and oppressive feelings within her subside, and she put on a cheery face as she continued to knead the dough for more of her favorite spice cakes and joined Emily in humming a song that the older woman had taught her over the years.

A smile lit up both women's faces, and all was right in the kitchen, and in the rest of the world, once again.

Abe sat at the head of the large gathering table, looking at the myriad of maps, planning notes, and lists of resources that he had at his disposal.

"So, what we were worried about has happened, correct Noah?" Abe asked his brother.

Noah seemed distracted by something, but his head rose as Abe asked him the question. He took his time to answer, and when he did, a chill ran through the room.

"Yes. Scouts reported back last week that Granger Mace's forces have joined with Hockley's, and they are all living in, or camped around, the old City," he said.

Abe nodded.

In his heart, he knew the final battle was upon them. The battle that would end this war.

A loud raucous sound came from further within the living quarters of the large building, and Abe's three daughters came running into the room, headed towards the kitchen area. Abe smiled.

They had smelled their mother's cakes.

All three girls laughing, running, and raising such a babble of noise that it shook the chill out of the room, made everyone at the table smile. The despair and gloom that had made the room seem darker than it really was dissipated, and a sigh of relief went through everyone.

The girls had always had that effect, Abe thought. And so did his wife.

And if he could focus on the good in what they were doing, and that there was a definite peace that could be achieved afterwards, he felt like he could make it through the coming conflict, along with everyone he loved.

He looked back at those sitting around the table. He would need all of these people, and they would need him. And that made him feel good too. They would do what needed doing. And they would all rejoice in the peace that would follow.

He was about to speak, to give commands on preparing the disembarkation of the joined armies of White Eyes, when his wife and his mother entered the room bearing refreshments.

The three girls, faces dirty with warm spice cake crumbs, followed their mother and grandmother. The girls still giggled together, and as one, walked up to their father, and planted wet and dirty kisses on his stubbled face.

And once again, just as the women in his life had felt a few moments before, all seemed right in the world.

He whispered his love to his daughters, and asked them to play outside, but to stay close by. He still remembered the day they had been taken by the dark creatures and had been cautious with the girls ever since.

The girls departed out of the room, spice cake held in increasingly dirty hands, and giggles followed them out.

Abe turned back to the people sitting around the table in the large, open room, sunlight streaming through the windows all around it. He saw a movement outside one of the windows closest to him and felt an even deeper sense of peace at knowing that the golden hawk, who his daughters had named Ariel, was outside, always nearby.

He smiled inwardly at the hawk's new name. The girls had unanimously named the hawk after an old story from the Before Time that he would tell them. His own father had told the story to Abe and his brothers. He didn't know what a mermaid was, but the girls enjoyed the stories just as he had.

A throat cleared, and Abe was brought back to the matter at hand.

"Alright, yes," he said to the room.

"If we start out by the end of this week, we should be able to arrive at the City, in full force, within a month. That puts us entrenched in the middle of summer," he said.

"Plenty of time to make ready," he finished.

The rest of his lieutenants, and the leaders of the combined worldly armies nodded along with him. All had ideas and plans for making this final battle successful, but to a person, they put their trust in Abe, and he in turn put his trust in them, to see all of the plans through to the very end.

This would all work out perfectly, he thought to himself. The enemy would never know what was coming until it was too late.

"And that would mean a single refueling stop for Cheese's aero-plane fleet, and if we hit the mark just right, he and his pilots will be right where we need them, right when we will need them the most," he said.

Abe looked down the table to Cheese, who was one of his oldest friends in the world, and Cheese looked back at Abe.

Cheese nodded to Abe, and Abe nodded back.

Another cloud out of nowhere obscured the sun shining into the windows around the room, and gloom once again settled on the group around the table.

Cheese's eyes never left Abe's face. And his own plans started forming in his mind as the man at the head of the table continued planning the battle to come.

Cheese raised a piece of Facecake's spice cake to his mouth, remembering better times, and memories of his childhood flooded his mind. He knew instinctively that he would be in the right when his plans came to fruition, and he could fix all of the wrongs perpetrated on him by the man at the head of table.

The man who was enjoying the same spice cake.

Facecake's spice cake that had never belonged to Abe in the first place, Cheese thought.

Chapter 39

"The troops are excited to be moving, Abe," Noah told his older brother.

They were seated on horseback once again, ready to head east. They sat atop a high ridge on the eastern rim of the valley they had called home for more than two decades. The long lines of White Eyed troops astride horses of their own, rode in double columns along the dusty road below them. Abe's chest swelled in

237

pride and happiness to be doing what he felt he had been made to do.

Other men, he knew, were tradesmen. Carpenters, builders, clay makers, engineers. Women made weapons, raised children, kept their homes. But Abe had been born for a single purpose.

To be a warrior poet. The first Memorist in recorded history to put the knowledge passed down through generations to actual use.

Every story, every battle, all the history stored in his mind and memories made him the perfect man to lead this army, and he knew it. A true Battle Lord was not only the best fighter in his army, but also the smartest, with the most knowledge of what lay ahead. And as he thought about it, he also realized that a true leader also worried the most, fretted for the longest time, and grieved over every single loss of life of those he was responsible for. And if that is what made up a true leader, he thought, then he was definitely the right man for the job, as he worried himself almost to paralysis most nights.

As if he had been made for that purpose, he thought, ideas and plans spinning through his mind, along with stresses and worry.

He felt, more than heard, Facecake ride up next to him. He marveled that their connection was so strong even after two decades. Hell, he thought, especially after the two decades they had gone through.

He looked over at his wife, and for a few glorious seconds, the world around them faded away, and he only saw her. Like a halo of light was behind her, she glowed in his sight, and in his memory.

He tried to picture his life before he had met her, and it would not come to mind. Everything washed out of his thoughts except for two things.

238

His wife, and the days of peace that they could share after this war was finished.

Oh, how he longed for that time.

And then the world, and the noise of it, came crashing back into his awareness, and he was once again ready to fight, and win, to have that day that he envisioned so strongly.

He looked to his left where his brother Noah was seated, still watching the troops march below. Abe looked back down on the army of White Eyes, from all corners of the world, and was grateful.

He could never have faced the coming conflict without the help of his brothers and sisters from across the oceans.

The rest of his command staff rode up soon after Facecake joined him at the rim of the valley. Abe looked to his left and to his right, and was thankful for all of the help, support, and trust that these blessed souls had given him to lead the army to victory.

Soon after, Abe turned back to the valley that he and his family had called home for so very long, and mentally wished it a fond farewell.

He was leaving his daughters and his mother behind with a group of trusted guards and protectors. He said a mental goodbye to his home and knew he would miss it.

But he was joyful to finally be setting off, to finish this fight that had consumed so much of his life.

That night, as the army of White Eye soldiers and the command staff found a large, open glen to camp well to the east and north of their home, Abe walked into the large tent that he shared with his wife and his brothers.

He had walked amongst the troops, gauging moods, and pumping up morale. Everyone knew where they were headed, and what would be expected of them.

From reading historical accounts of battles and warfare, Abe knew that as the Commander, it was critical to make sure that all of his men and women were ready for what was coming, without promising that they would live through it.

The worse thing he could do, he thought to himself, walking through the many campfires, with meat sizzling and broths being prepared for dinner, was to lie to his troops about the outcome of the coming conflict.

No, he thought. His job was simply to show strength and pass out hope.

And now he could enjoy his evening with his family. He smelled a wonderful stew coming from the camp pot in the middle of the large family tent. He glanced up at the roof of the tent to assure that the flap was open to vent the small campfire burning cheerfully in the middle of the open ground.

A wonder of engineering, Abe thought, as he watched the smoke rise up and out of the hole in the tent. His engineers had designed the vent to move the smoke out and keep the inside of the tent clear.

He looked at his beautiful wife once again, as she stirred the stew, and at his two brothers, who lounged on cots to either side of the small campfire. They were far enough away to not be in the way of the convection design in the middle of the tent. Abe was at peace.

He was so very full of love for his family, and did not let the small, biting worry that had been nagging in the back of his mind come to full fruition.

He would NOT lose anyone anymore. He couldn't handle anyone in this tent not enjoying the peace that they had all fought for so long to have. He needed both of his brothers, and his wife, which went without saying.

Suddenly, he heard laughter ringing out from the Head Tent, in the middle of the camp. Several smaller tents surrounded the Head Tent, since many White Eyes troops had partnered up, and husbands and wives shared camps, tents, and fighting.

An army of families, Abe thought to himself, as he settled into the double cot that he shared with his wife.

His brothers were around him, close by in the same tent. They shared his mindset. And his wife was wonderfully wrapped up in his arms.

All was well with the world, he thought, as he drifted off to sleep, hoping for just the same kind of day tomorrow, and the days after.

He would need this long, wonderful march, to be ready to fight the dark eyes in the way that he knew he would need to, as well as to be the example his troops would need him and his family to be.

The dark dream came to all three of the Simone brothers, who slumbered close together, on a forced march, towards a fate that they would not be able to believe, nor to stop.

In the dream, the three brothers all saw the same thing, but did not realize that the other two brothers were not in the dream. They were all seeing the dream through their own eyes, but alone, nonetheless.

A large, barren valley spread before each brother. It was dark, and the ground was cracked. Within the cracks, they could see glowing orange light. As if a fire burned just below the surface.

The rest of the valley felt like death, and an overwhelming presence pervaded their senses.

Within the very middle of the valley stood a monolith of a Tower. It was black, smooth as glass, and seemed to suck in all light.

The brother walked towards the middle of the barren valley, feeling evil emanating from the black monolith. But they were driven to it, nonetheless.

241

As the brothers approached the Tower, a light rose up from the very top of it.

It was a bright white light, and glowed brightly, straight up into the air, beyond what the brothers could see. The light felt slightly positive, but the same presence they had felt earlier seemed to emanate from the light as well.

It confused the brothers, who stood not far away from the tall Tower, looking up, towards the light.

They couldn't understand the feelings they had about the light. The emotions it caused directly opposed their feelings about the black monolith from which it had sprang forth.

The light seemed to also be a part of the evil presence within the Tower.

All of the brothers were as confused as they had ever been about emotions within them as they watched the light, but when they all glanced back down at the front façade of the Tower, their fears and their confused thoughts became overwhelmingly...

Familiar.

At the very front face of the large black monolithic Tower, where a door should normally be, was just a flat wall of expansive black rock. , A figure was chained to the wall.

And that figure gave all three boys the fears, mixed with comfort, that they had felt as very young boys, growing up in the caves.

The brothers ran towards that figure, at once recognizing who it was, and both terror and overwhelming joy sprang up in each of their chest.

They ran to the figure, seeing the chains holding his arms and feet grow tighter as they approached.

They looked into the eyes of the ragged, wizened figure. Recognition and shock were echoed on each face.

The chains pulled tighter, making the figure grunt in pain. All three brothers tried to pull the chains apart. They tried to find *something to break the chains, before the heavy chains could pull the figure's arms from his body.*

They tried with all of their might to break the chains free.

But they failed.

Seeing the defeat on the faces of the brothers, the figure finally spoke, uttering a single sentence, that rang in the ears of all three brothers who awoke in a panic, soon after.

"You have to destroy the Tower, boys. You have to destroy it right now, and you have to destroy me with it," their father, the Memorist Jerimiah Simone, whispered to them.

The chains pulled so tightly soon after, that his voice broke and stopped, and they heard ligaments and bones within their father's body start to snap and break.

All three brothers woke in a panic, sweat beading down each of their bodies. In the darkness of the large tent, they could see each other, sitting up on their cots. Anguish and fear enveloped their faces.

Facecake never stirred next to her husband, as the three Simone brothers looked at each other in shock and recognition.

Without a word, they all instinctively knew that they had each witnessed the same dream.

In silence, all three brothers arose from their cots, and walked out into the deep darkness of the summer night. They moved silently, stealthily, together to the edge of the camps, dodging the sentries and tired guards.

Finding a smaller glen not far away, they stopped at the familiar stream of water running through the middle of it. A sense of familiarity overrode all other emotions within the three, as they knelt at the edge of the water.

The three brothers joined hands as they had done their entire lives and bowed their heads in prayer.

A glowing, hidden figure looked down at the three kneeling brothers in the middle of the clearing.

A rainbow-colored glow surrounded the tall figure, as he looked over at the beautiful golden hawk perched in a tree branch next to him.

He knew that the plan was unfolding, and the end of this Mission was upon them all.

Raziel smiled, and felt joy fill his chest, at last.

His aura brightened, and he began plans for the conclusion of this particular mission.

Chapter 40

Cheese was a mess of confusion and anxiety. Nothing could settle him down, and he felt attacked by his thoughts. Hatred and anger beat out all other emotions. Even his wife and family could not keep the darkness from his mind.

The combined armies of the White Eyes had set out days prior, but he, and his pilots, were left behind for the couple of weeks it would take the foot soldiers to get into place around The City.

That was to be expected. Cheese's squadron of aero-planes could make the overland trip in a fraction of the time that the armies would need to march. But for some reason, that fact rankled Cheese's mind as well.

He found himself pacing the carpets in his family's living area. He couldn't get the incessant thoughts of revenge and violence he wished to take out on Abe, out of his mind. And it was getting worse.

For the days since the armies had marched East, Cheese's mind deteriorated. He felt in his soul that these feelings did not represent him. No, they came from an outside source. Regardless he could not put them at bay.

And now, days away from leaving with his cohort of pilots carrying as many incendiary devices and handheld bombs as they could, his mind was a cesspool of hatred.

Hatred, scorn, and fear. And he had no idea where it was all coming from.

He had been angry at his lot in life for a long time, he knew. But why now, when it was so close to the end of the war, did he feel it so overwhelmingly? He wondered if it was because everything would be so very real moving forward.

Once this war was over, and his friends and family, along with the man that he hated, had to face a future of certainty, instead of a constant state of stress and alertness, he would have to accept that Facecake had not chosen him, but rather had chosen the man who never had belonged.

And that, he knew, was what drove him to this constant place of hatred. When the war was over, he would have to see himself in a different light, and that light would be without Facecake.

He just couldn't handle that.

And so, his plans solidified in his mind. With barely a goodbye to his wife and family, he mustered his pilots, rode the line in his aero-plane along with his squadron, saluted the grounds crew, and rose into the air, feeling the same rushing adrenaline that he had the very first time he ever flew.

But it was all overridden by the hatred in his heart, and the plans that he made to destroy the man who had taken Facecake from him and ruined his life.

He flew east, along with his men in their own aero-planes, towards a destiny that none of them could foresee.

The three Simone brothers sat on horseback, covered in bits of leather armor, weapons sprouting from sheaths, and bows nocked and ready over their backs.

It was time for them to split up, each taking a third of the army with them, to converge on the City from three landward points of the compass. This was the moment they had been waiting for.

Since the night that the three of them shared the same dream about the Tower and their father, they had discussed it a few times, but mostly, they had prepared to end this war, once and for all.

The plan was simple, and easily executable. Abe knew his army's strengths and weaknesses, and so, had devised a plan to lean heavily on the former, and mitigate the latter.

At the moment, they stood miles from the City, but were within a quick horse ride to the middle of it. They would watch the full moon this very night. As the bright hunters moon reached its zenith, they would each lead their piece of the army to converge in cover of darkness on the heart of the enemy army.

They would kill and destroy as many Dark Eyes as they could overnight, and when the sun came up the following day, the plan was for Cheese's air force to meet them in the final stage of the battle, closest to the center of the crumbling City, to destroy their enemy once and for all.

They had departed their home along with the New Moon. The war would finally be finished by the Full.

Almost like Divine planning, Abe thought, as he nodded to his two brothers. They clasped arms and hands with several of their officers. Abe gave a last whispered word of encouragement to his wife, who would be following him, as always.

The day was dawning brightly, and they had to hurry to get into position.

This time tomorrow, Abe thought, the war may very well be over, and all of their lives would be changed.

At that moment, he had no idea, whatsoever, how real this thought would be.

Chapter 41

Facecake followed her husband, her love, her everything, towards a fight she hoped with all of her heart would be her last. Their last. She prayed to a Creator that she had learned to grow closer to, through knowing her husband for so many years.

But she also couldn't shake a funny feeling she had in her soul that things were not quite what she thought they were. Like a surprise was coming, and something was tugging at her mind and emotions for her to see it and prepare for it.

But she also knew that would be impossible. That was the Faith that Abe had shared with her so often. The idea of Faith was a foreign concept when she first heard of it. She had not grown up with people who knew what Faith was or would even have given it a thought if they had.

And so, she simply followed her husband, and the soldiers and friends and family that marched with them to the east of the City. They were heading as close to the water of the great ocean as they could. They would come from the east and meet the rest of their family at the center of the City. In victory, she prayed.

The pair of lovers led a group of close to two thousand White Eyes, all on horseback, and all moving as silently as thousands of horses could travel. They would quarter the animals away from the fighting when they were in position, but until then, they had to avoid being visible.. So, they stayed within the trees, and the crumbling ancient steel and stone buildings that they rode among.

Looking about her, Facecake wondered at the futility of it all. This world had perished, and here they were, trying to fight once more for it. She hoped that in the end, it would all be worth the effort.

Grasses, bushes, and trees grew through ground that was a bit too straight and even. She supposed that roads were buried under the land they traversed. This world had taken itself back centuries ago, she knew. Her husband had explained its history in many late night family gatherings, where he had given out the memories that his own father had taught him as a boy.

She looked at Abe. He was so tall and strong. In all the years that they had been married, and she had loved him fiercely, he had never wavered from his course, or failed to be the strength of all who knew him.

She felt even greater swells of love and pride gush through her chest.. She knew that she had chosen correctly so many years ago. Abe was the best man that she had ever known, and she had known it the first time that she had laid eyes on the too-tall young man.

The ruins of crumbling buildings and structures soon increased around the traveling army. Facecake knew that as the ruins started getting denser, and the vegetation around them became scarcer, they were getting closer to the borders of the Dark Eyes' City.

It was almost time.

Abe called a quiet halt to the traveling army using a raised fist that everyone was looking out for. As they came to a silent stop, a few horses nickered, and birds overhead called to each other.

There was no other sound from the White Eyes.

Many soldiers came and took the family's horses as Abe gathered his lieutenants around to hold a brief discussion about laying out the advanced scouts' routes, and where to stable the horses until the battle was finished.

Facecake began to worry that they had not kept the element of surprise, but looking at her husband gave her all the trust and faith that all would be well, just as she had felt earlier.

They all got into position, it was time to wait for nightfall, and the beginning of the final battle between the armies of the White Eyes, and the remnants of the Dark.

And at three separate points around the great City on the eastern coast of the land the White Eyes from the mountains in the west called home, the three Simone brothers thought over their shared dream. Every single night since they first had the dream, it had reappeared to them every time they closed their eyes.

The three brothers prepared their people, bedded them down to wait for the fall of night, and the rise of the full moon. They told the soldiers around them to try and sleep. To envision the coming battle in their minds and visualize the victory for all of their people.

251

And with that last message to the people around them, the three brothers all laid down their heads to rest and follow their own instructions.

They tried to visualize the coming conquest, and the end of all they had known since coming out of their ancestral home, the caves where they had been forged into the weapons that they were. They were destined to save the things they cherished most.

Each other.

Chapter 42

The darkness lay deep around the sleeping City, and the White Eye armies were ready to wreak havoc and death upon their enemies.

The White Eyes' ability to see in the darkness around them would benefit them mightily. The darkness was almost absolute, except for the full hunter's moon that would be overhead in a matter of hours. But until then, the White Eyes would have a deep advantage.

And they would use it.

Abe and Facecake led their group of soldiers through the dilapidated and crumbling buildings, which were all covered in grasses and weeds. They stayed in the shadows and moved as quietly as they could.

Abe had to lead Facecake by the hand through the darkness. This was an old habit, and Facecake was completely blind, yet trusted completely in her husband.

Abe knew it would take a few hours to get to the outside of the Dark Eye soldier lines, and so he walked quietly and cautiously, trying to go as fast as he could while remaining unseen.

He felt an overwhelming calm radiate from the middle of who he was, and what his purpose was in this world. And his men and women moved behind him with the same trust. He knew that they would be victorious, and that made him feel righteous in what he did.

It was that righteousness, that right-ness, that made him confident, along with the knowledge that the Creator and His ArchAngels would be with the White Eyes this night. It was a confidence that he knew he needed, and that his troops needed as well.

It was almost as if he could feel the presence of the Divine with him and his people, as they marched quietly to the middle of the great City.

And so, from three areas of the compass, the split forces of White Eyes converged on the City, and the bridges that led over to the island stronghold of the Dark Eyes.

All three crumbling bridges had been repaired for the Dark Eyes' use. Abe and his brothers had known this from advanced scout reports and thought to use the element of surprise to gain each bridge, overcome the Dark Eye sentries, and gain access to the very heart of the Dark Eyed army.

As the three brothers, leading their personal part of the White Eye army, approached the City from three directions. With stealth, and precise timing, each arrived at the pre-designated areas to begin their campaigns of death. All hell finally broke loose.

And that hell had begun with a light so bright, radiating from the middle of the great City, that it blinded every White Eyed soldier for miles around.

Chapter 43

Granger Mace hated the upstart idiot named Hockley. Always had, always would. But he needed the man, and the man's resources, to win this godforsaken war that the White Eye devils had brought to his doorstep.

His bones ached as he got up out of the poor excuse of the bed that he had been given to him in this wretched Tower. He was cold, and his insides rattled as he relieved himself out the window.

He was barely dressed, rousing himself with the cold water in the basin bowl in the room, when he felt the Shadow behind him.

Here we go, he thought to himself before the piercing pain hit his brain. It was always painful with the Shadow.

Always.

Why isn't it happening yet? the multi-chorused voice screamed in his mind.

"I..,I don't know, my lord. Hockley says they are coming," he whimpered back.

Sometimes the pain of the voice was too much, and he would pass out. Other times, a euphoric jolt would enter his mind and bring him momentary ecstasy, but those times were very short-lived.

He usually felt pain.

"I don't want excuses, or blame. I want the White Eyes killed, to a man!" The voice screamed in his head. And that scream was too much, Granger Mace thought, as he sunk down into unconsciousness.

A short time later, he never knew really how long, Granger Mace awoke to the sun in his eyes, and an ache in his back from falling to the hard stone floor.

But the Shadow was gone, and Granger had work to be about.

Granger Mace gathered himself after the onslaught and pain of the Shadow's visit and left his suite of rooms. He began to walk the halls, which had become a daily habit, dodging the Good People of the earth, and stepping over long black bundles of wires that snaked everywhere.

Those damn wires, he thought to himself, almost tripping over another bundle of them at a hallway crossing.

And that was why he had needed Hockley. God-forsaken hydroelectricity.

257

The Intelligence at the top of the Tower was powered by the electricity that Hockley's hydroelectric dams had created from the rivers surrounding the Island City. Those dams, and the water that was used to charge the generators that produced the power, was the only reason that Granger Mace had joined forces with this damn man, Hockley, and why Granger Mace put up with the man's designs of grandeur.

As soon as he could, he would kill the man, and take over all the Good People that were left in the world. That's what his people called themselves. The Good People.

And it was the war between the Good People and those damn White Eye devils that had made Granger Mace's life the hell it was. Well, the war, and the god-forsaken Shadow.

So, he had to put up with so much frustration and anger and felt out of control most days. But his people still followed him, and benefited from the technologies that he had created, and then perfected, from the memories of his prisoner.

His White Eye prisoner.

He stopped at another intersection, people moving around him, and stared down at the tie twist bundle of thick electrical wires. As if he could see the electricity coursing through the wires themselves, he remembered back to how this had all started.

And remembering, he changed his direction of travel suddenly, and started heading down the Tower, towards the man who had made all of this possible.

Granger Mace's prisoner of war.

Granger Mace hurried downward, towards the bottom floor of the tower, thinking about the man, and how he had helped in ways that would enable Granger Mace and Hockley to finally win this war, and wipe the White Eyes from the face of the Good People's world.

The world that they had made before those White Eyed devils had escaped from the bowels of the planet.

Every technological advancement that the Good People had created had come from the memories of the man chained to a wall at the base of the Tower.

Even the Artificial Intelligence at the top of the Tower, and the electrical power that had brought her back online, and the secrets and amazing things it had told them already, had been sourced from that man.

The man's knowledge included how to finally beat the White Eyes in this god-forsaken war.

All of that information had come from the mind of the man Granger Mace was heading to see, and probably get his anger and frustration out on, once again. He would feel better after torturing the man a little bit.

It had been such a long time since he had made the man scream.

He approached the cell door, set deep within the stone walls of the bottom most hallway of the Tower. He nodded to the single guard sitting, tired and lazy, next to the cell door. The guard was not one of Granger Mace's men. That made Granger Mace angry all over again.

That damn Hockley had taken everything that Granger Mace had created and worked towards for two decades and had made it his own.

All because he had the men and the natural ability to create the power that would be so damn critical for the future of the Good People.

Granger Mace took the ring of keys off of a metal hook set in the stone wall next to the heavy wooden cell door and turned the large rusty key in the lock. The door swung open on squeaky hinges, and he stepped into the darkness of the prison cell.

The smell in the cell made him almost lose a breakfast that he had not eaten. Rotten meat, refuse, and human excrement met his nose, and made him almost throw up. But he was stronger than bad smells.

The tall man was still manacled with a heavy chain that led from his right hand, and a cuff that cut the skin of his wrist, to another hook in the cell wall.

The older man had long, stringy gray hair, which was matted with dirt and grime. His left hand ended in a stump. And gray rags of clothing hung from his boney frame.

But the man still looked stronger and more able than Granger Mace had ever been. And that irritated him more than anything. And so, he thought about the torture, and gained back his confidence.

Years ago, Granger Mace had cut the man's left hand off, a finger at a time, and then the entire thing. He had to make sure the prisoner would be as helpful as possible.

Granger Mace smiled at the memory of the stubborn man's final submission and the treasure trove of information he had given him.

The prisoner's head was hanging down. He had not even raised it at the sound of the heavy door opening. Good, Granger Mace thought. The man was still submissive and beaten. That made him smile again.

He cleared his throat from the doorway, and the man finally looked up.

Granger Mace's spine turned to jelly at the fierce gaze from the pure white eyes that looked up at him from a face that showed defiance.

That was new, Granger Mace thought, and reconsidered his plan to torture the man even more.

He would need him, he thought, as the armies of White Eyes drew closer, and the final battle would commence.

He would need the man that the leader of the White Eyes had presumed was dead for two decades.

And Granger Mace would need this man even more to remove Hockley from his position of power once the war was over.

260

Granger Mace looked down with scorn, momentarily forgetting the fear that turned his spine to mush at the gaze from the prisoner chained up on the floor.

He would need this man more than he wanted to admit.

If only the man didn't scare him almost as much as the Shadow who constantly whispered to him to kill everyone, and to take over the world, once and for all.

"We need to talk," Granger Mace told the prisoner in a gravelly, tired voice.

Jerimiah Simone simply nodded.

Chapter 44

The bright light completely blinded Abe, and all he could do was duck down, and pull Facecake with him, while listening to his enemies approach.

Shit, he thought.

The Dark Eyes had known the White Eyes were coming. And the bright light had come from the very top of the Tower in the middle of the island City.

The White Eyed army had lost their main weapon, and advantage, against the Dark Eyes.

The next thing he heard was the whisper of arrows coming towards him and his troops. And soon-screams, grunts, and falling bodies all around him.

He felt Facecake's hand still in his own, gripping tightly. And then she stood, pulling him up, while he tried to regain his sight.

She moved him down a space between two dilapidated and falling structures, walking him into one of the buildings, and up a ragged stairwell. Only once did he trip on a fallen slab of stone.

Facecake held his hand, keeping him upright, and moving forward. The stairs were a struggle for Abe, but Facecake was confidently leading him.

As always, he marveled at her strength, and her willpower.

They arrived at what had once been a large window on the second floor, and Abe knew, and heard, that the enemy was below them, open to arrows and anything else his troops could use against the Dark People.

"Good job my love. Give me a few seconds," he told his wife.

She was the one who nodded at him now. He felt the movement more than heard it.

And within minutes, his eyesight was restored, and he had both of his long blades in his hands, while his wife exchanged arrows with the enemy. The look of determination and rage on her face told him that his army was still going to be alright.

From the second story window, Abe was able to see his troops now in the bright light from the Tower and could tell that they were recovering their sight. He figured that the enemy underestimated how long it would take the White Eyes to regain their vision after the onslaught of the bright light.

Abe watched his troops taking arrows and rocks from slings and got mad. He was full of rage and hate.

And then he jumped.

He landed in a cloud of dust and debris amongst his enemies, surprising them, and forcing a brief pause in the back-and-forth delivery of arrows.

He stood looking down at his feet for that brief second, ascertaining his enemies around him, feeling the quickened heartbeats, the dripping of sweat, the dank odor of fear. He smiled, his hair falling around his face, and looked up with pure white eyes that were full of hate, and purpose.

He moved first. And Dark People around him fell to the whirling 18-inch custom blades he held in both hands.

The feel of the leather cord-wrapped hilts in both of his dry hands was a comfort. The slow, steady heartbeats in his chest and temples sharpened him. And the memory of an arrow sticking out of his father's stomach two decades in the past kept him moving.

He was a storm of movement and death. He never stopped moving. He plunged his left knife into a surprised man's chest, and at the same time, kicked off the body that he had killed with his right hand.

He could feel his troops following him. And as he dealt out death with sharp, strong blades, many Dark People fell to his wife's arrows, saving him the effort of removing them from his path.

An arrow suddenly pierced a short man's right eye, and Abe leapt over his body, taking out two more Dark People who attacked him with drawn crossbows. His blades found fatal spots in both men.

And that's all he was aware of for the rest of the fight. He was a weapon, and nothing else bothered his thoughts except mowing down the next enemy.

His muscles bunched and expanded. Strength burst through his body more times than he could count, and he never faltered as he led his troops toward the tall, dark Tower in the middle of the island.

The Dark People never stood a chance against the determined, rage-filled Abraham Simone, and his people. Soon, he knew, he would meet up with his brothers, and they would finish this damn war, once and for all, by plunging his bloody, yet still sharp, long blade into the heart of Granger Mace.

It was a goal he kept in his mind as he stopped for a quick breath, and motioned for his wife, his protector, to join him.

As she walked up to Abe, breathing deeply, and looking more determined than even Abe felt, a shadow fell over her, and a strong, golden hawk landed on the outstretched arm of his little brother, Elijah, who somehow appeared on Abe's left, smiling with the satisfaction of being able to sneak up on Abe and surprise him.

"How did you get here so fast, little brother?" he asked the tall man. Elijah's smile never faltered as he soothed the hawk on his arm, ignoring Abe's question.

Finally, Elijah spoke.

"We got through the lines on the western flank pretty easily. After that, Ariel, here, led me to you. I think I need to stick as close to you as I can. Don't know why. Just a feeling I have," he told his oldest brother.

Abe felt a sense of relief as his wife, free of injury or wound, and his little brother, holding the ArchAngel hawk, surrounded him.

He turned, sheathing his bloody knives, and looked up at the Tower, less than half mile from where he stood. He only needed a final statement from his wife, to renew his determination to end this thing, once and for all.

"Let's get these bastards," she said.

He smiled at his beautiful wife. He wanted to hug and kiss her, but had to wait until the job was finished.

And so, he turned with the troops that remained with him, faced the large, tall Tower, and started moving forward.

He was the first one to hear the engines of aero-planes that were more than six hours early and sounded entirely too low.

Shit, he thought again.

Cheese was too early, and Abe didn't like what that meant for his chances of finishing this war before the night was over.

Chapter 45

Granger Mace stood on a balcony of sorts, at the very top of the Tower, looking down upon carnage and death.

Behind him, a hum was distractingly annoying. It was the Intelligence. And he hated talking to her. Like she could see into his soul and knew all of his secrets.

And then Jerimiah started talking to her again. The thing that rubbed Granger Mace the wrong way was that they were conversing in a language that he didn't understand, and he couldn't force a pain bad enough on the tall man to make him stop.

So, Granger Mace felt his impending doom, and he knew it was going to come from the White Eyed man talking to an ancient technology, probably about ways to end Granger's life.

Paranoia set in, and he turned quickly, walked up behind the chained man, and punched him as hard as he could in the back of the neck.

A satisfying grunt sounded from the man, and he sank to his knees.

"I told you," he spit at the taller man on his knees. "Talk to her so I can understand."

"She hasn't acclimated to the current tongue, Granger," Jerimiah said. "If you want real information and help, I must talk to her in ancient Spanish. To have clarity," he explained.

Granger Mace grinned maliciously. He wanted to rub in the fact that the taller man's people were dying below.

"The light above us worked perfectly, White Eye. What do you think of that?" Granger said into Jerimiah's ear.

The tall man did not answer.

"Now, ask her how to finish the weapon," Granger said. He reached down, grabbed the old, taller man under the armpits, and helped him to his feet. The chains connecting the man's leg rattled.

Speaking in the ancient language again, Jerimiah asked the Intelligence how to finish the weapon they had been working on for weeks. A r machine that repeatedly spit out small projectiles she had called "bullets."

The Good People's most industrious workers had been working on the bottom floors of the Tower to make both the machinery pieces and the bullets that the Intelligence instructed them to.

Jerimiah turned back to the machinery in front of him. She was humming loudly, and he knew from previous discussions with the AEMI that she was not at full capacity. Turning her back on had been a miracle, in Jerimiah's estimation.

But his ancestors had done a brilliant job preserving the machinery and banks of the computers that made up the Intelligence. Supplying electricity and changing a few blown capacitors that had been meticulously stored at the mountain fortress in the upper east part of this country, to Jerimiah, was a sign of the vastness of wonders that his ancestors had possessed.

But the Intelligence was also evil, and would destroy all humanity, once again, if given the chance.

And so he spoke to her about what had happened since she tried to destroy the human race. In somewhat broken Spanish, mixed with ancient English, he communicated to her the results and new processes his own people possessed in the current day and age.

"Computer," he said in the ancient tongue, "tell me again how my people evolved into the White Eyes that we are today."

The Intelligence answered him back in the same dual language that Granger Mace still could not decipher.

"It seems, Memorist, that in the darkness and close pressure of the caves where your ancestors sought refuge, certain physical and mental abilities were bred into your line, and the resulting mutations of the basic human pathology made you who you are," she said.

"I know that" Jerimiah answered. "But why, and for what purpose do you believe that we were made the way that we are?"

"Memorist, I cannot tell you the purpose of the mutations. I can only extrapolate the physical features that you have described to me, and in my banks of historical medical and physiological information, no such mutations had ever happened in the human race," she explained.

"Therefore, because you are a new classification of human, who you are and what you were made for are beyond my capacity to understand," she said.

Jerimiah simply nodded. These were much the same answers that the ArchAngels had given him when he had asked these questions as a younger man.

His quest to understand the purpose of his life, and the "why" of his existence, still eluded him.

He took his mind off of his own questions, and heard, once again, the clamor of the fighting that was happening in the brightened darkness of night, right outside the Tower he was standing in.

And he knew, instinctually, that his sons were out there, and they had no idea that he was in this Tower.

"How do the White Eyes defeat these remnants of humanity that never evolved, and have fought against us since we left the cave?" he asked the Intelligence. He refused to call her by the name his ancestors had given her.

"If what you have explained to me is true, and the darker people who existed outside the caves on this planet would eventually become the same humans that had almost destroyed this planet, I agree with you that they must be eliminated," she said.

"And so, I will teach you how to make a biological weapon that I believe will not affect the White Eyes, but will destroy the Dark People completely" she said.

"But first, you must be rescued from your captors, and to do that, I believe, once again, that I cannot be allowed to exist," she explained.

Jerimiah simply nodded at that wisdom. If the Dark People began to receive the information that this Intelligence could share with them, they would surely do the same to the earth that the ancient humans had done.

She continued to speak, and Jerimiah continued to memorize what she said. All the while, Granger Mace stood behind him, buzzing with frustration, and believing that the Intelligence was telling Jerimiah the secrets that the Good People would need in order to extinguish the plague of White Eyes on this planet, once and for all.

A noise, louder than the humming coming from the computer banks in the tall room around him, arose from outside the open doors leading to the balcony high above the battle below.

Granger Mace walked to that exact balcony to find out what the noise was and swore loudly when he realized that the White Eyes' fleet of aero-planes was flying in, and dropping bright, incendiary weapons. The Good People who were gathering to surround the White Eyes on the Island and take them from the rear were bearing the brunt of the aerial onslaught.

Damn it, Granger Mace thought to himself. He needed to tell Hockley and get the damn bullet machinery up and running. That's what the machinery was originally designed for. To blow those damn aero-planes out of the damn sky.

He turned, yelled a warning back to the tall White Eyed man to finish up and get the information they would need, and then hurried from the room. He ran down the tower as fast as his old legs would carry him, hellbent on rubbing the coming defeat in Hockley's face, and telling him that if Hockley didn't listen to Granger's advice for finishing this night, they would all die.

He had no idea that as he left the room, the Intelligence was explaining how to create a plague to Jerimiah. Then, without Granger knowing, a brighter light than the one at the top of the tower lit up the computer room, and an ArchAngel, seven feet tall, with full rainbow colored wings outstretched, entered.

And as the ArchAngel entered, the chains that had held Jerimiah prisoner for so many years fell away.

Jerimiah turned towards Raziel, smiling, and asked a single, simple question that would change the world forever.

"What took you so long?"

271

Chapter 46

"That damn Cheese," Abe yelled into the air. His wife flinched slightly but was just as full of rage as her husband.

Under cover of darkness, even with the bright light streaming in every direction from the top of the Tower, Cheese's aero-force was dropping their munitions on Dark People and White Eyes alike.

"This wasn't part of the plan!" Abe yelled again. And then he took off running.

With his foot-and-a-half-long blades whipping forward and backward, dodging arrows and crossbow bolts, Abe continued to forge a path forward through the mass of Dark People that came at him from all sides.

He was a harbinger of death, and those who followed him, were much the same.

This is how it should be, Abe thought to himself as he pulled a knife from the neck of a dirty Dark Eye, pushing the body away with a kick to the man's chest. He never stopped moving.

His lungs expanded, muscles constricted, and the physical gifts that he had been born with from the crucible of the caves made the killings seem almost child's play.

He finally came to an abrupt stop in a clearing close to the overbearing Tower, which rose into the encroaching dawn sky, a block away. All the other crumbling buildings, reduced to rubble around it, could not detract from the splendor and size of the thing.

And it radiated an evil that even Abe could feel. He knew that his wife, who soon joined him, breathless, could feel it too.

Abe looked to the brightening sky. Cheese's aero-planes circled close, still dropping explosive charges, and he cursed. But then he thought, maybe it wasn't as bad as it could have been.

That thought gave him a sense of peace.

Until Noah came running in from the West, surrounded by his own troops, heavily battered, bleeding, and holding each other up.

Abe and his own troops ran to give aid, as well as to help fight off the small horde of Dark Eyes that followed and harried Noah's troops.

A Divine rage filled Abe and he dispatched half of the enemy soldiers surrounding Noah's group himself. He felt almost invincible. It was a heady feeling, he thought, as he killed the final Dark Eye in a rather gruesome fountain of splattered blood.

He turned to his brother Noah and watched as the man fell to his knees. Abe knew that Noah had not had an easy time getting to the middle of the Island. But Noah was here now, and he was alive.

Both Facecake and Elijah were with Noah, and so Abe went to the other wounded White Eyes, ascertaining injuries, making mental tallies of how many troops he still had at his disposal.

About half, he figured. That was not a good thing.

He looked up when his name was called. The Generals from other lands on the earth were gathered in the shadows of an alleyway, or what had once been an alleyway. Now, it was a gloomy chamber-like area, surrounded by overgrown brick buildings, choked by vines and trees.

He walked over to the group of four. The tallest White Eye, the Nordic man named Paul, spoke first.

"We must finish this here, now, young Abraham," the man said with an accent that Abe found wonderfully lyrical.

He nodded back at the man, and then at the whole group of them.

Abe was thankful that the four leaders from other lands didn't hold him accountable for the soldiers that they had lost in this conflict. But he realized they had all known the risks. And the destruction of the Dark Eyes here, and now, and the removal of the technology that had destroyed the human race once already, needed to be done. All of his doubts from earlier in the year were gone.

"You're right. We need to storm that Tower," Abe said. He just hoped that they had killed off all of the Dark Eyed army. But if he knew his enemy, and he thought that he did, he knew that Granger Mace and Hockley both would have much more in store than what they had faced this night.

Abe looked up and saw the golden hawk soar above the growing group of White Eyes. More troops were stumbling, running, limping, or walking in as he watched the path of the hawk flying over them.

And that's when he realized that the aero-planes had fallen silent. They must have landed somewhere, Abe thought.

He searched for his top lieutenant, Jersey, and found the tall, dark-skinned man close by, as always. Abe beckoned Jersey over, and the man rushed to comply.

"Jersey, take a few men and go see where the aero-planes landed. And bring Cheese to me immediately," he told the tall man.

Jersey nodded, turned, and motioned to three other men, took off on a jog towards the east.

Good man, Abe thought before turning back towards the Tower.

Abe looked around at the crumbling row of buildings and saw open ground leading all the way up to the Tower. At that moment, he really liked the chances of ending this before he lost too many more men.

The avenue was clear, the grass-and tree-covered concrete was flat and straight, leading right up to the front doors of the dark Tower, which stood like an evil sentinel, looming into the morning sky overhead.

As Abe looked out at the clear and empty street,, the big doors at the base of the dark Tower opened, and a single man walked out.

Hockley, Abe thought to himself. How he hated the man. But not as much as he hated the man who jaunted out behind him.

Granger Mace, Abe could see, even at this distance, had a confident smirk on his face, and an air of victory about him.

Well, we'll see about that, Abe thought, as he gathered himself to start moving towards the two men.

And then the loudest sound that any of the White Eyes had ever heard lit up the morning stillness, and bullets started raining down amongst his men, scattering them, and trying to kill them all.

Chapter 47

Granger Mace stood next to Hockley, and smirked. He was very proud of himself, and how he had shown he was the real leader here, and not this overly large Hockley.

From Hockley's point of view, the battle that had raged throughout the night had not gone well at all. His plan, guided by the technology that the Intelligence had helped his men create, was for every single White Eye to have been killed in the night. But here it was, already morning, and more than half of them were still breathing.

He was beyond enraged. And this wasn't even his damn war.

Hockley looked over at the weasel, Granger Mace, and once again plotted how to rid himself of the little man. But he needed him. He needed the memories of the man that Granger Mace had held captive all these years.

Hockley looked up to the brightening sky, wishing to a higher being that this responsibility had not fallen on his shoulders. But he had needed a way to keep his people alive and fed through the long winters of the eastern parts of the land he had grown to love.

With Granger Mace's technology, the prisoner's memories, and a whole lot of ingenuity from his own people, he had managed to create enough power to sustain the people in the City, and had even been able to build a home that everyone could enjoy.

He looked up at his Tower, and felt pride swell within him. He had built floors of the structure with his own massive hands, and his family and friends had finished the rest. It was a home they would fight to the last man to protect.

All they had to do was destroy the White Eyes who were hellbent on eradicating it, along with all of his people, and his family. Hockley had not asked for this fate. But he would finish the deed, god willing.

No, he thought, still gazing at the sun-lit sky overhead, his thoughts all over the place. He had not asked for this responsibility.

And so, with Granger Mace smirking beside him in anticipation of using the technology that they had kept as secret as long as they could, Hockley raised his arm skyward, and brought it down in a swift movement.

The rail gun machinery behind him, which was pointed at the north at the moment, but was easily moveable to all points of the compass, opened up, and rained fire and death down upon the gathered White Eyes less than one hundred yards away.

Hockley closed his eyes at the sound, and at the carnage he could see spraying into the same air that he had so recently prayed to. The White Eyes would be killed down to a man, and it saddened Hockley immeasurably.

He could hear Granger Mace's maniacal laugh next to him, and he shuddered in suppressed rage.

By the time this day ended, he vowed to himself, he would kill the older man. He looked down at Granger Mace's psychotic face and felt both sadness and rage fill his chest.

The next few hours would determine which emotion would win the day.

The machinery was louder than he had expected, but it filled him with joy. He hoped it would very well be the thing that ended this ridiculous war between the White Eyes and Granger Mace.

Hockley just wished with all of his heart that his own people had not been caught up in this mess. But there was nothing he could do about it now.

If they wanted to survive, they had to win this war, right here, and right now.

Sadness and rage warred within him equally.

Granger Mace didn't care how Hockley looked at him. The war was about to be finished this very morning, after they unleashed the surprise he had kept secret all this time.

And as the blood and gore erupted from the gathered White Eyes down the flat area in front of the Tower, he laughed with glee.

The White Eyes all scattered, but the projectiles from the rail guns cut through brick and metal. There was no cover, no retreat for the White Eyed army. And as Granger Mace watched White Eyes collapse in pools of blood, he almost danced a jig.

Until he felt a vice-like grip on his throat, and turned to see Jerimiah Simone, out of chains for the first time in two decades, right behind him, his eyes shining with an internal light Granger Mace had never seen before.

It all happened so fast that even Hockley, who was the closest to Granger Mace, couldn't stop it.

Jerimiah Simone used his one free hand, as that was all he needed, to snap the thin neck of the man who had tortured him, beat him, starved him, and had gotten secrets out of him..

As soon as Granger Mace's limp body hit the grass under his feet, his large eyes staring blankly up at a sky he would never see again, Jerimiah Simone turned to Hockley and smiled.

Not even a full minute went by as they stood still, staring at each other. All sound was washed out by the roaring of the rail gun behind them.

And then silence, louder than the rail gun itself, covered everything.

Jerimiah smiled at Hockley again as the rail gun slowed and finally stopped once and for all.

Hockley knew the man had disabled the railgun in some way, but he was even more concerned with how he had gotten out of his chains with only one hand.

Someone in Granger Mace's group, or even in Hockley's own, had to have helped him.

Hockley lunged at the tall man, expecting to grab him, and wring some answers out of him, but Jerimiah was faster and stronger than he looked.

As Hockley's hand grabbed the ragged, threadbare shirt the man wore, Jerimiah chopped Hockley's hand with his own It felt like iron to the much larger man.

Hockley's hand became instantly numb, and he slowly looked up into the white eyes of the prisoner just as Jerimiah's hand shot out and crushed Hockley's windpipe.

Hockley fell to his knees and watched the older White Eyed man run away. No one stopped him. Hockley couldn't breathe, and he gasped for air like a landed fish.

And as life left Hockey's body, he wished once again that he had never met Granger Mace, had never tried to make his people's lives better, and had never tried to change the world.

Regret was the emotion that had actually won the day.

Chapter 48

Abe dove for cover behind a stack of loose bricks, pulling Facecake with him. All around him, his people looked for similar cover, but many were caught by the projectiles that moved too fast for them to see.

Blood erupted from the chest and head of two of the leaders from other parts of the world, and Abe's heart sank into his stomach.

He held Facecake close to him as the bullets hit all around him. He frantically looked for his brothers, finally seeing them

281

both behind a fallen wall. They appeared unscathed, but they stayed in the same position much like Abe himself.

Head down, behind cover, and protecting each other.

Death rained down on his people for what seemed like hours but was really only seconds. In those few seconds, dozens of his people were killed, right before his eyes. He couldn't handle it but knew there was nothing they could do about it.

They needed a miracle.

And then, the loud roar went silent, and he could hear his heartbeat in his temples.

Whatever machinery the Dark People had created was silenced, and nothing stirred around him for several seconds.

Finally, by some stroke of luck, or a miracle from the Creator himself, they were in the clear. The bullets seemed to have stopped.. Abe would use the lull in the death and destruction to make a final move.

He stood up, looking up at the Tower and not seeing a soul. In the silence of the morning, he could hear moans and cries from his own wounded but could see no movement from the Tower.

Abe looked around for Granger Mace and Hockley, but he could see nothing. He only saw a couple of bodies on the ground in front of the Tower. But that didn't make sense. He couldn't believe that those were the bodies of the leaders of the Dark People. That made no sense.

But he didn't have time to waste. He had to end this conflict here and now, and he could only think of one way to do that.

He had to destroy that Tower.

Abe reached down and pulled his wife to her feet. He started checking the men around him, making sure people were alright, and that those needing medical help were receiving it.

He motioned to his two brothers to join him behind the fallen wall. And as they trotted up to him and his wife, Abe cemented the plan he had in his mind.

It was time to end this, he thought, as he turned to his brothers and his wife.

"We have to destroy that Tower right now," he told them.

All three of the people closest to him nodded, understanding the threat if the machinery started back up again.

"The only way I know to destroy a Tower is to hit it high up, and hope it collapses on itself. Or, we can set charges at the base, and blow the bottom out, which will do the same thing," Abe said.

Noah and Elijah nodded at him. Facecake just waited to see what he was planning.

Abe took a deep breath and explained the rest of the plan.

"I want you three to stay here and lead the men in a full circle around that Tower. We have to kill any Dark Eye who comes out, or who's wandering these ruins," he told them.

"I'm going after Jersey and to have a word with Cheese. I want to fly over that Tower and drop everything we have on it, to see if we can bring it down," he told them. "I also want to find out why the hell he went against orders."

Facecake was the first to chime in. "I'm going with you," she told Abe.

He was about to argue with her, to tell her that she was safer here, helping to round up their troops and mop up the remaining Dark People. But he saw the look on her face, and knew it was a waste of time to argue with her.

He knew his wife so well that he could tell she wasn't going to change her mind.

So he just nodded at her in resignation and looked back at his brothers.

"When that Tower falls, we need to be ready for Granger Mace and Hockley to throw everything they have left at us," he said to the pair.

Noah clasped Abe on the shoulder, and Elijah clasped him on the other one. It was Elijah who spoke up first.

"We will, Abe, we will," he said.

"You take care of yourself. Join us as soon as you can. We'll need you," Noah said.

Abe nodded at them both, a flood of memories of the last twenty years together exploding in his mind.

"It ends here," he finally told them.

Abe was overcome with love for his family at that moment. He couldn't put a finger on the feeling, deep within the battle, as they had been in more situations like this than he cared to count. So he just grabbed his two brothers, pulled them in close, and hugged them as tightly as he could.

He pulled back, looked down at his brothers, and promised both inside his mind, and out loud, that he would be right back.

He gave Facecake time to hug the brothers as well, as he looked around for his weapons, which had fallen from his hands when the bullets first started falling.

When all was ready, and the machinery had still not started back up, he looked around at his troops, nodded to several of them, and grabbing Facecake by the hand, and with a last nod at his brothers, he started to jog away.

As he and Facecake got to the end of the row of dilapidated, overgrown buildings, Elijah yelled at them both.

"We love you guys," he yelled.

Abe stopped, turned around towards his brothers, and yelled the same reply as Facecake did, at the same time.

"Love you more!" they screamed in unison.

Abe, along with Facecake, headed east. They passed several more streets of overgrown steel structures and dodged piles of twisted metal and debris. The ancient people who had lived in this city centuries before had left a mess behind, Abe thought to himself.

On more than one occasion, the pair of lovers had to stop to handle small groups of Dark People who seemed to run at them, waving weapons, and going against their own self-preservation.

It was almost child's play to dispatch the tired, miserable-looking groups. But Abe and Facecake did just that with ruthless ease, relying on the skill and teamwork that they had honed over two decades of fighting and loving together.

And then they were clear of the dilapidated buildings and crumbling debris, and were jogging into a wide, open area, covered in soft grass, bright in the morning sunlight.

At the far end of the open grassy area, Abe could see the fleet of aero-planes parked together. It seemed as if Cheese had had his pilots land, and taxi close together, knowing that they would need to use most of the area to take off again.

At least Cheese is consistent and disciplined, Abe thought to himself, jogging with Facecake over to where several people were milling around together, amongst the aero-planes, all seeming to look at something on the ground.

As Abe and Facecake ran towards the group, Abe was formulating the plans for taking down the tower with incendiary devices thrown from the aero-planes.

One man moved away from the group of people, and walked towards the pair.

Abe could see it was Cheese, and something seemed wrong. He couldn't quite put his finger on it. Maybe the way the darker man was walking, or the way he held himself, or maybe even something in the air, but Abe was suddenly overcome with caution.

He stopped, and instinctually moved Facecake behind him. Something was seriously wrong.

285

He looked past Cheese, and saw that what lay on the ground catching everyone's attention were four bodies.

And then alarm and fear overcame Abe as he recognized the bodies belonged to his close friend and top lieutenant Jersey and the three men that he had grabbed earlier in the morning to find out why Cheese had come early to the attack.

Abe was suddenly calm. Something had been wrong with Cheese for a very long time, he knew. But he had ignored it.

And so, keeping Facecake behind him, he awaited his oldest friend.

Cheese sauntered up, wearing a grin from ear to ear.

"Cheese, what did you do?" Abe asked the man when he was within talking distance.

"What do you mean, what did I do?" Cheese responded with a question of his own.

The manic grin never left his dark face.

Abe could feel Facecake tense up behind him. She had known Cheese her entire life, and she had never heard that tone of voice come out of him before.

Abe was silent. He watched Cheese carefully. This would have to be handled extremely delicately, he knew.

But he also knew that there was no time. They had to destroy the Tower.

So Abe decided to get closer to Cheese. To see if he could unarm the smaller man. Cheese saw him coming, expecting Abe to move first, and so pulled out a long, serrated blade from the small of his back.

Abe drew his own blades in a whispering rush.

The two men didn't speak,, but volumes of understanding were about to rush between them.

They both tensed their bodies. They both leaned towards the other.

And they both started moving simultaneously.

Until Facecake ran between them suddenly, before Abe could stop her.

She moved faster than he had ever seen her move before.

She ran between the two men, intending to stop the coming fight. But both men were already moving towards each other. They were too close to stop, and Abe, looking back at the events later, knew in his heart that she must have known that too.

Abe stopped himself as Facecake ran between them. He was able to control his own body, with the gifts he had been born with.

But Cheese, who had always fallen well behind the tall White Eyed man, could not stop his forward momentum.

In half a blink of an eye, their entire worlds ended, right there, in that grassy glen amongst the ruined City.

Cheese's serrated blade, already well into a deep swing meant for the man who he had envied for decades, ended up buried in the chest of the woman that both men had loved.

The only two sounds heard in the large, open, grassy area that fateful morning were the screams of two men, pain and heartbreak exploding out of them both.

And the sound of Facecake's beautiful, broken body hitting the ground between them, already dead.

Chapter 49

Abe didn't hesitate a single second.

As Facecake's body hit the ground, he plunged his own blade into the heart of the man who he had seen as a brother for more years than he cared to think about.

Another scream sounded from the group of people who were still gathered around the bodies lying on the ground by the parked aero-planes.

Abe didn't even care. He only had eyes for his wife.

He bent over her, hugging her broken body to his own. He knew her blood was washing over his shirt and pants, but he didn't care.

He knew that people were running around him, calling his name. But he didn't care.

He felt hands on his shoulders, under his arms, lifting him, but he wouldn't budge, and he didn't care.

He only felt pain and heartbreak.

His Facecake, his wife, his Alexandria, was gone.

Sobs escaped his lips. Sounds he had never made in front of anyone else except the woman he still held to his chest. He didn't care who heard him then.

And as the sun reached the middle of the sky, and heat bore down on them all, he finally let the last tear he would ever shed fall from his face onto the hair of the only woman he would ever love.

He felt people surrounding him. He didn't know how much time had gone by. He looked up into a face he was surprised to see. A face that looked back at him with pity and heartbreak of its own.

"Moose," he whispered.

"Abe, I'm so sorry. I couldn't stop him," Moose said in his simple way.

Abe stood, finally letting other hands pull his wife's body from his arms. He looked squarely into the eyes of his second oldest friend and asked what he had wanted to ask the entire day.

"Why did Cheese turn on us?"

Moose just shrugged. To him, it was a simple matter that had turned deadly. But the wrong people had died, and now, he felt all alone in the world.

"He always loved her, Abe," he answered in his own way.

Abe's heartache and loss was suddenly replaced with rage and anger. He knew what he had to do.

289

"Moose," he said, "load up Cheese's plane with all the bombs it will carry."

The larger man looked into the stricken face of the man he had followed for two decades and didn't hesitate to nod and get to work.

Several years prior to that moment, when the engineers from the caves had outfitted and perfected the technology to allow the fleet of aero-planes to be larger than just the one that Cheese and Moose had found and fixed, Abe had asked Cheese to take him up into the air and show him how the planes worked.

Abe didn't remember much from that single trip, but afterwards he would sneak out to the airfield and sit in one of the planes and look over the controls, memorizing which buttons and which switches did what.

So, he felt confident that he would be able to accomplish what he had in mind.

He looked back once at the body of his wife. The other pilots, and White Eyed troops that had gathered close to the wide, open area, had placed her on a portable cot, ready to take her home. He knew, right then and there, that he would not be going home with her.

Moose was the last person he talked to as he climbed into the cockpit of the largest of the aero-planes.

"You sure about this, Abe? We can go with you, drop the bombs on the Tower together," he said.

"I've got to make this right, Moose. Just tell my brothers what happened here," he said. And then he started the aero-plane's loud engine.

It was a day for loud noises, and quiet pain, he thought, as he maneuvered the aero-plane at the end of the large open area and watched as a gathering crowd of White Eyes moved out of his way.

He opened the throttle like Cheese had showed him, gaining the speed he would need to rise into the air. He felt an overwhelming feeling of connectedness to his ancestors.

He remembered one of the stories that his father had told him when he was younger. About how his ancestor, Mark Simon, had been in an airplane about to travel out over the ocean to shut down the AEMI, when she had ended the world.

And here he was, in an airplane, on the same coast that his ancestor had been on, flying to do the same thing.

With that thought, and the pain he couldn't quite contain from the loss of his wife, his whole life, roaring louder in his mind than the aero-plane's engine, he rose into the air and flew towards open water.

Abe felt a deep calm settle deep within his chest and mind as he saw the coast fade away behind him. He was finally out, over the ocean that he had never traveled across, and ready to accomplish what came next.

He said a quiet prayer of safety for his friends, his family, and for the soul of his wife, who traveled to the Spiritual Realm that very day. Then he spun the yoke hard to the right and turned back towards the City.

Immediately in front of the aero-plane's glass windshield, he could see the tall Tower, shining in the sunlight. It was the tallest structure around by hundreds of feet. It was an easy target.

He said one last prayer under his breath for himself, and then pushed the throttle to full open. He felt the aero-plane pick up maximum speed.

Glancing over his shoulder, he saw the boxes of Contact Incendiary Devices, or as Noah liked to call them, SIDs, stacked up haphazardly in the open space behind the cockpit. Good, he thought. He would need every last one of them.

He just hoped his brothers and his soldiers would be out of the way of the blast like he had told them to be.

The tall, dark Tower was looming closer and closer in front of the aero-plane, and he didn't have any more time to remember. Or to feel.

He only had enough time to think that there were so many things that he wasn't thinking of.

His mother. His friends. His two little brothers.

His daughters who had looked so much like their mother.

The last thought that went through his mind before he flew the aero-plane full of explosive bombs and jet fuel into the very top of the Tower, was that he would be seeing his wife once again, in just a few short seconds.

The bright white light of the explosion at the top of the large Tower, where the AEMI data banks were housed, was the last thing Abraham Simone saw on this earth.

Chapter 50

Elijah and Noah were gathering their troops to surround the Tower as Abe had commanded. They followed their older brother unquestioningly. They always had.

As several more roving bands of Dark People were dispatched, and White Eyed troops were gathering together, the two brothers realized that they had not lost as many soldiers as Abe had first estimated.

That was the best news of the day.

Elijah finished pulling used arrows out of bodies to stick back into his quiver, and remembered the first time he had ever seen a bow used. Facecake had shot the deer that he was watching through an open glen, early one morning. That had taught him a good lesson. He still held respect for Facecake and her bow.

A breathless soldier ran up to him, and Elijah motioned for Noah to join him as the man steadied himself.

The man had caught his breath and told them what had happened in the open grassy area where the aero-planes had parked between Cheese and Abe. When he recounted what had happened to Facecake, both brothers spun towards the north, hoping to stop Abe from doing what he was hell bent on doing.

But it was too late.

A deep boom, an explosion larger than any they had heard that day, was followed a few moments later by an even louder explosion as the Tower fell. That was all the indication that the brothers needed to know that they had lost half their family in just a few short hours.

No one knew what to do for several minutes. Elijah and Noah simply held each other, sobs racking both of their bodies.

Their cries were cut short, however. Whispers surrounded them, and the sun beat down on their heads, dispelling all shadows around.

All of the White Eyed soldiers who were milling around them in a small, open area enclosed by larger crumbling structures moved out of the way. They cleared a space in the very middle, large enough for the two brothers to see what the whisperings had been about.

A tall, older White Eye was walking towards them, wearing ragged clothing. Gray hair hung limp and loose around his face. He was missing his left hand and walked with a limp.

But there was no mistaking the set of his shoulders, or the light behind his piercing white eyes. The whispers reached a crescendo when Elijah finally spoke up.

"It's my father, everyone," he called to the troops around them.

"It's the Memorist."

A few weeks later, the late summer sun was high in the sky, and a soft, calm breeze ruffled the trees around the orchard back in the deep valley where the White Eyes had made their home.

Emily Simone hummed an old tune that had been on her mind for a while.

And then she started singing as she picked summer apples.

"Country roads, take me home," she sang, dropping sweet apples into her basket. Three small voices around her picked up the song as well.

"To the place, I belong," the three Simone girls joined their grandmother.

"West Virginia, mountain momma, take me home, country roads." A deeper baritone joined the four females.

All sound cut off as Emily dropped the basket of apples at her feet, shock and dismay coloring her face. Her breath caught in her throat.

She knew that baritone voice as well as she knew her own.

Jerimiah Simone walked around from behind a grouping of smaller trees at the edge of the orchard, surrounded by two of his three sons.

Emily Simone almost fainted when she saw the face of the man that she thought she had lost forever. She then felt overwhelming sadness mixed with the excitement when she noticed who was not with her two remaining boys.

The family, and many other White Eyes who had known the famous couple, gathered around the clearing where the battle with the dark Beings had taken place what seemed like years ago.

A stone effigy had been erected in the months since the battle, listing the names of those lost that fateful evening. Including the ArchAngel, Azrael.

The gathered loved ones, standing together in a tight circle next to a swollen mound of fresh dirt, made no sound. They let the wind through the leaves sing their sorrow. They let their beating hearts and silent sobbing lift the dirge to the Creator for the loss that they all felt.

A new marker, bearing Alexandria and Abraham's names, was erected next to the effigy in the middle of the clearing.

And while Abe's body was not recovered, Facecake's remains would always be there, in the home they had built together.

Jerimiah, fresh from his reunion with his entire family, cleared his throat and reached into the satchel at his side. What he pulled out shocked the gathered family.

Jerimiah unrolled the pure white scroll that until that day had shown blank to the entire world. But it was now covered in bright gold writing.

He read aloud from the very last part of the scroll, which explained what had happened, and why it had to happen that way.

It was the same writing that he had read so many years ago, when he was first given the scroll. And it comforted everyone gathered around, just like it had done when he had read it for the first time.

Perched in a tree near the gathered family, eyes intent on the gathering, and the words finally spoken, a beautifully created golden hawk emanated peace to the gathered White Eyes.

Ariel would watch over this family for generations to come, both here in the Material Plane, and also in the Spiritual, where so many had reunited.

Later that night, gathered around the family fire, with dinner finished and cleaned away, the three Simone sisters sat at the feet of their grandfather Jerimiah as he started to speak.

Staring into the roaring flames, surrounded by family that he thought he would never see again, he told the three girls a story.

"Your mother and father were the bravest people I had ever known, or even heard of," he started.

It was difficult for him to tell the story of Abe and Facecake to their own children. But he did. And after that night, he told it as many times as the girls asked for it.

The three sisters, who had cried their hearts out most of that day were ready to hear it.

For most of the years of the rest of their peaceful lives, the Simone sisters never forgot what their grandfather told them that night. Remembering their parents, as well as hearing about their lives, would become easier as the years went by.

The pain never quite went away, but as the scroll explained, they would all be reunited again, one day. For all time after.

The family who had led the large group of White Eyes out of the caves so many years ago would go on to champion the cause that they were given.

To impart knowledge, and history, of the humans who had come before them, and who had made so many drastic mistakes and decisions that resulted in their own demise.

Now, the people left in the world, all with the white eyes that were so unique in all of Creation, would always first count the cost of any global decision.

And it had started that first night, at the feet of the man who had come back from the dead, and the lessons that he imparted to his granddaughters.

The three girls would grow up in a large, loving family, always missing their parents, who had sacrificed themselves to assure that peace would spread throughout all the earth.

Their living uncles, Elijah and Noah, would also both live long lives, finally settling down into the peace that was bought by the lives of their oldest brother and his wife.

And also by the lives of more White Eyes than they cared to count, whose sacrifices were no less important than Abe's and Facecake's.

The older Simone brother's own children would move out into the world that their fathers had first explored, and share the tales of the sacrifices of the few for the benefit of the many, which would go on to grow into legend.

It is what the final part of the scroll had told, and the secrets of the scroll, blank for so many years, were secrets no more.

Years later, as the Simone sisters imparted the memories and the legends to their own children and grandchildren, the original lessons would not be forgotten.

The three Simone sisters would grow up to make sure that the new, evolved, White Eyed human race would never again pay the bill for the choices of a few.

And all the while, a beautifully created golden hawk watched over them, assuring that the tale was told, and that war never gripped this planet, ever again.

The whole world would come to know what sacrifices were made to assure that technology would never kill off the human race again.

298

The Simone sisters would all grow up to be Memorists in their own right. They would never forget what their parents had died for, and kept their story alive so that their sacrifices would never be in vain.

And so that this world would never forget.

With that, this planet finally knew peace, and only peace, forevermore.

The End

Joshua Loyd Fox
Feb 2021 to Jan 2022

Epilogue

A rather tall, splendidly arrayed Being stood in the Spiritual Realm and looked down on a world full of soldiers.

The Mission that had been given from the Creator of All down to his Host was accomplished. To create an army of enhanced, evolved humans to serve as companions to the Heavenly Armies of Light.

And in a few short centuries, the tall Being knew, this world below would produce billions of the White Eyed humans.

Those billions would serve the Creator in the battle that the entire Heavens now knew was coming.

They had lost a sister. And that did not sit well with the Host. It was inevitable that a conflict was coming. They just had no idea who they would be going to war against.

Raziel felt a presence surround him, and knew his Father was near. That fact alone gave the tall, rainbow-hued ArchAngel peace.

A peace that overrode the unease he felt at the loss of Azrael. But then, he thought, they didn't really lose her.

He turned, and watched his Father approach, holding out His arm. On it was perched, a large, perfectly made golden hawk.

The Creator of All smiled at the hawk, and she flew away, back to the throne room, where she existed both in this plane, and the Material.

It was a confusing idea, Raziel knew, but the Creator seemed at ease with it.

His Father stood next to him, looking down on the same world that Raziel had just spent centuries honing to the completion of the Mission, and his Father was glad.

Not a word was spoken by either Being, but a sense of completion, and of accomplishment, pervaded Raziel's senses, and he knew that it was time for him to rest.

To rest and prepare for the conflict that was soon to be amongst them all.

A loud voice boomed into Raziel's mind, but it wasn't painful. Quite the opposite, actually.

"WELL DONE, GOOD AND FAITHFUL SON," the Father's voice said.

Raziel nodded his gratitude, and took his leave from the Father, off to take a rest after so many centuries in the Material Realm.

Very close by, though separated by centuries in the Material Plane, another tall, beautiful Being stood on a cliff, overlooking normalcy.

The same presence that had given Raziel so much peace earlier, also surrounded the ArchAngel Jeremiel.

He smiled up at his Father.

As an ArchAngel of the Younger Ilk, this was to be his very first Mission alone.

He was not to be mentored, nor led, by one of the Older Ilk. And for that, Jeremiel was thankful.

The Father's presence made him know that it was time.

It was time to manipulate and form the life of a single man below.

A normal man, with nothing about him distinguishing him in the world below except for a single gift of the Father.

The man below, when he was born, was given Favor. And with that Favor, the man below, who, in his present life was as normal, and forgetful as possible, could shape existence forever.

The Father laid a hand onto Jeremiel's shoulder. The ArchAngel Jeremiel smiled again and set his sights on a point in the Material World.

Before the ArchAngel of the next mission departed, a final thought leapt from his mind to the mind of his Father, and made the Creator of the Universe smile Himself.

"Oh, this was going to be great fun!"

As His child winked out of the Spiritual Plane, the Father of All, the Alpha and the Omega, looked down with a Face that no one in the Material Plane had ever seen.

He would need the Fate Maker that the man below was destined to become. That much The Father knew.

But what He didn't know gave Him pause.

He didn't know WHY a Fate Maker was needed.

And for the Creator of All, not knowing something.....was a horrifyingly new feeling.

From the Author

Almost three years ago, I set off on a journey that I had zero idea where it would lead. For those of you, Happy Readers, who have read all of the novels so far, starting with my autobiography, "I Won't Be Shaken," all the way through the conclusion of this book, you've seen the progression of my daily life go from homelessness and brokenness, up to today, where I am whole, full of joy, and blessed beyond belief.

And while writing a novel is supposed to be a very lonely job, and it sometimes can be, to get it out into the world in a professional, fully realized way, takes a whole team. And there is zero chance I would have gotten where I am today without some of the most amazing people on this planet. I want to take time, after this, my fourth novel, to thank and acknowledge all those who have made my books, and frankly, my life, so much more than I had ever hoped, or really deserve.

First and foremost, I want to thank my children and their mothers. When I wrote "Shaken," I had to protect everyone by changing names and distinguishing features. Maybe it will be fun for those outside of my life to try and go back and match real names with fictional.

Avan Graham, Nathaniel Channing, and Ethan Riley are my three oldest sons, and their personalities and qualities make up the three brothers in this book. I haven't always been the best father, and most times down right horrible, but they have always been the best sons a father could ask for. They are all amazing men, successful and brilliant in their own lives and futures, and they give me hope that I may have done one or two things right in this life so far. I love you all boys, and I am so very proud of each of you. I cannot wait to see what you do in your own futures, and how you surpass even the small dreams your dad has for his own.

My four youngest children, while not being old enough to have read my books, have nonetheless inspired me to be the best version of myself. Brenden, Chloe, Hannah, and Luke, just like your older brothers, you are such amazing and beautiful souls. I am daily reminded of just how blessed a man can be in his children, and the four of you will change the world in ways I can't even imagine. I love you all more than you will ever know, and while I haven't always been the best father, you have all been the most beautiful and amazing children I could ask for. You all give me hope for the future, and that all that I have done was not in vain.

I have learned in this journey that not everyone you start out with, you end up with. A famous quote says that the bigger your circle is, the more fake you are, and the more real you become, the smaller your circle becomes. That is more true than I originally gave credence to.

With all of my heart and soul I want to acknowledge and thank my three best friends in the whole world, and their families.

Liz Drummond-Spinhirne, you saved my life twice. Once, when I was in the seventh grade by becoming my friend, and the second, which was outlined in the Foreword's of "Shaken." Without you, your husband Jarett, and your children, I would not know what family really is. My love for you and for your family is something I could never measure. Every single thing that has come from that day almost three years ago, and everything that comes after this, is because of you. I thought as I was growing up that I would never know what unconditional love looks like, but it was always there, right in front of my face. I love you all as unconditionally as you love me. (and put up with me!)

Cheryl Zamora-McCormick, I meant what I put in the dedication of "Had I Not Chosen." You taught me a lesson twenty-five years ago that I still use every single day. You are the hardest working, most loving, loyal, and dedicated person I know. Your goodness, and your big heart inspire me every single day to be better than I already am. You've brightened up this journey that I have been on, every time we talk. Laughing together with you on the phone, planning the growth of both of our platforms, and sharing advice back and forth, is always the highlight of my day. Your family is so beautiful, you should be on the cover of a magazine every month. Chris McCormick, my brother in arms, and the husband of my best friend, thank you for your service, your love for Cheryl, and the inspiration you are to all those who know you. I look forward, Cheryl, to seeing you and your family grow and reach all you deserve to be.

One last person I want to acknowledge and thank here, at the beginning where you list the most important people in your life, my best guy friend, and brother from another mother, Marc Dannemiller. Man, you supported me in more ways than I could ever thank you for. You gave me a roof when I was homeless, a best friend and an ear when I thought I didn't have anyone else, and inspiration for the kindness that makes you who you are, every single day. I will never forget our "Popcorn Socials" at work, on the flightline for the Navy, and I will never forget all that you have done for me since. You truly are one of the kindest souls I will ever know. I love watching your family grow, and I can't wait until you and Amanda Stovall mesh your lives together completely. Your children I adopt as my own, obviously, and I am so very proud of you all. I love you all as the family I never had, but am surrounded with, every single day now. Amanda, thank you from the bottom of my heart for all you have done for me on this journey as well, but even more so, for how you have completed Marc's life in only the way you could. I've always said that everything you two have gone through, you both deserve each other in the most positive and amazing ways! I love you guys, Cakes, Gwyn, and Ryder completely. (and can't forget Girr!) Thank you for everything!

I would also like to thank members of my family that, while not being a part of this journey, per se, still gave me encouragement and strength in other ways. My brother, Jason, who supported me when no one else would. My sisters, Jennifer, Josie, and Veezie. You are the most beautiful women in the world, and I marvel at each of you.

My family on my Fox side, Aunt Liz and her husband Steve, their daughters, Michelle, and Laura, and their son, Eric. My mother's other siblings, Aunt Leslie, and uncle Ken, and your wonderful children. Your beautiful families always make me smile.

And on my father's side, my aunt and uncle, Ann and Jerrel Gardner, their children, Cory, Terry, and Gina. I love and miss you all. Memories of my childhood were the most positive when I had you in my life. I'm sorry that things don't always turn out in a positive way, but I hope that if you ever read this, you'll know that you all did an amazing job, and I am ok. Better than ok, most days.

The members of my family who are no longer with us, but made an impact on me, at some point in my life, or at least, in who I am, and who I was born to be. My mother, Glenet, my father, Herbert, and my step-mother, Linda. My grandparents, Lester and Wanda Fox, and all that they taught me in the short time I knew them. Thank you all for making me who I am.

And now for the team who has made these books and this amazing journey that God started me on, almost three years ago, but which I had been preparing for my entire life, possible.

My editor, Dasha Bultova shows me with each consecutive book just how amazing and gifted she is. I was blessed beyond belief to have met you, and that you chose to take me and my writing on, very early on. You allow me my own voice, and while you have to routinely correct me in my somewhat conservative and sexist views, you do so with grace and understanding. You have made my books better than I ever could, and without you, I know my voice wouldn't shine the way it does. Thank you again, and I can't wait to work on the next project with you. And of course, any mistakes in all of my books are mine and mine alone.

The artist who has made the visual representation of not only my books, but my online presence as well is Rogue Blackwood of In the Blackwood Designs. Rogue is not only the best graphic artist I have ever known, she is also a writer, a designer, a spiritual guru, and all around amazing human being. I am blessed to know her, work with her, be corrected by her, and to come to understand many other perspectives than my own, through the people, like Rogue, who have come into my life the last several years. Thank you for putting up with me Rogue, and for always being yourself. You are my hero.

As the progression of this journey sped up, and I started gaining confidence in my writing, as well as how my life was shaping up, there were so many people from my past, present, and for sure, going to be in my future, that read the books as I wrote them, and gave encouragement when I needed them the most. I call my Beta Team my "Happy Readers." And as the books were developed, and released, the team changed many times. But a lot of folks stayed with me throughout the process.

Lenel Dillon Robinson has always been a true friend, and an amazing mother. She also has the most amazing parents. I learned so much, early in my adulthood, from Vernon and Betsy Dillon. But I learned more about strength and resilience from Lenel herself. Thank you, Lenel, for your support, and your constant love and attention to Brenden, and everyone who knows you. You truly have a healer's soul.

Michelle Denning, I have known you since I was a young teenager, and you've always constantly been yourself. Thank you for reading along, always giving support, encouragement, and an ear. I wish you the happiest future, wherever that takes you.

Aniko Samu Kuschatka, thank you from the bottom of my heart for reading along, your amazing outlook on life, my stories, your own stories, and for being a really good friend when I wasn't always one. You daily surprise me with your strength, your "I'm never giving up, no matter what," attitude, and your outlook on life. You are truly one of God's angels on this earth.

Two other late-arriving yet lovingly wonderful Beta Readers are Mariella Curmi and Tony Brooks. Mariella has become a constant friend and supporter. Her lovely outlook on life lifts me up on dark days. She is on another continent, but constantly here with me in spirit. And I met Tony years ago while I worked as a contractor for the Navy at Test and Evaluation Squadron VX-20. He always had a joke and made me laugh. Now, he is an amazing supporter and has even started a Book Club where they are reading these novels. It is people like this that every author needs. Beautiful people like Mariella and Tony keep authors pushing forward.

Other Beta Team readers included Michelle Cronin, Sarah Zhang, Tracy Ennis (and Abigail Ennis, thank you for buying my books early on and sharing them with your amazing family! I can't wait to see how our families join together!), Dianna Malone, Sherry Neil (Mrs. Neil, even when I was a child you were the best example of a surrogate mother to so many Boy's Ranchers!), Ruby Godfrey (also an amazing surrogate mother to the Ranchers), Michelle Richards (love you cousin), Shane and Angel Storrs, (see you guys soon! Love you so much! And tell Cayden he only has one job!), Sandra D'Ambroise (love you my cousin and spiritual guru), Brandi (Brassy) Fox-Young, Brian Clince, and his wife, Rachel, (thank you Moose, for allowing me to use you, your family, and your amazing town in two of my books now), Katie Bitz, Krystall Williams, Katy Orawsky, Marina Aris (an amazing publisher, writer, and all around wonderful human being and mother in her own right), Michelle Templin, and many others who came and went like the tides.

I want to thank the Southern Maryland Literary Group, headed by Mr. Tony Brooks. Big "thank you guys!" to Lori Ann Thomas (The headbanging metalhead, herself), Chastity Lawson (the coolest Halloween decorator, ever!), Angela Villa (sorry for the human emotions when you read Shaken, Angela), Angela James Wood, Brianna Marshall, Dawn Rose Beck (Dawn, we go so far back, I can't even remember when we met except you took me for my first pedicure, and of course, the Edwin McCain concert at Rams Head! LOL), Grayce Solskin, Leighanne VanderHeyden, and Maddison VanderHeyden. We all need more coffee meetings, and Used Book scavenger hunts, guys!

There are also thousands of people on multiple platforms and social media sites that have given some small encouragement when it was needed most, and who are on the same kind of road that I have been on for so long. I do all of this for you as well. I hope that when it gets really tough, when the night is darkest, and the cold wind is shaking your bones, you can see that we can accomplish anything together. We are a global family, and what happens to one, affects all others in some small way. That's always been the truth of this life. So, thank you all, my fellow Warriors, for helping me get to this place.

And then there are people who I would like to take a moment to thank, not for encouragement, or love, or even support. But for making me stronger in lessons learned. Jeannine Carr, Janean Byrne, Jami Harmon, Dina Grasso, and Kristel Ruch. I don't see any of you as enemies, quite the opposite in fact, but that isn't how you see me. And that's ok. I'm still here, I'm still doing what God has made me to do, and I appreciate you all more than almost anyone else the last four years, as I got strong as hell from each of you. So, thank you for those lessons in life, love and pain, and I wish you all the happiness you can find.

And finally, as I have told everyone who has come in contact with me during this entire journey, I wouldn't be here if it wasn't for God's constant hand on my life, directing me, opening doors, and straightening my steps. Some days, when the words don't come as easy as others, it's a simple meditation and prayer, and they appear like a miracle. When resources are thin, and I was trying to figure out how to keep a roof over my head, I was always provided for. When emotions and pain threatened to overtake me, over and over again, peace flooded me like a river.

I told God that if He would get me here, I would tell everyone it was all because of Him. And it was. I give it all back now, because it was first given to me.

Thank you all, Happy Readers, for getting to this place with me, and thank you to all those listed here, and the many that I did not mention. I will write another one of these as we go along, and get everyone in here somewhere.

The magic of this life is that we are never, truly, alone; and love surrounds us all, whether we see it or not. We are all connected, and in that connection, grace and mercy is plentiful. Thank you all for making me the man I am today, and as I'm fond of saying, "There is so much more to come, hold onto your butts!"

J.L.F
2/2/22

Joshua Loyd Fox is the author of four novels to date. *I Won't Be Shaken*, *Had I Not Chosen*, *Amongst You*, and *To Build a Tower*. All four novels are available on multiple platforms and in several styles from Watertower Hill Publishing, LLC.

He is also the author of one book of poetry, *I Don't Write Poetry: a Collection,* available Summer of 2022, and a short story anthology, *Book of the Tower and Traitor*, available Christmas, 2022.

All of Joshua Loyd Fox's novels can be found and ordered at www.jlfoxbooks.com.

Look for his next installation of the ArchAngel Missions, *One Becomes a Thousand*, available from Watertower Hill Publishing, arriving spring, 2023.

This work of fiction was formatted using 11-point Times New Roman font, the author's favorite, on 55lb cream stock paper. The page size is 5.06" x 7.81". The custom margins are industry standard, 0.5" all around, and 0.00" inside, with no bleed, and 0.635" gutter, with mirrored pages. Headers and footers are standard.

The cover is full color paperback in a glossy finish.

The binding is 'perfect.'